# NELL HARLEY

BY
THEODORE GOODRIDGE ROBERTS

INTRODUCTION BY
VALERIE M. LATUS

Formac Publishing Company Limited
Halifax

Copyright © 2003 Formac Publishing Company Limited

All rights reserved. No part of this book may be reproduced or transmitted in any form or by any means, electronic or mechanical, including photocopying, or by any information storage or retrieval system, without permission in writing from the publisher.

Formac Publishing Company Limited acknowledges the support of the Cultural Affairs Section, Nova Scotia Department of Tourism and Culture. We acknowledge the financial support of the Government of Canada through the Book Publishing Industry Development Program (BPIDP) for our publishing activities.

We acknowledge the support of the Canada Council for the Arts for our publishing program.

**National Library of Canada Cataloguing in Publication**

Roberts, Theodore Goodridge, 1877-1953.
[Rayton]
    Nell Harley : a backwoods mystery / by Theodore Goodridge Roberts ;
introduction by Valerie Latus.

(Formac fiction treasures)
First published Boston : L.C. Page, 1912 under title: Rayton : a backwoods mystery.
ISBN 0-88780-605-8

    I. Title. II. Title: Rayton. III. Series.

PS8535.O267R37 2003      C813'.52      C2003-905186-2

Formac Publishing Company Limited
5502 Atlantic Street
Halifax, Nova Scotia
B3H 1G4
www.formac.ca

Series editor: Gwendolyn Davies

Printed and bound in Canada

# Presenting Formac Fiction Treasures
*Series Editor: Gwendolyn Davies*

A taste for reading popular fiction expanded in the nineteenth century with the mass marketing of books and magazines. People read rousing adventure stories aloud at night around the fireside; they bought entertaining romances to read while travelling on trains and curled up with the latest serial novel in their leisure moments. Novelists were important cultural figures, with devotees who eagerly awaited their next work.

Among the many successful popular English language novelists of the late 19th and early 20th centuries were a group of Maritimers who found in their own education, travel and sense of history, events and characters capable of entertaining readers on both sides of the Atlantic. They emerged from well-established communities which valued education and culture, for women as well as men. Faced with limited publishing opportunities in the Maritimes, successful writers sought magazine and book publishers in the major cultural centres: New York, Boston, Philadelphia, London, and sometimes Montreal and Toronto. They often enjoyed much success with readers 'at home' but the best of these writers found large audiences across Canada and in the United States and Great Britain.

The Formac Fiction Treasures series is aimed at offering contemporary readers access to books that were successful, often huge bestsellers in their time, but which are now little known and often hard to find. The authors and titles selected are chosen first of all as enjoyable to read, and secondly for the light they shine on historical events and on attitudes and views of the culture from which they emerged. These complete original texts reflect values which are sometimes in conflict with those of today: for example, racism is often evident, and bluntly expressed. This collection of novels is offered as a step towards rediscovering a surprisingly diverse and not nearly well enough known popular cultural heritage of the Maritime provinces and of Canada.

# INTRODUCTION

THROUGHOUT his professional life, Theodore Goodridge Roberts was a prolific writer and notable for the variety of his work. His novels can be classified as backwoods adventures and mysteries, such as *Nell Harley*, historical romances, wartime escapades, South Sea adventures, aboriginal stories and tales specific to Newfoundland and Labrador. He is particularly esteemed for the quality of his poetry. However, his poetry, as well as his fiction, was overshadowed by the literary stature of his brother, Charles G.D. Roberts and of his cousin, Bliss Carman, as well as by the changing tastes of the era in which he wrote. When Theodore was only three, Charles published his seminal work, *Orion*. Perhaps this event inspired the younger Roberts to begin his literary career; at the age of eleven he had a poem published in a prominent New York magazine, *The Century*. During his career, Theodore published thirty-five novels, four books of poetry, and more than a hundred articles. While some of his writing is directed at young readers, most of it has energy and an interest level that appeal to people of all ages. Although much of his work has been found only in university library stacks and special collections, there is, nevertheless, a selection still available.

The challenge that Theodore Goodridge Roberts faced was that strong family ties both benefited and hampered him. In 1897, Charles contrived to find employment for both his brothers, Will and Theodore, and they were appointed sub-editors of *The Independent* in New York; in addition, they all lived in the same boarding house. There were many examples of Charles demonstrating the solicitude of a big brother for his siblings. In 1931, he wrote to several friends requesting "a little 'show'" for Theodore in Toronto where the latter was giving a public lecture. In 1933, Charles was again writing to friends on Theodore's behalf, this time to solicit support for Theodore's candidacy as a fellow of the Royal Society of Canada. Charles had a true regard for his brother's literary talents, calling Theodore's newly published book of verse, *The Lost Shipmate*, "exquisite stuff" and declaring that "in authentic *essentially poetic* quality he ranks with our very best."

During their literary careers, both Charles and Theodore experienced the distress associated with lack of adequate remuneration for their efforts. Charles, at his lowest financial point, was "living largely on porridge" and said bluntly that he would prefer a pension to a knighthood (he eventually received both). Thus it is hardly surprising that during more lucrative times, Charles helped alleviate Theodore's own financial embarrassments with loans. Despite being very different in temperament, they enjoyed each other's company. (Charles was, according to biographer John Coldwell Adams, more optimistic, whereas Thede — the family's

## Introduction                vii

name for Theodore — was more cynical and difficult to please.) The brothers spent several periods of their adult lives in close physical proximity. During the First World War, both Theodore and Charles enlisted, and were mutually concerned about each other's health and safety. Charles discouraged another family member from enlisting, saying that he and Theodore were enough sacrifice for the family.

Despite the inherent affection between the two brothers, Theodore in his later years resented the recognition given his older brother — sometimes rather stringently. When journalist Wilfred Eggleston met Thede in 1931 he was shocked by the vehemence with which the writer "deflated the popular image of his famous older brother in a diatribe which lasted several minutes."

Theodore's older brother was not the only family member who was renowned for literary and academic abilities and achievements. His grandfather was the headmaster of Fredericton Collegiate for forty years, while his father was the Rector of St. Ann's Parish and Canon of Christ Church Cathedral. In addition to the literary feats of Charles, and his cousin Bliss Carman, Theodore's other brother, William Carman, and his sister, Jane Elizabeth, published a book of verse, *Northland Lyrics*, with Theodore. The artistic tradition continued in Theodore's own family; of his four children, one became a well-known artist, while another achieved prominence as a poet.

Theodore Goodridge Roberts' own life provided him

with much of the material and knowledge to lay the foundations of his novels; his fertile imagination did the rest. While Theodore did attend university from 1894 to 1896, he did not complete his degree; the lure of the publishing world proved too strong for him. After he took the post of sub-editor at *The Independent*, he went as a war correspondent to cover the Cuban conflict. While there, he contracted a severe case of malaria and was sent home to Fredericton with a pessimistic prognosis. Several operations followed and his recovery owed much to the devoted nursing of Frances Seymour Allen whom he married some years later.

After recovering from malaria, Roberts moved to St. John's, Newfoundland, where he established and edited *The Newfoundland Magazine*. He seized the opportunity to travel around the coast of Newfoundland and Labrador, and also to voyage into the interior of the country. In the summer of 1901 the author made a five-month round-trip voyage on the full-rigged barkentine *The Flora* from St. John's to Pernambuco, Brazil.

After their marriage in 1904, Frances and Theodore travelled to Barbados but decided it was not an appropriate place to bring up a family. Roberts then made a conscious decision not to remain near the literary mecca of New York, but instead based his family in Fredericton. Nevertheless, Theodore seems to have inherited the same wanderlust as his brother Charles, and the family moved frequently. In 1909 they lived in England; in 1910 they spent time in France, at Pontlevoy. This latter sojourn was at the suggestion of

# Introduction

Charles, who felt it would be a suitable place for Theodore to write.

In 1914 he enlisted in the $12^{th}$ Battalion of the Canadian Expeditionary Force. Salisbury Plain was his temporary home, but he was fortunate to be joined in England by his wife and children. However, the effect of his war-time experiences in Europe was later evident in poems reflecting the horrors he witnessed during those four years. In time, the family lived in Quebec, in Ontario and in Nova Scotia. In 1932 they also travelled to the Caribbean and the Panama Canal.

In *Nell Harley*, the reader is taken into the world Theodore knew and loved best of all. While the city of Fredericton always maintained a place in his heart (he is buried in Forest Hill Cemetery in Fredericton), the author also loved the rural areas of New Brunswick, in particular the St. John River Valley. Like Rayton, in *Nell Harley*, the "peace of the frost-nipped, sun-steeped wilderness soothed and healed his spirit.... He loved it all — every stump, shadow, sound, and soaring wall of it, every flickering wing and furtive call, every scent, tone and silence." Nevertheless, Theodore was not sentimental about life in the backwoods. He understood that hunting, fishing and trapping were businesses from which people earn their livelihoods.

*Nell Harley* was published in 1912 under the title *Rayton, A Backwoods Mystery*. By that time hunting and fishing camps were well established in several areas of New Brunswick by outfitters who could earn a good stipend for guiding wealthy Americans around the lakes and forests. In the novel, Davy Marsh does just that; he caters to hunters like Mr. Banks with his "patent range finders and seventeen different kinds of rifles." In both fiction and non-fiction great care was taken to preserve the desirability of the New Brunswick camps for rich Americans. For example, when Mr. Banks goes missing, not only are the locals concerned about the man, they also understand that to protect their reputation they must find him "or there'll be terrible things printed in the New York papers about this here settlement."

In 1900, Canada consisted of seven provinces and two territories. The Laurier government had begun an ambitious plan to promote settlement in the country and Clifford Sifton, a Manitoban, was charged with the tasks of expansion and western settlement. Between 1900 and 1914, of three million immigrants to Canada almost one million were from Great Britain, 750,000 were from the United States (many were returning Canadians), and more than 500,000 were from continental Europe. While Sifton focussed on the western provinces, echoes of this plan were evident in New Brunswick, with the intention of attracting farmers. However, the lack of arable land was a problem that turned settlers to other occupations, such as lumbering. Also significant were ship building and fishing. Many settlers, in a manner similar to the fictional Jim Harley in this novel, farmed in summer but made their livelihoods in lumber camps in winter. Early settlers in New Brunswick were not driven by religious persecution, economic distress or resistance to the Crown. These factors produced a population that was conservative in general character although still pioneer in spirit and North American in outlook.

This novel reflects contemporary views on class and race. Being called a gentleman, or a gentlewoman, was valued, as was a love of tradition. Rayton, an Englishman, reflects this approach in his remarks to Captain Wigmore, also an outsider: "You seem to be — if you'll pardon my saying it — of quite another world than these simple people."

In rural New Brunswick, women were to be protected and were expected to marry to suit their respective stations in life. David Marsh is vehemently defensive about being viewed by Nell's brother Jim as an unworthy match for Nell. He muses that anyone "with half an eye could see that she and Jim came of a stock that was pretty special. That would attract the Englishman, no doubt, for he, too, looked and talked like something extra in the way of breed." Jim declares that while Dick Goodine may be a good-hearted fellow he is neither refined nor educated enough to marry Nell. Dick Goodine holds no illusions; he says to Rayton, "But don't think that I'm even expectin' to be good enough for her.... You are more the kind she ought to marry."

While Nell Harley exhibits some 'spunk,' it is the men who dominate the action. Nell acts impetuously enough when she goes to visit Rayton after his accident, but her conduct, which is described half-seriously as "brazen" by her sister in law, is tempered by averted glances and the occasional tear. The inherent propriety of Nell's actions is contrasted with the trickery of Maggie Leblanc, who is of French, English and Maliseet descent.

In *Nell Harley*, the characters who grew up in Samson's Mill Settlement typify the native New Brunswicker of Roberts' era; Rayton and Captain Wigmore are the interlopers in that world. The locals have an "absolute respectability" whereas the outsiders, Rayton and Wigmore, are "absolutely at their ease" and either enhance or threaten the conservative life of the local people. The standards set for gentlemen were based on bravery, loyalty, truth, and fair play. When he feels Jim has been unfairly stigmatized by Nash, Rayton, the quintessential gentleman, calls Nash a "bounder" and a liar. Although Nash throws the first punch and Rayton is victorious, Rayton feels that he has let himself down by forgetting his manners. While the gentlemanly Rayton is an asset to the neighbourhood, the mysterious Wigmore brings insecurity. He is not, in fact, an outsider in origin but a deviant native element. Rather than benefitting him, exotic travel has warped Wigmore. Here is the motif of the crazed seaman, which Roberts uses elsewhere in his writing. It occurs, for example, in *Comrades of the Trails* and is also the focus of his poem "The Mad Sailor." As Martin Ware writes in *That Far River: Selected Poems of Theodore Goodridge Roberts*, there is an "intense romanticism and the same painful but sometimes funny awareness of a culture which on occasion is fiercely philistine."

## Introduction xiii

Evidence of how incursion by outsiders from overseas may be either positive or negative appears again in the author's *Comrades of the Trails*, a novel which includes elements similar to those found in *Nell Harley*. In *Comrades*, Dick Ramsey's voyage to New Brunswick is detailed, at first by comfort, with "snug and speedy railway carriages" across England, then a "great Canadian liner"; he recalls steaming up the St. Lawrence River to Quebec and reaching the "unknown land of his dreams by means of three railways." The trip becomes harder in the new world, however: Wolf's Landing to McDodd's Camp, a distance of twenty-five miles by sled, takes two days; both men and horses arrive covered in black mud from the difficulties of that journey. It is in a lumber camp, in the forests of New Brunswick, and through the assistance of the aboriginal Sober Sam, that Dick Ramsey comes to manhood. He learns survival skills and how to suffer with fortitude. Similarly, the gentlemanly Rayton, being already endowed with the necessary codes, has them honed in the forests of New Brunswick. He shows common sense and decency, an aptitude for woodland skills and a readiness to accept the quiet life he will share with Nell.

Although the language of *Nell Harley* may seem antiquated in some instances (pasteboards for playing cards, haw-haw for laughter), and some attitudes archaic (notably those toward women and people of other cultures, as well as the idea that fairly copious quantities of alcohol can restore one's physical health after some deprivation), those were the prevailing attitudes when the novel was written. The reader can revel in a gripping tale in which the natural world is resplendent — though not to be taken lightly — and qualities of loyalty, truthfulness, bravery and fair play are valued. *Nell Harley* portrays life in Goodridge Roberts' beloved New Brunswick and reflects an era in which settlers added to the well-being and growth of both a community and of a province, while enriching their own lives in the process.

> Valerie M. Latus
> Windsor, Nova Scotia
> 2003

# CONTENTS

| CHAPTER | | PAGE |
|---|---|---|
| I. | THE GAME THAT WAS NOT FINISHED | 1 |
| II. | JIM HARLEY TELLS AN OLD STORY | 17 |
| III. | DAVID MARSH DECIDES TO SPEAK — AND DOESN'T | 33 |
| IV. | THE TRAPPER'S CONFESSION | 46 |
| V. | DOCTOR NASH'S SUSPICIONS — YOUNG MARSH'S MISFORTUNE | 61 |
| VI. | DAVID TAKES A MISFORTUNE IN A POOR SPIRIT | 76 |
| VII. | MR. BANKS TAKES A HAND IN THE GAME | 91 |
| VIII. | RAYTON GOES TO BORROW A SAUCEPAN | 107 |
| IX. | RAYTON CONFESSES | 122 |
| X. | RED CROSSES AGAIN | 138 |
| XI. | AN UNFORTUNATE MOMENT FOR THE DOCTOR | 154 |
| XII. | RAYTON IS REMINDED OF THE RED CROSSES | 169 |
| XIII. | CAPTAIN WIGMORE SUGGESTS AN AMAZING THING | 184 |
| XIV. | FEAR FORGOTTEN — AND RECALLED | 200 |
| XV. | MR. BANKS IS STUNG | 215 |
| XVI. | THE LITTLE CAT AND THE BIG MOUSE | 230 |
| XVII. | AN ASTONISHING DISCOVERY | 245 |
| XVIII. | DICK GOODINE RETURNS UNEXPECTEDLY | 260 |
| XIX. | THE CAPTAIN'S CHARGE | 275 |
| XX. | THE CHOSEN INSTRUMENT OF FATE | 291 |
| XXI. | THE DEATH OF THE CURSE | 302 |
| XXII. | IN THE WAY OF HAPPINESS | 312 |

# LIST OF ILLUSTRATIONS

| | |
|---|---|
| Nell Harley | Frontispiece |
| "Jim Harley snatched up the card" | 4 |
| "He advanced slowly, painfully, a pitiful figure" | 72 |
| "Plunged at Rayton, with his fists flying" | 164 |
| "Then he halted and recoiled, clutching at the cold walls!" | 232 |

# CHAPTER I

### THE GAME THAT WAS NOT FINISHED

SAMSON's Mill Settlement had, for the past fifteen years, prided itself on its absolute respectability; and then came Reginald Baynes Rayton, with his unfailing good humor, his riding breeches, and constant "haw-haw" — and corrupted the community. So it happened that five representative men of the settlement, and Mr. Rayton, sat and played poker one October night in Rayton's snug living room. They had done it before — only last week, in fact — but the sense of guilty novelty had not yet worn off. Only Rayton and old Wigmore were absolutely at their ease. White beans had to do in the place of the usual chips. The standard of play was very moderate — a one-cent *ante* and a five-cent *limit* — but it seemed reckless to some of those representative citizens.

"Jane questioned me pretty sharp, to-night," said Benjamin Samson, the owner of the mill that sawed lumber and ground buckwheat for the whole Beaver Brook valley; "but I give her a bagful of evasive answers. Yes, sir-ee! I guess she suspicioned something. She's been kinder expectin' me to fall from grace ever since she first married me."

"Haw-haw!" brayed Mr. Rayton. "Mrs. Samson is a clever woman. She knows a bad egg, Benjamin, without having to break the shell."

The others chuckled.

"She ain't as smart as you think," replied Samson, awkwardly shuffling the cards, "for at last I said to her, 'I'm goin' to see Rayton,' says I. 'He's started a kinder lit'ry club for his male friends.' 'Then you'll learn no harm from him,' says she, 'for I'm sure his morals is as good as his manners. The way he lifts his hat to me is a regular treat. *He* knows what's my due, even if some other folks don't,' says she."

Five men, including Samson himself, roared at this; but Rayton's haw-haw lacked, for once, its usual heartiness.

# The Game That Was Not Finished 3

"Oh, come now," he protested shamefacedly. "It's not just the thing to — to be making fun of a lady. Of course I raise my hat to Mrs. Samson. Proud to do it, I'm sure; and I'm glad she appreciates it. Harley, you are banker, I think. Pass me over fifty beans. Benjamin, when you've finished shoveling those cards about — I don't call it shuffling — give us a chance to cut for deal."

Jim Harley, a shrewd man of about thirty years of age, who farmed in the summer and operated in the lumber woods, on a small but paying scale, in the winter months, counted out beans to the company in return for quarters and dimes. Samson shot the cards across the table, backs up, and every one drew. Old Captain Wigmore won the deal. He brought the cards together in a neat pile with one sweep of the hand, shuffled them swiftly and skillfully, and dealt so fast as to keep three in the air at once. It was a pleasure to watch him. Even Rayton was a fumbler with the pasteboards beside him.

The six picked up their cards and looked at them, each in a way characteristic of him. Honest Benjamin, catching sight of two kings and feeling Doctor Nash's prying glance upon him, struggled to hide a smirk of satisfaction that was too strong for him. Rayton beamed; but that might mean anything. Old Wigmore's bewhiskered face expressed nothing, as usual. The other visages showed hope or disgust as plainly as if the words were printed across them. Discards were thrown to the centre of the table, and Wigmore distributed others.

"What—?" queried young David Marsh, and immediately relapsed into silence.

"What *what?*" asked Rayton.

"Oh, it will keep," replied Marsh.

"Davy wants to know if four aces are any good?" suggested the doctor, winking at Rayton.

Benjamin Samson, torn with doubt, ventured three beans on the chances of his pair of kings. That started things briskly; but on the second round David Marsh went the limit. That brought things to a standstill, and the pool went to David without a challenge; but he showed his cards for all that.

"What I want to know is, who's marked this six of clubs?" he asked. "That's what I began to ask, a minute back," he added, looking at Doctor Nash.

"Four of a kind," murmured Samson enviously.

"But look at the six of clubs," urged Marsh.

*"Jim Harley snatched up the card"*

"Look at the two red crosses in the middle of it, will you!"

All got to their feet and stared down at the card.

"What's it for?" demanded David Marsh. "If it was marked on the back, now, it might be of some use. I've heard of such things."

"The marks weren't there last night," said Rayton, "for I was playing patience with this very pack and would have seen them."

At that moment Jim Harley snatched up the card and held it close to his eyes. "Hell!" he exclaimed. "The red crosses!"

They gazed at him in astonishment, and saw that his face was colorless under the tan. The stout, excitable Benjamin laughed hysterically and fingered a pocket of his curving vest to make sure that his watch was still there. He felt very uneasy; but perhaps Jim was only playing a trick on them? That was not like Jim — but who can say what a man may not do who has fallen to poker playing? Old Captain Wigmore shared this suspicion evidently.

"Very amusing, James," he said. "You would have made a first-rate actor. But suppose we go on with the game. Have you another deck, Reginald — one that our smart young friend has not had a chance to monkey with?"

"Do you mean that I marked this one?" cried Harley. "What the devil would I do that for? Why, you — you old idiot, I'd sooner break my leg than see —— But what's the good of talkin'?"

Old Wigmore sighed patiently, sat down, and began to fill his pipe. The others stared at Jim Harley in amazed consternation. They saw that he was not joking and so thought that he had suddenly become insane.

"Yes, I quite agree with you, Jim," said Doctor Nash soothingly. "Captain Wigmore is an old idiot, beyond a doubt, and it is a most remarkable thing that the card should be marked with two red crosses. Sit down and tell me all about it, like a good fellow."

"You go chase yourself, doc," returned the other unpleasantly. "You think I'm off my nut, I guess; but I'm saner than *you* are — by a long sight."

"I never knew you to act so queer before, Jim," complained Benjamin Samson. "You give me the twists, you do. Wish I'd stayed home, after all. This card playin' ain't healthy, I guess."

"Have a drink, Jim. Something has upset you," said Rayton.

## The Game That Was Not Finished 7

Harley accepted a glass of whisky and water. Then he sat down and again examined the six of clubs, the others watching him keenly.

"Oh, of course it's all foolishness!" he exclaimed. "But it gave me a turn, I must say — and it being dealt to Dave, and all that. Looked queer, for a minute, I must say. But I guess Mr. Rayton just marked it with red ink and forgot all about it."

Rayton shook his head. "Sorry," he replied, "but there's not a drop of red ink in the house."

"Then some one else did it," said Harley. "It just *happened*, that's all. No good in talking about it! Go on with the game, boys. I'll just go home and get to bed."

"No, you don't, my son," cried Doctor Nash. "You'll just sit where you are and tell us what all this rot is about. You've interrupted our game, and now you have to explain things. You hinted that it was strange that the marked card should go to Davy Marsh. Now what did you mean by that? You've got something on your mind, I'll bet a dollar."

"I'm going home," repeated Harley firmly. "Are you stepping, too, Davy? I want to have a word with you."

"Yes, I'll come," replied Marsh. He turned to the doctor and whispered: "Safer to have somebody along with him, I guess. He don't seem himself, to-night."

"I'm off, too," said Samson. "I don't feel right, I can tell you. Jim, your queer actions has upset me. Wish I'd stayed quietly at home, with Jane, and read last week's newspaper like a respectable Christian."

"I'm stepping, too," said the doctor. "It's my duty to keep an eye on him, Rayton," he added, in an aside to his host.

The man who had caused the disturbance went over to Rayton and shook his hand. His tanned cheeks had not yet regained the glow of health and vitality that was usual to them.

"I guess I've broken up your party by my foolishness," he said, "and I'm all-fired sorry. I wasn't myself, for a minute — nor I don't feel quite right, even now. I don't know that I'm free to explain my actions. If I am I'll let you know just how it was, next time I see you."

"Not another word, my dear fellow," returned Rayton. "I'm sorry you have to go, of course — but don't worry about it. And hang explaining! Don't tell me a word you don't want to. No doubt

## The Game That Was Not Finished 9

it's a private superstition of some kind — or something of that sort. Why, there was my poor old pater — and he was a parson — always got into a funk if three rooks perched on top of his hat — or something of that kind. So I understand, Jim. I'll look at the cards, next time, before we begin playing."

Reginald Baynes Rayton did not often say so much in one burst. It cost him a serious effort.

"I believe you *do* understand," said Harley gratefully. "You've shot mighty close to the mark, anyhow. I guess you're smarter than some people give you credit for, Mr. Rayton."

It was not until four of his guests had been sped into the night with kindly words, that Rayton realized Jim Harley's tactless but well-meant remark.

"Hah-hah!" he laughed. "That was too bad. Hah-hah!"

"What are you braying about, now, Reginald?" asked old Wigmore, who still sat at the table, smoking his pipe and gazing at the scattered cards.

"A joke of Harley's. It was quite unintentional, I think," returned Rayton.

The old man shot a keen glance at the other from

under his shaggy eyebrows. "Those marks on the card seemed to hit him hard," he remarked. "I can't make it out. He is a prosperous, steady-going chap, without any crazy notions or troubles, and very clear-headed, I have always heard. Now, why should two red marks on the six of clubs cause him to make a fool of himself? It was young Marsh, I believe, who had the card dealt to him."

"Yes, David Marsh got the card," replied Rayton.

"Then why didn't he raise a row, if there's anything terrible in those marks?"

"It did not mean anything to him, evidently; but I'd swear it did to Harley. I've heard of such things at home in England. I don't take any stock in them myself."

"Neither do I. But it's queer that the marks should have been there."

"Yes," said Rayton, and stepped over to the table.

"You needn't look for the card," said the old man. "Nash took it away with him. Last fall he tracked a moose across a plowed field, and he has considered himself something of a detective ever since."

The young Englishman laughed with a pre-

## The Game That Was Not Finished 11

occupied note. He stood in front of the open stove, warming the seat of his London-cut breeches.

"It is queer that those marks should be there," he said, "but it is still queerer that they should put Harley in such a wax. Suppose *I* had put the crosses there, for instance — well, the thing would be just as queer, wouldn't it? A knowledge of how the marks got on the card would not explain Harley's behavior."

"You are right," returned the old man dryly. "'And Harley was right, too, when he said that you are not such a fool as the people of Samson's Mill Settlement think you."

Rayton laughed frankly.

"You spoke of not having a drop of red ink in the house; but you did not mention — to me, at least — a drop of anything else," continued the other.

"I beg your pardon!" exclaimed Rayton. "This mystery has quite muddled me. I'm awfully sorry, really."

He bustled about and placed a bottle of whisky, a jug of fresh water, and two glasses on the table.

"Don't apologize, Reginald," said Wigmore, with a thin smile. "It is not often you forget to offer hospitality. The fact is, you are a bit too hospitable. You'll be giving away the clothes off your back next — even those elegant looking pants, perhaps."

"Oh, come now!" remonstrated the younger man, pulling at his straw-colored mustache, and grinning sheepishly.

"You must have a pot of money, Reginald," said the other.

"Heavens! No!"

"Then why did you give all that tea and sugar to that old squaw, Molly Canadian — and two barrels of potatoes to Frank Gorman?"

"How do you know that?" cried Rayton, astonished.

The captain helped himself to whisky. "I keep my eyes about me," he said complacently. "I know pretty much everything that goes on 'round this settlement."

"Then I wish you knew the secret of Jim Harley's queer behavior to-night — and how that card came to be marked," replied Rayton.

The old man laughed aloud — a thing that was rare with him. "That is asking too much," he said. "I'm not a wizard, Reginald. But I venture to say that, if I gave my mind to it, I'd have the

## The Game That Was Not Finished

mystery entirely solved before that Smart Alec of a Nash has so much as picked up the right scent."

"I quite believe you," returned Rayton. "Do you know, captain," he added, smiling frankly, "I wonder at your living in this place. You seem to be — if you'll pardon my saying it — of quite another world than these simple people."

"And what about you, Reginald?"

"Oh, I'm just an ordinary chap. Came out here to farm — and here I am. All this suits me to the tick — working in the fields, fishing, feeding cattle, and moose shooting. But you are not a farmer, and why you should have selected Samson's Mill Settlement to live in, after the life you must have lived, beats me. You have no relations here. I can't understand it, captain."

Old Wigmore got to his feet, his gray beard aquiver with anger. "Really, sir," he cried, "what business is it of yours where I choose to live? Damn it all! — really, I did not expect you, at least, of prying into my affairs. Where are my hat and coat? Thanks for your whisky — which might be better — and good night to you."

"Oh, I say! Don't go, captain!" cried the good-natured Rayton; but the old man had already stepped briskly from the room. In another moment, the door banged behind him.

"Now that's too bad, really," soliloquized the Englishman. "Gad! I wouldn't have offended him, intentionally, for fifty dollars. But he is a cranky old Johnny, I must say."

He filled his pipe, cleared the cards from the table, and sat down before the crackling stove. Old Wigmore's show of temper soon gave way, in his mind, to the more startling and mysterious events of the evening. The marks on the card were strange enough; but the way in which the sight of those marks had affected Jim Harley was altogether extraordinary. It was not what he would have expected from Harley — or from any one in the settlement, for that matter. The incident smacked of the Wild West of fiction rather than of the real backwoods of New Brunswick. And Harley was such a sensible fellow, too; hard-working, prosperous, with a fine wife, two children, and such a delightful sister. Yes, a charming sister! And yet he had flown clean off the handle at sight of two little red marks on the face of the six of clubs. Really, it was preposterous! Idiotic! Perhaps the poor chap was ill — on the verge of a nervous breakdown from overwork? Or perhaps some silly

## The Game That Was Not Finished 15

old superstition was to blame for the distressing incident?

"Well, it beats me to a standstill," he murmured, at last; "but I think Jim Harley will feel like a fool when he wakes up to-morrow morning and remembers what an ass he has made of himself. I hope the other fellows have kept him from making a scene at home and frightening that fine little sister of his — or his wife, either, of course."

Then Mr. Rayton closed the drafts of the stove, fastened doors and windows, and went upstairs to bed.

In the meantime, Jim Harley had walked up and down the country roads for an hour and a half before he had convinced Doctor Nash and Benjamin Samson that he was not insane, not feverish, and not to be forced into an explanation of his remarkable behavior at Rayton's. They went off to their homes at last, Samson disheartened, Nash sarcastic. Then Harley turned to young David Marsh.

"Davy," he said, "I don't want you to think I have gone cracked in the upper story; but I can't tell you, just now, why I've been acting so queer to-night. I got a scare — but I guess there's nothing to it. Anyhow, I want you to keep clear of my place for a day or two — to keep clear of Nell."

"What's that!" exclaimed Marsh indignantly. "Keep clear of your place, is it? What the devil is the matter with me — or with you? You think I ain't good enough for your sister, do you — because you've got some money and I haven't. Damn your place!"

## CHAPTER II

#### JIM HARLEY TELLS AN OLD STORY

Jim Harley groaned. "Davy, you are all wrong," he said gloomily. "Hang it all, man, don't be a fool! Don't go and make things worse for me. I don't know just how Nell feels for you, but I like you first-rate — pretty near as well as any young fellow I've ever met. But — but it's for your own good, Davy. It's about that card going to you, don't you see? That sounds crazy — but I'm not crazy."

"The card? Dang the card!" returned David. "What d'ye take me for, Jim Harley, to try to scare me with such fool talk as that? You acted darn well to-night, I must say; but I guess I see your game. You've invented some sort of fairy story to try to scare me away from Nell. And so you marked that card. Red crosses on a card! D'ye take me for a darn, ignorant Injun or half-breed? Oh, you can't fool me! You want to catch that hee-haw Englishman for Nell, I guess."

Harley grabbed the younger man by the shoulder with fingers like the jaws of a fox trap for strength. "You blasted young idiot!" he cried, his voice trembling with anger. "D'ye think I'd take the trouble to monkey with cards, and all that sort of tommyrot, if I wanted to scare you away from my sister? No, David Marsh, I'd just tell you to keep clear — and if you didn't I'd knock the stuffin' out of you. I guess you know me well enough to believe *that*."

"I don't know what to believe," returned David sulkily, "except that you're actin' more like a darn, crazy half-breed than a white man, to-night. Let go my shoulder, anyhow, or maybe you'll learn that two can play at that game."

Jim loosed his grip, and let his arm fall to his side. For a full minute they faced each other in silence in the chill half dark of the October night, there on the desolate backwoods road. David Marsh broke the silence:

"I don't want to fight with you, Jim," he said, "but — but I must say this talk of yours about that confounded card, and the way you are actin' to-night, and — and what you just said about Nell — makes me mad as a bobcat. If you can tell me what it is you're drivin' at, for Heaven's sake tell

## Jim Harley Tells an Old Story 19

me quick! I don't want to think you've gone nutty, Jim, and no more do I want to think — to think——"

"What?" asked Harley sharply.

"That you're a liar."

"If you think that, you'd better keep it to yourself!"

"Well, then, I don't think it. But, jumpin' Moses, I must think *something!*"

"I've asked you to keep away from my house, and my sister," returned Harley, "so perhaps I had better explain things to you, as well as I can. Then you can judge for yourself if I'm doing right or not. You'll laugh, I guess — and maybe I'll laugh myself, to-morrow morning. But, first of all, Davy, you must give me your word to keep what I tell you to yourself. Maybe I'll have to tell it to Rayton, if Nell don't object, because of the row I kicked up in his house. That would be only polite, I suppose."

"I'll keep quiet, Jim."

"Let's walk along, to keep warm," said Harley. "It's a long story, Davy, and I guess you'll think it a mighty foolish one."

"Fire away," returned Marsh. "Foolishness is in the air to-night, I reckon."

"Well," began the other slowly, "it starts with my mother's mother. That's kind of a long jump backward, but it can't be helped. It's the way it was told to me. My mother's mother was a pretty fine young woman, I guess, and her parents weren't just the common run — they came from Boston and settled in St. John about the time George Washington got up and hit the other George that smack over the head which we've all read about. Well, the girl grew up a regular beauty, to judge by the way the young fellows carried on about her. Two men led all the others in the running, though. One was a Spaniard, and t'other was an Englishman; and, after a while, it looked as if the Englishman was getting along with the girl better than the Spaniard. The Spaniard called himself a count, or something of that kind.

"One night, at one of those parties the men used to have in those days, after they'd all eaten and drunk about as much as they could hold, they sat down to play cards. I don't know what the game was, but I do know that they used to bet a horse, or a gold watch, or a few acres of land as quick as us fellows will bet five white beans. Well, it happened that the Spanish count and the young Englishman — he was a navy officer, I've heard —

and two more were at the same table. Pretty soon the navy officer got a card dealt to him with *two red crosses* marked on it. I forgot what card it was.

"Well, they didn't make any fuss about it, and went on with the game; but when they were thinking of going home the count got the young fellow by the elbow and whispered something in his ear. The other men didn't hear what it was that he whispered, but every one in the room heard the navy officer's answer — and the lad who afterward married my mother's mother was one of the fellows that heard it. What the Englishman yelled was: 'That's what it means in your country, is it! The devil take you, and your lies, and your damn monkey tricks!' Yes, that's what he yelled, right into the count's yellow face. They drank a terrible lot of liquor in those days. More than was good for them, I reckon."

Jim Harley paused. "It sounds like a crazy sort of yarn to be telling," he said apologetically.

"Go ahead," said David Marsh. "It's a fine yarn, Jim — and your folks must have been pretty big potatoes. It's better than a book. What was it the count whispered to the navy officer?"

"*That* they never found out," replied Jim. "But

the officer told a friend of his — the fellow who got the girl, after all — that the Spaniard was trying to bluff him out of the game — not out of the game of cards, but away from the girl. Anyhow, the count up and let fly a glass of liquor fair into the Englishman's face, just the way it's written in stories. Then there was a rumpus, the Spaniard spitting like a cat, and the other lad trying to smack him in the eye with his fist. But fists weren't considered good enough to fight with, in those days, and it wasn't polite just to pitch in when you felt like it. So they went right out, and off to a field at the edge of the town, and fought a duel with pistols. It was a moonlight night. It looked as if the Spanish count fired half a second too soon — anyhow, he put a hole smash through the Englishman's head. Well, that was too much for the other lads, drunk as most of them were, and they went up to the count and told him that if he wasn't out of the country before sunrise they'd hang him up by the neck like any common murderer. So he went. And he never came back again, as far as I ever heard."

"I guess that happened quite a while ago," said Marsh.

"Yes, a good many years ago. But I've heard

that the old lady talked about it to the day of her death."

"And who was the man she married?"

"Just my grandfather — my mother's father. He was a young lawyer, or something of that kind."

"Well," said Marsh, with a sigh of relief, "that's nothing but ancient history. I wouldn't believe more than half of that even if I had been taught it in school, out of a book. If that's all you've got to say against the red crosses then they don't worry me a mite. Anyway, where's the Spanish count? You'll have to dig up a Spanish count, Jim, afore you can get any change out of me with little red crosses on a playin' card."

"Yes, that is ancient history," replied Harley, "and I won't swear to the truth of it. The duel is true enough, though, for my own father saw it written down in the records. But you've not heard the whole story yet, Davy. The real thing — the part that bothers me — is yet to come."

"By the great horn spoon!" exclaimed Marsh. "And it must be near ten o'clock! Hurry up with the rest of it, Jim — and if it's not any worse than what you've told I'll think you've been makin' a fool of me."

"The rest of the story is about my own **father**

— and my own mother," said Harley. "Nell and I don't talk about it, even to each other; and this is the first time it's been told to any one outside the family. I'd almost forgotten it — till I saw that card to-night. Then it jumped into my mind like — like a flash from hell's flames."

David Marsh felt a sudden embarrassment, and quick chill at his heart.

"Maybe you'd rather not tell it, Jim," he said. "If it's anything bad I'll take your word for it."

"It is bad enough," returned the other, "but it is not disgraceful. I must tell it to you, Davy, and then you can think over what happened tonight and work it out for yourself. It's only right that you should know all that I can tell you — and then, if you think it all foolishness, it's your own funeral."

David could not see his companion's face in the darkness, though he fairly strained his eyes to make it out. He wet his dry lips with his tongue. "I'm listening," he said, and forced an uneasy laugh.

"My mother lived in St. John with her parents, until she married, and moved over to the Miramichi," began Harley. "My father's home was in St. John, too, when he was a young fellow; but he was a sailor in those days and so spent most of his time at sea. He was a smart lad, and no mistake

## Jim Harley Tells an Old Story

— mate of a foreign-goin' bark when he was nineteen and skipper when he was twenty-one. His schooling had been good, and he owned some shares in the ship, so he wasn't one of the common run of shellbacks.

"When he first met my mother he was layin' off a voyage to recover from a dose of malarial fever that had got into his blood down in Brazil. He saw her at a party of some kind; and, not being troubled with shyness, he went right after her. She was a beauty, I guess, like her mother before her — and, like her mother again, there was a whole bunch of young fellows courting her. My father, though, was a fine, upstanding lad, with good looks, fine manners, and a dashing way in everything he did. So he sailed right in; but he didn't have everything all his own way, at first.

"I've heard my mother say that, Sunday evenings, as many as six young men would call at her father's house — and she was the only girl, mind you. But they'd all pretend to be pleased to see each other, and there would be singing, and piano playing, and cake and wine — yes, and the old gent would invite one or two of them into his library to smoke his cigars, and the old lady would talk away to the rest of them about the grand times in

St. John when she was young. Sometimes she'd tell about how the navy officer and the Spanish count fought about her — and, of course, she'd mention the queer marks on the card. She called it a romantic story.

"Well, it wasn't long before my father thought he had the other fellows beaten out, so he popped the question. My mother said 'Yes' — and so the old people announced the engagement. They were pretty stylish, you see. My father was all cured of his malarial fever, by this time, and ready for sea again. About a week after my mother had given him her promise, and only a few days before he expected to have his ship ready for a voyage to the West Indies, he was walking home about ten o'clock in the evening and met a bunch of his friends. They were going to have supper at a hotel and then finish the night at card playing. Well, my father was a light-hearted lad, with a pocketful of money and a taste for jolly company; so he joined the gang. The game they played was whist. Suddenly my father jumped to his feet, his face as red as fire, and tore one of the cards into little bits and flung them on the floor.

"'You may consider that a joke — whoever did

## Jim Harley Tells an Old Story 27

it — but it's a damn poor joke!' he cried. He was a good man, but sometimes he got boiling mad. Some of the lads asked him what was the trouble, and one young fellow picked up the scraps of the torn card and found the two red crosses. 'Some one here knows what the trouble is,' yelled my father, 'and if he'll just stand up and confess to his ungentlemanly joke, I'll smack him across the face for his trouble.'

"Nobody stood up, you may bet your hat on that; but when the lad who had picked up the scraps of card began handing them around, a lot of them began to laugh and jeer, and make fun of the sailor. Most of them had heard the old lady tell about the Spanish count, you know. 'Better make your will,' said one. 'That's a dangerous family to monkey with,' said another. 'Glad I'm not in your boots.' 'It's the Spaniard's ghost.' 'Better break it off, Tom, and look 'round for a safer wife.' 'The other chap who got the red marks was a sailor, too.'

"And so they shouted things at him until he was mad enough to kill somebody. But he couldn't tackle them all. So he called them a lot of hard names. He told them that the sailors aboard his ship had a better idea of a joke and better manners than they had. They began to quiet down, then, and some of them looked mighty red in the face, for every lad there considered himself something pretty extra when it came to style and manners. My father finished by saying that the trick they had played and the things they had said to him were insults to two ladies who had never done any of them a shadow of harm. Most of them jumped up and yelled that they knew nothing about any trick, and hadn't meant to insult any one; but my father just glared and sneered at them, and left the room. He was just a skipper of a sailing ship, but he had been brought up with pretty strict notions about manners, and insults, and those kinds of things.

"He had just reached the street when one of the others — a lad called Jackson — came jumping after him and grabbed him by the back of the neck. This Jackson was as white as paper, he was that mad. 'I'll teach you your proper place, you damn fo'castle swine!' he yelled, striking my father in the face with his free hand. Well, my father jerked himself clear and give him one on the jaw that put him to sleep for an hour or two."

At this, Harley halted in his talk, and his walk,

## Jim Harley Tells an Old Story

at one and the same moment, and began to cut tobacco for his pipe.

"Go ahead!" exclaimed young Marsh.

"Well, all that row was kept quiet," continued Harley. "My father sailed away — and then came a report that pieces of the wreck of his ship had gone ashore on the Bahamas. Then people who knew about the marked card began to talk. It looked as if what the Spanish count had said, in the old days — or what people supposed he had said — had some truth in it. His girl — she who was afterward my mother — nearly went crazy. Then, one fine day, my father turned up, sound as a bell — the only survivor of the wreck of his ship. He got his share of the underwriter's money, and invested it in a one-third interest in another and smaller vessel. He had no trouble in getting the job of skipper of her; but he had plenty of trouble with his sweetheart and her parents, for they were all sure that the red crosses were really the marks of the devil and had caused the loss of his ship. My father laughed at them; and well he might, since his ship had gone down in a hurricane that had wrecked half a dozen other vessels, and he was the only man to be saved from all his crew. 'If the devil had anything to do with it,' he said, 'he certainly made a mess of it.' But it took him a whole week to calm them down and get the girl's promise to marry him on his return from his next voyage.

"On the very night before he was to sail, when he was on his way to the ship from saying good-by to my mother and the old people, a man sprang out from behind a pile of lumber on one of the wharves, and struck at him; but my father jumped back in time and struck in return with a loaded stick which he carried. The man let a yelp of pain out of him, and ran up the wharf to the dark streets of the city. My father struck a light and presently found something that he had heard drop on the planks when the fellow yelped — a long knife with a point sharp as a needle.

"He went aboard his ship, wrote a letter, packed up the knife in a box, and first thing in the morning sent both letter and knife ashore to a magistrate. Then he sailed away. He returned after three months, with a cargo of sugar and molasses — and his left arm in a sling. He had been stabbed, one night, in Bridgetown, Barbados. That was a thing that did not often happen in Barbados.

"Immediately upon his return, he made quiet inquiries for young Mr. Jackson. But Jackson had

## Jim Harley Tells an Old Story 31

gone away, months before. There had been some talk about the police going to look for Jackson too, just about the time my father had sailed away. My father never gave the red crosses two thoughts; but he often remembered the look in Jackson's face that night they had fought in the street after the game of cards.

"Well, they married, and my father gave up the sea, moved to the mouth of the Miramichi, and started shipbuilding. That was on my mother's account. He did a good business, and they were happy. I was their first child. Five years later, Nell came. About six months after that an envelope was left at the house for him by a poor old half-witted character in the town, who had once been a sailor. When my father came home from the office he opened the envelope — and out fell a blue-backed playing card onto the carpet. My mother went into a dead faint, without waiting to see the face of it. When my father turned it over, there were the two red crosses!"

"Did they catch Jackson?" asked David Marsh.

"No," returned Harley. "My father ran out of the house, maybe to find the poor half-wit who had brought it to him, and he was shot dead within ten yards of his own door."

"By Jackson?" cried David, in a husky voice.

"It must have been. No one was caught. The shock killed my mother. That is the story, Davy. There wasn't much money for Nell and me, by the time I was old enough to notice things — and we came here, as you know, nine years ago."

"But — who'd want to play the old trick on me?" asked Marsh anxiously. "And who is there here that knows anything about it? Jackson? What would *he* care about Nell and me?"

"Some rival, perhaps," suggested Harley. "The devil only knows! Perhaps some one who dislikes you knows the old story; but — don't ask me," he added nervously.

"There is Dick Goodine, the trapper," said Marsh. "He is sweet on Nell. But what does he know — and how could he do it? Hell! Jim, it beats me!"

## CHAPTER III

DAVID MARSH DECIDES TO SPEAK — AND DOESN'T

JIM HARLEY decided, before morning, that he must tell the tragic story to Rayton. He also decided that there was no need, at present, of telling either Nell or his wife of the mysterious advent of the two red marks into Samson's Mill Settlement.

Young David Marsh spent a restless night, going over and over all that Jim had told him. He came to the conclusion, at last, that the red crosses themselves were harmless, and utterly foolish, and that the real danger and tragedy lay in the human fate that had always inspired their appearance. Then his active mind quested far and near in search of an enemy of his own to correspond with the Spanish count of the first tragedy, and with young Jackson of the second — and not only that, but he must find an enemy who was in love with Nell Harley, and who knew the story of the red crosses. He thought of every man he had ever met, young and middle-aged; but he soon saw that this was too wide a field to explore. He could only bring to mind one man who, to his certain knowledge, had paid any attention to Nell Harley — and this was Dick Goodine. Likewise, he could think of only one man in the community with whom he was not on fairly friendly terms — and this, too, was Goodine.

Goodine had French blood in his veins, and was known to be eccentric; but he had never been considered dangerous in any way. He was a good-looking young woodsman who spent his summers in idleness, and his winters in trapping furs. Sometimes he did a little business in David Marsh's own chosen field, and guided "sports" into the wilderness after moose and caribou. But this was not often, for Dick Goodine's pride was even quicker than his temper. "It's not white men's work," he had said to David, not long before, in the course of the very argument that had caused the coolness that now existed between them. "It's Injun's work — or nigger's. The guidin' is good enough; but when it comes to cookin' for them, and pullin' off their wet boots at night — oh, t' hell with it! It may suit you, but it don't suit me."

But how should Dick Goodine know anything

about the story of the red crosses, even if the state of his feelings had become sufficiently violent to incite him to make use of them? And he had not been at Rayton's, last night. How could he have marked the card? So David dismissed the trapper from his mind, for the time, and turned elsewhere for a solution of the mystery.

There was young Rayton, the Englishman. The thing had happened in his house, and the marked card belonged to him. He was a stranger to the settlement, for he had been only six months in the place. He seemed honest and harmless — but that was not enough to clear him. The dazzling smile, clear, gray eyes, and ready haw-haw might cover an unscrupulous and vicious nature. What was known in Samson's Mill Settlement of his past? Nothing but a few unlikely sounding anecdotes of his own telling. He had traveled in other parts of the province, looking for a farm that suited both his tastes and his purse, so he might very easily have heard something of the fate of Jim Harley's father.

So far, so good! But was he in love with Nell Harley? He had shown no signs of it, certainly; and yet if he took an interest in any young woman in the settlement, or within ten miles of it in any direction, it would naturally be in Nell Harley. She was well educated — and so was the Englishman, seemingly. No one had ever denied her quiet beauty. Any one with half an eye could see that she and Jim came of a stock that was pretty special. That would attract the Englishman, no doubt, for he, too, looked and talked like something extra in the way of breed. But, in spite of all this, David had to admit to himself that he had neither heard nor seen anything to lead him to suppose that Rayton was his rival.

Well, who else, then? What about Doctor Nash? Nash was a bachelor, and a great hand at making himself agreeable with the women. But David knew that Nell did not like Nash; but, of course, a little thing like that wouldn't bother Nash if he had taken a fancy in that direction. Yes, the doctor might be the man. The idea was worth keeping in sight. David could not bring any other suspect to mind. Benjamin Samson and old Wigmore had been there when the marked card made its appearance, 'tis true; but, in spite of his anxiety to solve the mystery, David put these two harmless gentlemen from his thoughts with a chuckle.

At last David Marsh was on the verge of sleep

## David Marsh Decides to Speak

when a sudden, galling question flashed into his mind and prodded him wide awake again. Why should anybody who might be in love with Nell Harley look upon him — upon David Marsh — as a dangerous rival? Why, indeed! He was sweet on Nell, there was no denying it, and had been for the past three years or more, and no doubt there had been talk about his frequent calls at Jim's house; but had she ever treated him as anything but just a good friend? Not once. He was honest enough with himself to admit this, but it hurt his vanity. And had he ever told her that he loved her? No. He had meant to, over and over again; but, somehow, things had never seemed to be exactly in line for the confession. The fact is, there was something in the young woman's frank manner with him, and in the straightforward glance of her eyes, that always made him feel that next time would do. He had never even found sufficient courage to try to hold her hand.

"I guess she likes me, though," he murmured. "I'll go to-morrow and tell her how I feel toward her. Yes, by thunder! I'll show the fellow who fixed that card trick on me that I ain't scared of him — nor of her, neither. Why should I be scared of her? I'm honest — and I'm making good money — and Jim likes me, all right. That card trick settles it, by ginger! I'll go and tell her to-morrow. I'll give that skunk a run for his money, whoever he may be."

As much in the dark as ever about the mystery of the marked card, but fully determined on his course of action as regards Miss Harley, David Marsh fell asleep at last. His alarm clock had been set for six, however, as he had a busy day before him; so he was soon awake again. He sat up, grumbling, and lit the little oil lamp that stood on a chair beside his bed. There was no turning over and going to sleep again for him, for he had to get a load of provisions and some kit in to his camp on Teakettle Brook before night; for he was expecting a sportsman from the States along in a few days. From the nearer camp be would have to portage a lot of grub across a half mile of bad trail and take it up, by canoe, to his shack on the headwaters of Dan's River.

"I've got to hustle!" he exclaimed, and jumped courageously out of his warm bed; but the instant his feet struck the cold floor, the queer happenings and stories of the previous night flashed into his mind. "Hell!" he exclaimed. "I must see Nell,

## David Marsh Decides to Speak

I guess — but I've simply got to get that jay of stuff in to the Teakettle by dark."

He grumbled steadily while he dressed. Dawn was breaking, and the world outside looked depressingly cold and rough. He had a hard day before him and a hard to-morrow after that; but he must snatch a half hour for his interview with Nell. He shaved in cold water, with a razor that needed honing — and this did not lighten his spirits. "The devil take that foolishness!" he grumbled. "Why can't things leave me alone?" He went downstairs in his sock feet, pulled on his heavy boots in the kitchen, and lit the fire. He was a handy young fellow — as a guide and woodsman needs to be — and set briskly to work to cook his own breakfast. He was sitting up to his tea and bacon, close to the crackling stove, and the world outside was looking considerably brighter, when his mother entered the room.

"What is worryin' you, Davy?" she inquired anxiously. "I heard you tossin' and turnin' last night."

"Nothing much," he replied. "I was just planning things. I've a heap to do before Mr. Banks lands here with his patent range finders, and seventeen different kinds of rifles. He's not the kind to kick at hard hunting, and he's generous; but he likes to have everything tidy and handy."

"I'm sure he'll have nothin' to complain of, Davy, so long as you look after him," returned Mrs. Marsh. "But what kept you out so late last night?"

"I was talking to Jim Harley."

"Oh, you were at the Harleys' place, were you? You seem to be gettin' along fine in that quarter, Davy."

The young man blushed. "I wasn't at the house, mother," he said. "I met Jim over at Rayton's, and we went for a walk together. He had a regular talking fit on, I can tell you."

"I didn't know Jim was ever took that way," returned the mother. "So you saw young Mr. Rayton, did you? And how is he?"

"He's all right, I guess."

"He's a very polite, agreeable young man."

"Oh, yes, he's polite enough."

Mrs. Marsh looked at him sharply.

"What have you got against Mr. Rayton?" she demanded.

"Nothing," replied David. "Nothing at all, mother. I don't know anything about him, good or bad. But it's easy enough to be polite, I guess — and it don't cost anything."

The mother sighed and smiled at the same time. "If it's so easy," she said, "then I wish more folks about here would try it."

David drained his cup, and got to his feet. "Well, I must hustle along, mother," he said. "I've got to run over to Harley's before I load up for Teakettle Brook."

"Jim goin' with you?"

"No. Oh, no!"

"You wouldn't go callin' on a young lady this time in the morning, surely?"

"Oh, quit your fooling, mother! I've simply *got* to speak to Nell this morning."

The moment the door had shut behind David, Mrs. Marsh went to the foot of the stairs. "Wake up, pa!" she called.

"Wake up!" repeated a voice from above bitterly. "Bless my soul, I've been awake an hour and up this last fifteen minutes; but I'm stuck for want of my pants! D'ye expect me to chase 'round in the mud in my Sunday-go-to-meetin's, ma?"

"Dear me!" exclaimed Mrs. Marsh. "I was patchin' them last night and left them in the sittin' room." She ran and got her husband's required garments, and threw them, flapping ungracefully, up the narrow back staircase to him.

Soon after that old Davy appeared. "Where's the boy?" he asked.

"He's had his breakfast, and now he's run over to see Nell Harley," replied Mrs. Marsh, beaming.

"Then the more fool him!" said old Davy. "It's time he cut that out. Ain't he got an eye in his head? He's got no more chance of marryin' her than I'd have if I was into the game."

"D'ye mean that she don't think him good enough for her?" asked the other sharply.

"I guess she don't think anything about him at all, from what I can see. He's good enough for any girl — but he ain't got the *character* to catch Nell Harley. That's it — he ain't got the character."

"He's got as good a character as any young man in the province — as good as *you* had, at his age, David Marsh!"

The old man shook his head, smiling. "He's a good lad. I've nothin' to say against our youngest son, ma. But he's all for his sportsmen and his savings-bank account — all for himself. He's smart and he's honest — but he's all for Number

## David Marsh Decides to Speak 43

One. To catch a girl like Nell Harley a man would want to jump right into the job with both feet, hell bent for election, holusbolus and hokus-pokus and never say die — like I done when I went a-courtin' you, ma."

Mrs. Marsh's face recovered its usual expression of good humor. "Maybe you're right, pa," she said. "He don't seem to give his hull mind to his courtin', I must say."

In the meantime, young David had tramped the half mile of road that lay between the Marsh farm and Jim Harley's place. The sun had come up white and clean in a clear sky, promising a fine day. A few vivid red and yellow leaves still hung in the maples and birches, and the frost sparkled like diamonds in the stubble, and shone like powdered glass along the fence rails. The air went tingling to heart and head like a wine of an immortal vintage. David felt fairly reckless under the influence of it; but when he came face to face with Nell Harley, in the kitchen door, his recklessness turned to confusion.

"You are out early, Davy," said the young woman, smiling pleasantly. "Do you want to see Jim?"

"Well — yes, I guess I do, Nell."

"Nothing the matter over at your house, I hope?"

"No. Everything's all right."

"Come in. We've finished breakfast, but Jim is not down yet. He was out until late, last night, and I don't think he slept well."

David followed her as far as the dining-room door, but there he halted.

"I guess I won't trouble him, Nell," he said. "I'm in a hurry, too. I have to get a load in to my camp on the Teakettle to-day."

"Can I give him a message?"

"Oh, no! It ain't important. Good morning, Nell."

He was halfway home, thoroughly disgusted with himself, when a voice hailed him. Looking up, he saw old Captain Wigmore approaching.

"Good morning to you, David," said the captain, halting in front of him. "Did James Harley explain his extraordinary behavior to you, last night?"

"Yes."

"Ah! And what was the explanation?"

"You'd better ask him yourself, cap. He told me not to tell."

The old man drew himself up and rapped his

stick on the ground. "Confound his impertinence!" he exclaimed. "I shall ask him, certainly. He owes me an explanation. Queer way to behave before a man of my age and position! And he called me an old idiot!"

## CHAPTER IV

#### THE TRAPPER'S CONFESSION

OLD Captain Wigmore returned to his lonely but well-furnished and well-painted house, ate a reflective breakfast, smoked a cigar, and then set out to find Jim Harley. Wigmore lived with a servant or companion — a very old, grizzled, silent fellow, who did not seem to be "all there." It was from this old chap, Timothy Fletcher by name, that the people of the settlement had learned to give Wigmore the title of captain. As to what kind of a captain he had been, opinions differed.

Wigmore found Harley in the farm-yard helping a teamster get away with a wagonload of pork, flour, and oats for his lumber camp on Harley Brook, five miles away. As soon as man and load were gone, the captain addressed the lumber operator.

"James," said he, slowly and with dignity, "I feel that you owe me an explanation of your strange behavior of last night."

## The Trapper's Confession

Harley sighed. "I can't explain it to you, captain," he said. "It has to do with — with a purely family matter; but I beg your pardon for anything amiss that I may have said to you in my excitement."

"Granted, James! Granted!" returned Wigmore, with a fine gesture of the left hand. "But I am sorry, of course, that you — but it does not matter; I am old, more or less of a stranger, and of no importance. You explained your agitation to young Marsh, I understand?"

"Yes, I felt that I owed it to him."

"Very good, James. Of course I am anxious, and fairly itching with curiosity — but my curiosity does not matter in the least. It struck me as a most remarkable thing, though."

"I was foolish," said the other; "but should it happen that — that it turns out to be serious — to really mean anything — may I confide in you, captain? May I ask your advice?"

"Please do so, my dear boy," replied Wigmore cordially. "I shall be only too happy to do anything for you — or for any member of your family. But now I'll not keep you from your work any longer, James. If I may, I'll just step over to the house and pay my respects to the ladies. I have a new book in my pocket that they may be interested in."

"They'll be glad to see you, captain," said Jim sincerely. "They always are."

So the captain went to the house and Mrs. Harley and Nell were glad to see him, in spite of the fact that it was rather a busy time of day for them to receive a caller. But the captain could be very entertaining when he took the trouble to try — and he always took the required amount of trouble when he met the Harley women. Now he produced the new book from his pocket, and laid it on the table. It was a volume of literary essays; and Nell took it up eagerly. The captain talked a little of books, lightly and gracefully, and a little of travel and big cities. He had a pretty wit. Except for the gray in his beard and mustache and neatly brushed, thick hair, he did not look to be more than middle-aged while he talked. Though he always walked with a slight limp, now he stood very straight. His bright, dark eyes turned to Nell when she looked away from him. He remained for about twenty minutes, and then went away, leaving a very pleasant impression in the minds of both young women.

"What a catch he would be if he wasn't so old!" said Jim's wife, laughing.

Nell shook her head seriously. "He is very entertaining," she replied, "and has read a great deal and seen a great deal; but there is something about his eyes that — well, that is not attractive."

"Most eccentric people have eyes like that," returned Mrs. Harley — who, by the way, was not a native of the settlement — "and I do not think them unattractive. Now there is poor Dick Goodine. His eyes are like that, too — so bright and quick."

"But Dick's are honest — and Captain Wigmore's look sly."

"Oh! You *like* Dick's eyes, Nell? Well, I think you might find eyes to admire belonging to some one more worth while than Dick Goodine."

"Don't be silly, Kate, *please!*" cried Nell. "I am no more interested in the eyes of the young men of this place than you are."

"What about David Marsh?"

"Poor David. He is not amusing; and, though he looks so simple, I must say that I cannot understand him."

Jim Harley went to see Rayton, and found him bringing his horses in from the fields just at the fall of the dusk. The Englishman had been doing a last bit of fall plowing before the frost gripped the land in earnest. He was muddy, but cheerful; and as hospitable as ever. Harley stayed to supper — a very good supper of his host's own cooking. Then they lit their pipes and went into the sitting room, where a fine fire was crackling in the open stove. Harley told Rayton the same story that he had told, the night before, to young Marsh.

"Good heavens! That is very tragic!" exclaimed the Englishman. "But I must say that I think last night's incident was nothing but chance. The card had become marked in some way, quite by accident — and there you are."

They talked for an hour or two, and Rayton would not give way an inch in his argument, that the affair of the previous night had been nothing but blind chance. He was much more impressed by the other's story of the past, and felt a new interest in Jim Harley.

"I wish I could look at it as you do," said Jim, as he was leaving for home. "But it seems to be more than chance to me — it looks like that same damnable hate that killed my father."

"But why should it descend upon young Marsh? Surely he is not — that is, Miss Harley does not ——"

"I don't know," replied Jim. "I don't think so — but I don't know. The thing worries me, anyhow — worries me like the devil! I'll keep my eyes open, you may bet on that; and I'd consider it mighty friendly of you to do the same."

"I'll do it, then, Jim, though I must say I'm not much of a hand at solving mysteries or catching sinners. But I'll keep my peepers open, you may gamble on that."

Reginald Baynes Rayton returned to his warm chair by the fire, and fixed his mind, with an effort, on the solving of the mystery. He liked Jim Harley, so he'd get to the bottom of that card trick if it burst his brain. Suddenly he slapped his hand on his knee.

"I have it!" he cried. "By George, I have it! It's that blithering bounder, Nash. He's always up to some rotten joke or other; and he's heard that story about the mother and grandmother somewhere, and so marked that card to take a rise out of Jim. He hasn't enough sense to know if a thing is sacred or not. He's one of those dashed fools who enjoy jumping in where angels fear to tread. That's it. By George, it didn't take me long to work out that puzzle! But I'll just keep it to myself for a while — to make sure, you know."

So he put the incident of the previous night out of his mind, and thought of Harley's story, and of Harley's sister, instead. He knew Nell, of course, but had not talked with her more than half a dozen times. He admired her greatly; and now, since hearing this story of her parents and her grandmother, he felt an extraordinary stirring of tenderness toward her. He sighed, lit another pipe, and went up to bed. He wanted to be up in the morning at even an earlier hour than usual, for he had planned a long day in the woods. He had arranged with a lad on the next farm to tend the stock for him during the day.

Rayton gave the animals their morning feed and breakfasted himself by lantern light. Then, with the pockets of his shooting coat stored with sandwiches and a flask of whisky and water, and with his grown spaniel, Turk, wriggling about his feet, he set out for the big timber that crowded right up to his back pastures from the hundreds of square miles of wilderness beyond. A heavy frost had gripped the earth during the night. The buckwheat stubble was crisp with it.

Dawn was spreading over the southeastern sky as he came to the edge of the forest. He halted there, called Turk to heel, and filled and started his pipe. His equipment was remarkable, and it would bother some people to say what game he intended to go after with a dog and a rifle. But Rayton knew what he was about. He wanted to bag a few brace of ruffled grouse; but he did not want to miss any good chance that might offer at moose, caribou, or deer. And he could not carry both shot-gun and rifle. The dog was well trained and could be depended upon not to trail, rush, or startle any big game. So it was Rayton's method to let Turk flush the birds from the ground into the trees, from which he would then shoot them with the rifle. He always fired at the head. Of course, he missed the mark frequently, in which case the bird flew away uninjured, as it is almost impossible to catch sight of a flying bird in the high and thick covers of that country, this was a good and sportsmanlike plan; and then he always had his rifle with him in case he came across something bigger than grouse.

Rayton carried a compass, and was not above consulting it now and again. Men have been lost in less formidable wildernesses than that — and have never been found. By noon he had five grouse attached to his belt — each minus its head — and had failed to get a clean shot at a bull moose.

He had crossed two small streams, and was now close to the Teakettle. He sat down on a fallen hemlock, and brought a bone for Turk, and half the sandwiches from his pocket. Suddenly the spaniel jumped to his feet with a low, inquiring yap. Rayton turned and beheld Dick Goodine.

"Hello, Goodine, you're just in time," he cried cheerfully.

At that, Turk lay down again and gnawed at the bone.

"Good day, Mr. Rayton," replied the trapper.

He carried a rifle under his arm, and an axe and small pack on his shoulder. He advanced, laid his axe and pack on the ground, and shook hands with the Englishman. He was a handsome man, younger than the farmer by a year or two, perhaps, and not so tall by a couple of inches. His eyes were large and dark, and just now had a somewhat sullen light in their depths. His face was swarthy and clean-shaven. He leaned his rifle against an upheaved root, and sat down on the log beside Rayton.

"Any luck?" he asked.

"No," replied the Englishman, "How about you?"

"I've shot my three head already. I'm just

## The Trapper's Confession

cruisin' now, keepin' an eye open for b'ar and fixin' up a few dead falls. Plenty of signs of fur this year."

"Glad to hear it; but you don't look as gay as usual for all that. But help yourself, Dick. Help yourself, and here's the flask."

Goodine removed his wide felt hat, smiling reflectively. "Thank'e," he said, and took up a sandwich. Half of it was gone — and he ate slowly — before he spoke again. "Well, I don't feel gay," he said.

"What's the trouble?"

"Oh, I have my troubles — like most of us, I guess. But just for the moment it's Davy Marsh is kinder stickin' in my crop."

The other started, almost upsetting the flask which stood on the log beside him.

"What's the matter with Davy?" he asked.

"I saw him this mornin', yonder at his camp on the Teakettle," replied the trapper. "We had an argyment about guidin', a month or two ago — only a word or two — an' he holds it against me. He was loadin' his canoe, for Dan's River, when I sighted him. I sung out to him, friendly as you please — and he didn't much more than answer me. Well, I've always put up with Davy, because he can't help his manners, I guess, so I kep' right along and helped him trim his canoe and get away downstream. But he was sulky as a b'ar with a bee in his ear all the time, and kep' lookin' at me as if I was dangerous. He was darn uncivil — an' that's a thing I can't stand. I've bin sorter chewin' on it, ever since."

"Cheer up, Dick," returned Rayton, and laughed heartily. "You mustn't let Davy Marsh's bad manners hump you. Take a drink and forget it." He offered the flask.

Goodine shook his head. "I guess not, thank'e all the same," he said. "I know your liquor is good. I've drunk it before, and there's no man in the country I'd sooner take a *smile* with than you, Mr. Rayton; but I'm leavin' the stuff alone, now."

"Right you are, Dick," replied the other, returning the flask to his pocket without quenching his own thirst.

"You see," said the trapper, "it makes a beast of me. If I got a taste of it, now, I'd go out to the settlement and get some more, and keep at it till I was a regular beast. So I reckon I'll cut it out." He looked keenly at the Englishman. "Last time I was cornered," he continued, "*she* saw me!"

"Ah!" exclaimed Rayton. "Who saw you?"

"Nell Harley — the whitest woman on top the earth! *She* saw me when I was more like a hog than a man. I was shamed. I'm sick with the shame of it this very minute."

Rayton looked embarrassed.

"Oh! I'm a fool to be talkin'," continued the other bitterly; "but I can't keep wrestlin' with myself all the time. She's treated me right — but I know she don't care a damn for me. And why should she? Oh! I ain't *quite* a fool! But I want her to think well of me — I want to show her that I'm as decent as most men 'round these parts, and decenter than some. Yes, I want her to see that — and I *can* be decent, if I try. I'm poor — but that's no disgrace in this country, thank God! My old man was a drunkard; but my mother is a good woman, and honest. She is French, from up Quebec way. I reckon some folks 'round here think that's something for me to be ashamed of."

"Think *what* is something to be ashamed of?"

"Bein' half French."

"The devil!" exclaimed Rayton indignantly. "Then they show their ignorance, Dick. French blood is glorious blood. I'm pure English myself, but I say that and stick to it. What was your mother's name?"

"Julie Lemoyne was her maiden name."

"That was a great name in Quebec, in the old days," replied Rayton enthusiastically; "and it may still be, for all I know. There have been great soldiers by that name, and some famous scholars, too." He clipped a hand on the trapper's knee. "So cheer up!" he cried. "Very likely you are descended from soldiers and scholars. Take it for granted, anyway, and act accordingly — and you'll be the equal of anybody in this province. Never mind Davy's bad manners, but take them for a warning. And if — if you care for some one you consider to be too good for you, just show her, by your actions — and by your life — that it is an honor to enjoy your regard and friendship."

Dick Goodine looked at the speaker with glowing eyes. "You've done me good!" he cried. "I feel more like a man, already. You're a wonder, Mr. Rayton — a livin' wonder. Shake on it! I'm your friend, by damn! from now till hell freezes over."

"Thanks. And I'm your friend," said Rayton, shaking the proffered hand vigorously. "And I hope you'll forgive me for preaching," he added.

"Forgive you? I'll bless you for it, more likely," returned Dick.

They were about to part — for the trapper meant to spend the night in the woods and the farmer wanted to get home before dark — when Goodine turned again, a daring and attractive figure with axe and pack on his right shoulder and the rifle in his left hand. "But don't think that I'm even expectin' to be good enough for her," he said. "I'll try to be decent, God knows! — but I'll still be just a poor, ignorant bushwhacker. You are more the kind she ought to marry."

"Me! What are you thinking of, Dick?" cried Rayton.

"That's all right," replied the trapper, and vanished in the underbrush.

Rayton tramped and scrambled along with his mind so busy with thoughts of Dick Goodine, of Nell Harley, and of David Marsh that, when he arrived at his own pasture fence shortly after sunset, he discovered that he had not added so much as one bird to his bag.

"The devil!" he exclaimed. "That comes of woolgathering. But never mind, Turk, we'll do better to-morrow."

When he reached the house he found Doctor

Nash's buggy in front of the door, and the doctor inside.

"I thought I'd drop in and have a talk over that queer business of a couple of nights ago," said Nash.

This dealt a blow to Rayton's suspicion. "Drive 'round and we'll put the nag under cover, and give her a feed," he said.

## CHAPTER V

#### DOCTOR NASH'S SUSPICIONS — YOUNG MARSH'S MISFORTUNE

DOCTOR NASH was a gentleman blessed with the deportment of early and untrained youth, and with the years of middle age. His manners were those of a first-year medical student, though he considered himself to be a polished and sophisticated man of the world. He had practised in four different parts of the country, but had nowhere impressed the people favorably by his cures, or his personality. He was a bachelor. He was narrow and lanky of build, but fat and ruddy of face. His hair was carroty on top of his head, but of a darker shade in mustache and close-trimmed beard. His eyes were small and light, and over the left, the lid drooped in a remarkable way. Whenever he happened to remember the dignity of his profession he became ridiculously consequential — and even when he forgot it he continued to make a fool of himself.

These traits of character did not endear Doctor Nash to Mr. Rayton, but they did not mar the perfection of the farmer's simple hospitality. He produced a cold venison pie for supper, made coffee and buttered toast, and flanked these things with a decanter of whisky on one side and a jug of sweet cider on the other.

"Cold meat pie," remarked Nash slightingly — and immediately began to devour it. After saying that he had never heard of such a thing as buttered toast for supper he ate more than half the supply. He lost no time in informing the other that he had always *dined* in the evening before fate had thrown him away on a backwoods practice.

Rayton haw-hawed regularly, finding this the easiest way of hiding his feelings.

"Whisky!" exclaimed Nash, after his second cup of coffee with cream. "I believe you live for it, Rayton. I never have it in my own house except for medicinal purposes." Then he helped himself to a bumper that fairly outraged his host's sense of proportions.

"I saw Miss Harley to-day," he said. "She told me that Jim had been to see you, last night."

"Well?" queried Rayton, puzzled. "She does not object, does she?" His mind had been furtively busy with the young woman throughout the meal.

## Doctor Nash's Suspicions 63

"So I thought that he may have explained his queer behavior to you," said the other.

"Yes, he did."

"What did he say?"

"Really, Nash, I don't know that I have any right to repeat what he told me."

"Did he ask you not to?"

"No; but perhaps he intended to do so and forgot."

Nash laughed uproariously. "You are the limit!" he exclaimed. "You beat the band! Why should he tell you a thing that he would not want me to know?"

Rayton suspected several reasons; but he did not want to offend his guest by advancing them.

"Have you seen Jim since that night?" he asked.

"No."

"But saw his sister?"

"Yes. Jim wasn't at home."

Rayton lit his pipe, reflected for half a minute, and then gave his guest a brief and colorless version of the story. He told it grudgingly, wishing all the while that Harley had asked him not to repeat it.

Nash straddled his long, thin legs toward the

fire. "So that's the yarn, is it?" he sneered. "And do you believe it?"

"Believe it? What Harley told me?"

"Yes."

"Certainly I do."

"Then you are more of a fool than I took you for. Don't you see it's all a game of Harley's to keep that young cub away from his sister? He doesn't want to have such a lout hanging 'round all the time for fear it may scare some one else away — some one who'd be a better catch. So he rigged the card and invented the fine story."

Rayton withdrew his pipe from his lips and stared at his guest blankly.

"Oh! that was easy," continued Nash complacently. "I thought, until you told me that yarn, that I really had hold of a problem worth solving. But it is easy as rolling off a log. Here is the marked card. See, it is marked in red chalk. A man could do that in two winks, right under our noses." He handed the card to Rayton — the cross-marked six of clubs. Rayton took it, but did not even glance at it. His gaze was fixed steadily upon his guest.

"I don't quite follow you," he said — "or, at least, I hope I don't."

## Doctor Nash's Suspicions

"Hope you don't follow me? What do you mean?"

"I mean just this, Doctor Nash. When you happen to be in my house be careful what you say about my friends."

Nash stared. Then he laughed unpleasantly. "Are you bitten, too?" he asked.

Rayton got to his feet. "See here, Nash, I don't want to cut up rusty, or be rude, or anything of that kind," he exclaimed, "but I warn you that if you don't drop this personal strain there'll be trouble."

"Personal strain!" retorted the other. "How the devil are we to talk about that card trick, and the cause of it, without becoming personal?"

Rayton was silent.

"But you know what I think about it," continued Nash, "so you can make what you please of it. I'll be going now. I'm not used to be jawed at by a — by a farmer."

The Englishman laughed, helped his offended guest into his overcoat, followed him to the stable, and hitched-in the nag for him.

"A word of advice to you," said Nash, when he was all ready to drive away. "If you have your eye on Miss Harley, take it off. Don't run away with any idea that Jim is trying to scare young Marsh out so as to clear the road for *you*."

Then the whip snapped and away he rolled into the darkness.

Rayton stood in the empty barnyard for a long time, as motionless as if he had taken root. "I'll keep a grip on my temper," he said at last. "For a while, anyway. When I *do* let myself out at that silly ass it'll be once and for all."

Then he returned to the sitting-room fire and thought about Nell Harley.

"Goodine, Marsh, and Nash — they're all in love with her," he muttered. "So it looks as if some one was up to some sort of dirty game with that marked card, after all; but who the devil can it be? It's utter nonsense to suspect poor Dick Goodine — or Jim; but it will do no harm to keep my first idea about Nash in my mind. If he did it, though, I don't believe it was in the way of a joke, after all."

Now to go back to the morning, and David Marsh. At break of day the guide had started the horses and wagon back along the muddy twelve-mile road to the settlement, in charge of a young nephew. They had been gone an hour when Dick Goodine appeared. At that appearance it had immediately jumped into his mind that the trapper was spying on him; but he had kept the thought to himself. He had been greatly relieved, however, to get away from the trapper's company and unsolicited assistance. There was plenty of water in the brook, so he paddled swiftly down the brown current for a mile or two. Then, feeling that he had got clear of Goodine, he let the heavily loaded canoe run with the current and filled his pipe.

"The more I see of that Goodine," he reflected, "the more I mistrust him. And the cheek of him, poor and shiftless, to think about Nell. I bet it was him put the marks on that card, somehow or other. The dirty French blood in him would teach him how to do them kinder tricks. Why, he ain't much better than a half-breed — and yet *he* talks about bein' above cookin' for sports, and lookin' after them in camp. He's too lazy to do honest work, that's what's the matter. So long's he can raise enough money to go on a spree now and then, he's happy. I don't trust him. I don't like them black eyes of his. I bet he's been spying on me ever since I got to the camp last night. Let him spy! He'd be scared to try anything on with me; and if he thinks a girl like Nell would have anything to do with a darn jumpin' Frenchman like him, he better go soak his head."

So as the stream carried him farther and farther away from the spot where he had left the trapper, his indignation against that young man increased and his uneasiness subsided.

"I wish I'd up and asked him what the devil he wanted," he muttered, "I'd ought to let him see, straight, what I think of him. But maybe he was just lookin' for trouble — for a chance to get out his knife at me. He wouldn't mind killin' a man, I guess — by the looks of him. No, he wouldn't go so far as that, yet a while. That would cook his goose, for sure."

Three miles below the camp, the Teakettle emptied into a larger stream that was known as Dan's River. It was on the headwaters of this river that Marsh had his second and more important sporting camp in a region full of game. On reaching Dan's River, Marsh swung the bow of his canoe upstream, keeping within a yard or two of the right bank. He laid his paddle aside, took up a long pole of spruce, and got to his feet, perfectly balanced. For the first quarter of a mile it was lazy work, and then he came to a piece of swift and broken water called Little Rapids. This was

## Doctor Nash's Suspicions

a stiff piece of poling, though not stiff enough under any circumstances to drive an experienced canoe man to portaging around it. David Marsh had mastered it, both ways, at all depths of water, more than a dozen times. The channel was in midstream. The canoe shot across the current and then headed up into that long rush and clatter of waters. The young man set his feet more firmly and put his body into his work.

The slim, deep-loaded craft crawled upward, foot by foot, the clashing waters snarling along her gunwales and curling white at her gleaming bow. Now David threw every ounce of his strength, from heel to neck, into the steady thrust. The long pole bent under the weight, curved valiantly — and broke clean with a report like a rifle shot. David was flung outward, struggling to regain his balance; and, at the same moment, the canoe swung side-on to the roaring water and then rolled over.

David Marsh fought the whirling, buffeting waters with frantic energy. He was struggling for his life. That was his only thought. He struck out to steady himself, to keep clear of the boiling eddies where the black rocks seemed to lift and sink, and to keep his head above the smother. The beating, roaring, and slopping of the rapids almost deafened him, and filled him with a shuddering dread of those raging, clamorous surfaces, and silent, spinning depths. Now he saw the clear, blue sky with a hawk adrift in the sunshine — and now he glimpsed one shore or the other, with dark green of spruce, and a spot or two of frost-bitten red — and now black sinews and twisting ribbons crossed his vision, and torn spray beat against his sight with white hands. The deathly chill of the water bit into blood and bone.

It seemed to him that he was smothered, spun and hammered in this hell of choking tumult for hours. At last the roar and clatter began to soften in his ears — to soften and sweeten to a low song. Wonderful lights swam across his eyes — red, clearest green, and the blue of the rainbow. A swift, grinding agony in his right arm aroused him. He was among the rocks at the tail of the rapids. For a minute he fought desperately; and then he dragged himself out of the shouting river and lay still.

Marsh was young and strong, and had not swallowed a serious amount of water. For ten minutes he lay under the leafless willows, unconsciously struggling for his breath. Then he sat up, swayed

## Doctor Nash's Suspicions 71

dizzily, and screamed suddenly with the pain in his arm. It was that excruciating pain, burning and stabbing from wrist to shoulder, that brought him fully to his senses. He staggered to his feet and gazed up and down the bright course of the river. He shivered with cold and weakness.

"Arm smashed!" he cried, almost sobbing. "Outfit lost! My God!"

He sank again, easing himself to the ground by the willows with his left hand. With the bandanna handkerchief from his neck, a piece of cord from his pocket, a few handfuls of dry grass, and a thin slip of driftwood he made a rough support for his arm and fastened it securely to his side. This took him fully half an hour, and caused him intense pain and severe nervous fatigue. He was shaking and gasping by the time it was done — yes, and on the verge of tears.

"The pole broke," he whimpered. "And it was a good pole — the best I could find. It never happened before."

He got to his feet again, and started painfully along the shore. The bank was steep, with only a narrow fringe of rocky beach. In some places the overhanging thicket forced him to wade knee-deep in the water. He stumbled along, groaning with the pain of his arm. His cheeks were bloodless under the tan, and there was a haunted look in his eyes. Fear still gripped him — not the violent, sickening horror that he had felt while struggling in the eddies of the rapid, but a quiet, vague fear that he could give no name to.

Marsh rested for a few minutes on a little grassy flat at the mouth of the Teakettle. By this time the sun, and his own exertions, had warmed him a little; but still the shadow of fear was in his eyes. "It was a strong pole," he kept muttering. "I cut it myself — and tested it. How did it come to break!"

He found the footing along the smaller stream even more difficult than that which he had left behind. Both banks were flanked with impenetrable snarls of underbrush that overhung the gliding current, and so he was forced to wade, knee-deep. The bottom was rocky and slippery, and the swift water dragged mercilessly at his weary legs. He advanced slowly, painfully, a pitiful figure. Sometimes he stumbled, almost fell, and jarred his shattered arm in his recovery. Sometimes he groaned. Sometimes he cursed aloud. "My luck's gone!" he cried. "The pole broke on me — and it was a good pole. Never

*"He advanced slowly, painfully, a pitiful figure"*

broke a pole before! Never got spilled before! Something damn queer about that!" He was forced to rest frequently, sitting on a stranded log or flat rock, or perhaps standing and clinging to the alders and willows. His arm ached numbly now. Now showers of silver sparks streamed across his vision, and again he saw little blue and red dots dancing in the sunlight.

It took him a long time to cover the three miles from the mouth of the Teakettle up to the little camp that he had sped so swiftly away from early that morning. It was long past noon when he dragged himself up the steep path, unfastened the door, and stumbled into the shack. After a few minutes' rest on the floor, he managed to light a fire in the stove and put a kettle of water on to boil. He needed tea — tea, hot and strong. That would pull him together for the twelve-mile journey that lay between him and Doctor Nash. But he'd lie down until the water boiled. He pulled off his moccasins and crawled into a bunk, drawing two pairs of heavy blankets over him. He was too tired to think — too tired even to continue his whimpering and cursing. After a minute he dozed off.

David Marsh was awakened shortly by a touch

on his injured arm. He yelled with the pain of it even before he opened his eyes. Then he stared, for there stood a young woman named Maggie Leblanc, gazing at him in astonishment. She was a fine-looking young woman in a striking, but rather coarse red and black way. She was roughly dressed, and had an old muzzle-loading gun by her side, and five partridges hanging at her belt. She was the eldest of many children belonging to a worthless couple who lived about two miles from the Marsh farm, in a poor community called French Corner. It was in that same part of the settlement that Dick Goodine's mother lived.

"Hell!" exclaimed Marsh. "Where'd you come from, Maggie?"

"What are you yelling about?" asked the girl. "An' what are you layin' there for, this time o' day?"

"I'm hurt," returned David. "My arm is broke, I guess." Then he told her all about his morning's misfortune.

"And Dick Goodine was here, was he!" cried the girl. "He helped you load the canoe, did he! And then your pole broke! Are you good friends with Dick Goodine?"

David looked at her eagerly. "Not particular," he answered. "What are you drivin' at?"

"He's after your girl, ain't he?" she asked, her black eyes glistening.

"Look here, what are you drivin' at, Maggie?"

She came close to the edge of the bunk. "Maybe he knows what made the pole break! I've heard o' that trick before. He put it in the canoe for you, didn't he?"

"Yes!" cried the young man furiously. "Yes, he did. Damn him!—if he played that dirty trick on me."

"You lay quiet," said Maggie Leblanc. "I'll cook you a bite o' dinner, an' then I'll light out for Doctor Nash. You ain't fit to travel another step."

## CHAPTER VI

##### DAVID TAKES A MISFORTUNE IN A POOR SPIRIT

David drank tea, Maggie Leblanc holding the tin mug to his lips. The pain in his arm became more intense as his strength returned. His temper was raw. He refused the bacon which the girl fried for him.

"Hell!" he exclaimed, "I feel too bad to eat. I feel like the very devil, Maggie. Arm busted, canoe and outfit lost! Hell!"

"I guess that skunk, Dick Goodine, done you pretty brown," remarked the girl. "Dick's cute. Always was. He bested you just like he'd best a mink or a fox. You ain't no match for Dick Goodine, Davy."

David Marsh cursed bitterly.

"That durn half-breed!" he cried. "Me no match for him! You wait and see, Maggie. I'll get square with him, one of these days."

"Dick ain't no half-breed," retorted the girl. "He's French and English — and that mixture

## A Misfortune

don't made a breed. Got to have Injin blood, like me, to make a breed."

"Injin blood's better'n his mixture," said David.

"Hell, yes! Dick Goodine's pure skunk. But I'll do him yet. You just watch, Maggie. Arm busted! Canoe busted and outfit sunk! He'll pay me for that."

"You think a heap o' yer money, Davy," said Maggie Leblanc.

"You go get the doctor," returned the young woodsman sullenly, "and leave my affairs alone. Money? Well, I guess I make it hard enough. You go 'long now, Maggie, like a good girl, and get Doctor Nash — or maybe I'll never have the use o' this arm again. It's stiffenin' up terrible quick. I'll make it worth yer while, Maggie. Five dollars! How'll five dollars do?"

"I'm goin'," answered Maggie. "But you keep yer money. I don't want yer five dollars. I'll fetch the doc, and I'll help you get square with that skunk Dick Goodine, all for nothin'. You bet! Lay still, now, and I'll light out for the settlement."

"I thought you was sweet on Dick Goodine; but you don't seem much that way now, Maggie. What's he bin doin' to you?" asked David.

"Yer mind yer own business, Davy Marsh," retorted the young woman, "and don't you give none o' yer cheek to me. I'm helpin' you, ain't I? Then mind yer manners!"

Then, with a toss of her handsome head, she hurried from the shack.

Left alone under that low roof in the quiet forest, with the afternoon sunshine flooding in by open door and window, David gave his mind unreservedly to his accident, considering it from many points of view. He had accepted Maggie Leblanc's suggestion without question — that Goodine had caused the disaster by injuring his canoe pole in some way. Now, alone in the silent forest, he thought of the marks on the card, and remembered the story that Jim Harley had confided to him. It was foolishness, of course, to set any store by two red crosses on a playing card — and yet — and yet——

Queer things happen, he reflected. The devil still takes a hand in the games of men. The idea of the blow being the work of a supernatural agency, directed by the marked card, grew upon him. But even so, what more likely than that Dick Goodine had cut his canoe pole — had been chosen as the instrument of fate? One has strange fancies when lying faint and hurt in a silent wilderness, in a golden, empty afternoon.

The sunlight gradually died away from window and door. David thought of his loss and counted the money that would slip from his fingers, owing to the broken arm. This was bitter food for the mind of such a man as David Marsh. Mr. Banks, the rich and generous American sportsman, would soon be at Samson's Mill Settlement — only, alas, for the profit of some other than the unfortunate Davy. It was a hard fact to consider, but at last the sullen young man fell asleep with the weight of it on his mind.

He dreamed of a life-and-death struggle with a Spanish count, who looked like Dick Goodine dressed up in queer clothes. The Spanish nobleman ran a knife into his arm and the pain was sickening. The count vanished, and beside him stood a young man in a blue coat with brass buttons, whom they called Jackson. This Mr. Jackson had a terrible leer on his face, and a huge pistol in his right hand. Seizing David by the collar, he hammered him with the pistol upon the wound made by the Spaniard's knife. David yelled with the pain of it — and woke up! Above him leaned Doctor Nash, holding a lantern, and with a finger on the broken arm. "Quit it!" cried David. "Quit it, doc! That's the busted place yer pinchin'."

A painful period of twenty minutes followed, and at the end of it David's arm was in splints and bandages, and David's face was absolutely colorless. Nash brought him 'round with a long drink of brandy.

"Hell!" said David. "That's all I want to see of you for the rest o' my life, doc."

The doctor grinned, mopped his heated brow, and set the lantern on the table. "Oh, that's nothing," he said. "Booh! I've done ten times as much as that before breakfast. Keep still, now, and give it a chance. Your arm will be as good as new in a few months."

David groaned. Nash built up the fire.

"I'm hungry," he said. "Where d'you keep your grub? Got anything fit to eat?"

"I reckon yes," returned the woodsman. "There's plenty of grub in this camp, and every durn ounce of it is fit for anybody to eat. Well, I guess! There's eggs in that there box on the floor, and bacon in the cupboard, and tea and coffee, and everything. Help yourself, doc. It was bought to feed Mr. Banks — so I guess you'll find it good enough for you."

## A Misfortune 81

"Don't get excited, David," retorted the doctor. "Keep your hair on, or maybe you'll keep your arm from knitting."

He cooked a good meal, gave a little of it to his patient, and devoured the choicer, and by far the larger, share of it himself. Then he lit his pipe and drew a stool close up to the bunk in which David lay.

"You are not fit to move to-night," he said, "so I'll stay here and take you in to-morrow morning. I managed to get my rig through the mud-holes without breaking anything, I guess."

David moved his feet uneasily.

"Guess you'll be chargin' me pretty heavy for this, doc," he returned.

"Don't you worry," returned Nash. "I'll only charge what's fair, Davy. Of course it was quite a serious operation, and a long drive — but don't you worry."

He drew at his pipe for a little while in silence. At last he said: "Maggie Leblanc tells me it was Dick Goodine who worked the dirty trick on you. Is that so?"

"I guess so. Don't see what else. The pole was a good one, far's I know."

"What's the trouble between you and Dick? I didn't know he was that kind."

"Well, we had an argyment a while back. Nothin' serious; but he's a spiteful kind of cuss. Dirty blood in him, I guess."

Nash nodded. "And perhaps you think the marks on that card had something to do with it. Isn't that so, Davy? I guess Jim Hariey has told you what those marks mean."

"That's all durned foolishness. Marks on a card! How'd them little crosses break my pole and upset me into the rapids?"

"Sounds fine, Davy; but you are scared of that marked card, all the same. Don't lie to me — for it's no use. I think the marks on the card have something to do with your broken arm."

"How, doc? No, yer foolin'! Yer tryin' to make game of me. I ain't a scholar, like you, doc, but I ain't fool enough to believe in ghosts, just the same."

"I am not saying anything about ghosts, Davy. You just keep your hair on, and I'll tell you what I think. In the first place, just remember that I am a man with a trained mind and a wide knowledge of life."

"Guess yer right, doc. Fire away!"

## A Misfortune

"Jim Harley told you that long story of his about his grandmother?"

"That's so."

"Do you believe it?"

"Maybe I do — and maybe I don't. What's that to you?"

"Of course you believe it! That's because your mind is untrained, and you don't know anything of the ways of the world."

"You just leave my mind alone, doc. It ain't hurtin' you, I guess. You talk as if I hadn't any more brains than a sheep."

Nash grinned, and rubbed his long hands briskly together. He enjoyed this sort of thing.

"Right you are. You believe Jim's story — and I don't. What I think is this: Jim Harley marked the card, dealt it to you, and then invented the yarn. He is trying to scare you away — away from fooling around his sister."

"You just let his sister alone, doc! And mind yer own business, too!"

"Keep cool, my boy. Well, he scares you a bit with his story. Then he has a talk to Dick Goodine. He knows Dick and you are not very good friends. So he fixes Dick, and Dick fixes your canoe pole — and there you are! Jim and

Dick do the busting, and I do the mending. What do you think of that?"

"Durned foolishness!" retorted David. "Maybe Goodine done it; but Jim didn't set him to it. I guess I know Jim Harley a durn sight better'n you do."

"Oh, yes! You are a devilish clever chap, David — in your own opinion. Just the same, my smart young friend, take the hint from me and stop thinking about Nell Harley. You are not wanted 'round that vicinity, and if Jim can't scare you away with his card trick and his silly story, he'll scare you with something else."

David Marsh was raging; but he was helpless in the bunk, with a broken arm to remember. He swore like the proverbial trooper — and Doctor Nash sat and smoked, with his sneering grin broad on his fat face. He did not say a word in reply to the woodsman's tirade. At last David lay back weakly, breathless, and empty of oaths. Nash refilled his pipe.

"Think it over quietly," he said. "Are the red marks after you? Or is Dick Goodine after you, on his own trick? Or is Jim Harley working a game on you? Think it over, Davy, and don't swear at your friends."

## A Misfortune 85

David's reply was a grunt; but he spent half the night in thinking it over. The harder he thought the more hopelessly confused he became.

During the drive to the Marsh farm next morning, Doctor Nash carefully avoided the subject of the marked cards and his suspicions. As there was not much else to talk of in Samson's Mill Settlement, just then, the drive was a quiet one. After helping his patient into the house the doctor drove away.

Jim Harley came over to see David in the afternoon. The sufferer received him with open suspicion, but Harley's manner soon drove the shadow away. He listened to the story of the accident with every sign of distress, and was impressed by the fact that Dick Goodine had helped load and launch the canoe. He knew that David and the trapper were not on friendly terms, and he believed the latter to be dangerously quick-tempered; but he could scarcely bring himself to believe that he would carry a grudge so far as to endanger a man's life.

"Have you and Dick had words about anything else?" he asked, "anything more than that argument about guiding sportsmen?"

"I guess he holds something else against me," admitted the guide.

"What is it? What have you ever done to him?" asked Harley.

David shifted about uneasily in his chair, and became very red in the face. In the depth of his heart he feared Jim Harley.

"I ain't done anything to him," he said falteringly. "I — I ain't said one uncivil word to him, except that time we had the tongue fight. He just don't like me, that's all. He don't like me because I'm a smarter guide than him, and get hold of all the rich sports; and — and I guess he thinks — well, he thinks —— "

"What? What does he think?" demanded Harley.

"Well, you see, Jim, he — I guess he kinder thinks I've got the — the inside track, so to speak."

"Inside track? You mean with the sportsmen? You have the best camps, and all that sort of thing. I guess he's right, Davy."

"That ain't just exactly what I mean, Jim. I ain't talking about guidin' and campin' now. Lookee here, you know as how I'm kinder — well, as how I am almighty fond o' Nell. You know that, Jim, for I've told you before. Well, Dick

Goodine's struck a bit that way, too, far's I can make out. Durned cheek; but that's the truth. So I guess that's maybe why he's got an axe behind his back for me."

Jim Harley sighed and shook his head mournfully.

"I hadn't thought about that," he said; "but now that you mention it, Davy, I see that it may be so. I've always found Dick a good-hearted fellow — but I guess he goes on the rip now and again. Not extra steady — and not the kind to marry my sister. He's not steady, you see — and he's so danged ignorant."

Jim made these last remarks in a low, reflective voice, as if he were talking only to himself. Tone and words fanned David's old suspicions into sudden flame.

"Yes, he's danged ignorant!" he cried. "Danged ignorant, just like me. That's what you mean, ain't it? You don't want Nell to marry a bushwhacker like Dick Goodine — nor like me. That's about right, ain't it, Jim? My first guess was right t'other night, I do believe."

Harley stared at him in angry amazement.

"You are talking like a blasted fool!" he exclaimed. "You were on the same string before, and I went to a good deal of trouble to set you right. Too much trouble, I see now. But I tell you again, if I objected seriously to you, David, you'd damn soon know it. You make me tired."

"I didn't mean to rile you, Jim," returned the guide, "but what with the gnawin' pain in my arm, and — and that story you told me about them marks on the card — and them marks being dealt to me — I tell you, Jim, I don't feel easy. I feel jumpy as a cat. Here I am with my arm busted already, and a canoe and outfit gone clear to the devil. I never lost a canoe before — nor bust my arm before."

"I am sorry, David. I am mighty sorry," said Harley. "It is hard luck, no mistake about that, but all I can say is, I don't wish you any harm, and never have. If you think Goodine is laying for you, keep your eye on him. If you think there is anything in those marks on the card — well, you know the story. Act as you think best for yourself, Davy."

"Thankee. I'll keep my eye skinned; but I tell you now, Jim, I ain't scart o' them marks on the card. I believe all you told me — but I guess it was just luck that brought them marks to this settlement and handed them out to me. I don't think fer one minute they busted my arm or upset my canoe."

After the evening meal, Jim Harley visited Rayton. The Englishman was in his sitting room, writing letters before a good fire. He pushed his papers aside and received his visitor with that manner of perfect hospitality which was as natural to him as his frequent laughter. He had already heard rumors of David's accident, but when Jim told the full story, he replied in forceful terms that Dick Goodine had no part in it.

"But it looks queer," persisted Jim Harley.

"Looks!" retorted the Englishman. "My dear Harley, didn't a canoe pole ever break before? Is this the first man who ever smashed his arm? Rot! I know Goodine, and he's the right sort. He's a man."

Harley had great faith in Reginald Rayton's opinions; but he could not get his suspicions of the trapper out of his head.

"Don't think any more about it," urged his host. "You might as well suspect Ben Samson — or old Wigmore. Drop it — and have a drink."

So Jim dropped it and had a drink. But he was worried and preoccupied throughout the evening.

When he was about to leave, however, he shook himself together.

"If you are ever lonely," he said, "come over and see us."

"Thanks very much," returned Rayton, gripping his hand. "I get a bit lonely, sometimes. Ah — perhaps you'll see me to-morrow night, if that will be convenient."

At that moment Turk jumped to his feet, uttered a low growl, and ran to the window. Rayton jumped after him and snatched the curtain aside. Nothing was to be seen, though a pale half-moon was shining clearly.

"That's queer," said Rayton. "Turk never gives false alarms."

## CHAPTER VII

#### MR. BANKS TAKES A HAND IN THE GAME

MR. HARVEY P. BANKS, of New York, was an angry and dejected man when he arrived at Samson's Mill Settlement, only to learn that his guide of several past seasons — in fact, the only available professional guide in the district — was laid up with a broken arm. He poured the full stream of his wrath upon the unfortunate David Marsh. He was a big man — tall, thick, broad, and big of face and hand, big of voice, foot, and outlook upon life — and his size seemed to fill the little farmhouse bedroom and press poor David against the wall. After expressing himself at length, he asked why the guide had not wired to him, so as to give him time to make other arrangements.

Now that was a question that David had asked himself, too late. He answered truthfully, his courage reviving as he realized that his excuse was a pretty good one. He told of his accident in detail, of his suspicion of Dick Goodine, and then, after another question or two, he went back and described the game of poker, the marked card, and told Jim Harley's story. Thus he explained a state of mind that had turned big business considerations into unimportant shadows and meaningless whisperings.

Through it all Mr. Harvey P. Banks sat in a splint-bottomed chair — bulging generously over the edges of the seat — smoking a long cigar, and gazing unblinkingly at the young woodsman. He nodded his big head when David finished, and flipped a two-inch white ash from the end of his cigar to the hooked mat at his feet.

"That's good enough for me, Marsh," he said. "I take back the hard names I called you a few minutes ago. No wonder you forgot to send me a wire."

He turned his head and gazed through the window at a field of buckwheat stubble, rusty-red, and a green-black wall of spruces and firs.

"Jim Harley told you the story, you say?"

"Yes, sir; Jim Harley. Doctor Nash don't believe it."

"Nash be blowed! And you say Jim acted very strangely when he saw the marks on the card in your hand."

## Mr. Banks Takes a Hand

"Yes, sir; he acted mighty queer. Doctor Nash says it was all a bluff, though."

"T'hell with Nash! How did the others take the sight of the red crosses?"

"Quiet enough, sir. They was all took up with Jim's queer look and words."

"And Rayton?"

"He just looked like an astonished horse, Mr. Banks. That's his natural look."

"And Captain Wigmore?"

"Oh, it didn't bother him none, you can bet yer hat on that."

Mr. Banks nodded again. "It wouldn't," he said reflectively. "A mark on a card wouldn't interest that old clam, I imagine, unless it was on the back, where it might be of some use to him."

He asked several more questions about the chances of obtaining good heads of moose and caribou in the Beaver Brook, Teakettle, and Dan's River country this season, talked of past adventures which he had shared with the young woodsman, and slipped in more than one query concerning Maggie Leblanc. Then, promising to see David again in a day or two, he lit another cigar and took his departure.

Ten minutes later, on the road, Harvey P. Banks met Reginald Baynes Rayton. The Englishman wore his oldest pair of breeches, but their cut was undeniable. Banks' eyes were sharp, though their expression was usually exceedingly mild.

"You are Mr. Rayton, who is farming the old Bill Hooker place, I am sure," he said.

"Yes. And you are Mr. Banks, of New York, I'm quite positive," returned Rayton, lifting a shabby felt hat, and laughing pleasantly. There was nothing to laugh at — but Reginald had a way of laughing politely at everything and nothing. It meant nothing, but it covered profound meanings.

Mr. Banks returned the unexpected salute with a fine gesture of his tweed cap, and then the two shook hands.

"I have just been to see poor David Marsh," said Banks. "I blew him up pretty high, at first, but I melted when I heard what he has on his mind."

"Yes, he seems to be in a funk about one thing and another," returned Rayton. "But it is rough on you, too. But — ah — I think I can help you — if you don't consider it cheeky of me to — to make a suggestion."

## Mr. Banks Takes a Hand

"Cheeky! My dear Mr. Rayton, I'll bless you for a likely suggestion."

"Then let me put you on to some good shooting. I know this country fairly well, considering I'm a new settler, and this is my slack season on the farm. I can help you to a couple of good heads, I'm positive. We can make my house our headquarters, for the game is very close in this year. The house is snug, and I am something quite special in the cooking line. What do you say?"

"It sounds mighty tempting, but — well, Mr. Rayton, I am a business man, and I like to see the business end of every proposition before I start in."

Rayton laughed freely, but politely.

"Of course," he said. "I am a farmer — and I see what you mean. The business end of some propositions is like the hinder end of a wasp, isn't it? Hah-hah! But — if you don't mind — well, I don't see how we can put any business end to this. Ah — if you will be so kind as just to consider yourself my guest. Hope you don't think it cheeky of me!"

"Well! 'Pon my word, Mr. Rayton, you are very kind. Why should you befriend me like this? It is astonishing."

"Not at all. We can have some good talks, you see. I am a bit lonely, sometimes. It is all serene, isn't it? Good. Where are your traps? Come along."

So they turned and walked side by side along the road and across the empty fields to Rayton's house. Mr. Banks glanced frequently and wonderingly at his new friend. Never before, in all his wide and active life, had his confidence been captured so quickly.

"And he seems to take me quite as a matter of course," he reflected.

That afternoon the two new friends, with Turk's assistance, shot a few brace of woodcocks and grouse, in quiet swales and corners around the outskirts of the farm. Then, together, they cooked supper. Shortly after supper, while they were playing a game of chess, and smoking two of Mr. Banks' long and superior cigars, old Captain Wigmore knocked on the front door, and entered without waiting for it to be opened for him. Rayton welcomed him as affably as if they had last parted on the most polite terms. He introduced the small old man to the big middle-aged one.

"We have met before," said the captain.

## Mr. Banks Takes a Hand

"Yes, I knew Captain Wigmore last year," said Banks.

Wigmore accepted a cigar from the New Yorker's bulging case.

"That is the real thing — the real leaf," he said. He looked at the chessmen.

"Reginald, when are we to have another game of poker? I am sure Mr. Banks plays the game of his nation. We must sit in again soon. We must not be frightened away from a harmless amusement by that silly trick Jim Harley played on us a few nights ago."

Mr. Banks feigned astonishment. "What was the trick?" he asked. "I should never have suspected Harley of playing a trick — especially a card trick. He has always seemed to me a very serious chap."

"Rather a queer thing happened a few nights ago, while we were playing poker, here," said Rayton. "Captain Wigmore thinks Harley was at the bottom of it; but I don't. Tell about it, captain."

So for the second time, Banks heard of the card marked with two red crosses and dealt to young David Marsh. He watched Wigmore throughout the telling as intently as he had watched the guide.

"Very interesting? Jim Harley is not such a

serious fellow as I thought," he said, by way of comment. And that was all until after Wigmore took his leave, at half-past ten. Wigmore had not mentioned the tradition behind the two red marks. When the door had closed upon the queer old captain, Rayton and Banks talked for nearly an hour about Harley's story of the red crosses, and David Marsh's experience of them. The Englishman convinced the New Yorker that Dick Goodine had played no part in David's accident. Mr. Banks, like Jim Harley, found it natural to accept Rayton's readings of men and things.

Mr. Banks lay awake in his comfortable bed for a full hour after turning in, his mind busy with the mystery of Samson's Mill Settlement. He decided that whoever marked the card had known the tragic story of the Harley family. He did not take much stock in David's accident. That had been nothing more nor less than a piece of bad luck. Canoe poles break frequently, owing to some hidden flaw in the white wood. But he felt sure that the two red crosses on the face of the card were not matters of chance.

"I'll work this thing out if it drives me crazy. I have always had an itch to do a bit of detective work," he murmured.

## Mr. Banks Takes a Hand 99

Then he sank into deep and peaceful slumber.

When Banks entered the kitchen next morning, at an early hour, he found the porridge neglected and sullenly boiling over the brim of the pot onto the top of the stove, and his host standing with drooped shoulders gazing mournfully at a five-foot length of spruce pole that stood in the corner. Banks jumped ponderously and rescued the porridge.

"What's the trouble?" he asked. "Are you thinking of beating some one with that stick?"

Rayton laughed joylessly. "This is too bad!" he said. "Molly Canadian, the busy old idiot, brought this in to me only a few minutes ago. Silly old chump!"

"What is it? And who is Molly Canadian?"

"She's an old squaw — and a great pal of mine. This thing is a piece of a canoe pole."

"Ah! Piece of a pole. Why does it interest and depress you so?"

"She found it at the foot of the rapids in which young Marsh came to grief. Yesterday, she says. If you look at the broken end of it you'll notice that the surface is remarkably smooth for about halfway across."

"Ah! It has been cut! Cut halfway through! Do you think it is David's pole?"

"I am afraid it is the one he broke. It was found at the foot of the rapids."

Mr. Banks scratched his clean-shaven chin.

"Looks as if you had put your trust in a lame horse," he said.

"Yes, it looks that way," admitted the Englishman, "but I don't believe Dick Goodine cut that pole! I know Goodine — but I'm not so sure of this pole. Sounds silly; but that's the way I feel. I'm not much on reasoning things out, but I've a few pretty clear ideas on this subject. From what you tell me that Marsh told you, it is quite evident that Maggie Leblanc is anxious to get Dick into a mess. Well?"

"You think the girl cut the pole?"

"Yes. Why not? She has Maliseet blood in her, you know — English, French, and Maliseet. She is a fine looking girl, in her way and of her kind, but I've seen two devils shining in her eyes."

"Would she run the risk of killing one man, just on the chance of getting another into trouble?"

"I won't say that of her, Banks, but there'd be no need for her to run that risk. Finding David in his camp, with a broken arm, evidently suggested

## Mr. Banks Takes a Hand

to her the chance of making trouble for Goodine. Then why shouldn't she travel over to the rapids and hunt for the pole — or a part of it? With luck, she'd find it. Then she could trim the broken end a little, and leave it where it would be most likely to be found."

"Where was it found? In an eddy?"

"No. High and dry on top of a flat rock."

"That certainly looks fishy!" exclaimed the New Yorker. "I'm with you, Rayton, no matter how severely you test my — my imagination. Shake on it, old man!"

They shook.

"I am greatly relieved," said the Englishman. "You see, unless I get outside opinion, I am never quite sure if the things I think of all by myself have any sense in them or not. Well, I am mighty glad you see it the same way I do. As soon as Molly told me where she had found the piece of pole, I smelt a rat. Of course I'd never have thought of all that about Maggie Leblanc, except for my thorough belief in Dick Goodine. That set me to work. Now we had better have breakfast."

Mr. Banks nodded.

"Why don't you set seriously to work to

straighten out the marked card business?" he asked.

"I have; but it just takes me 'round and 'round," said Rayton.

They had just finished their breakfast when Dick Goodine appeared, ready to take them into the woods for a day, after moose. He brought a boy with him to look after the place and the live stock, in case the sportsmen should be kept out all night. The three left the house shortly after seven o'clock.

Early in the afternoon Banks shot an old bull moose carrying a fine pair of antlers. They skinned and dressed it, and hung hide, flesh, and antlers in a tree; they pressed forward, for they were near a great square of barren land, where the chances of finding caribou were good. They reached the barren, sighted a small herd, and Rayton dropped a fair-sized stag, and after making packs of the antlers, hide, and the best cuts, they struck the homeward trail.

It was dark by the time the tree in which the remains of the moose was hung was reached, so they made camp there for the night. At the first break of dawn they were up and afoot again, and though heavily loaded, they made good time. They

## Mr. Banks Takes a Hand 103

halted only half an hour for their midday meal, and reached Rayton's farm shortly after three o'clock in the afternoon. Old Captain Wigmore was there to welcome them. They found him in the sitting room, very much at his ease, with a decanter of the Englishman's whisky on the table in front of him. Rayton laughed good-humoredly, shook his hand cordially, and invited him to stay for the remainder of the day.

"Gladly, my dear boy," returned the captain. He seemed to be in a much better humor than was usual with him. The sportsmen washed, changed, and had a long and quiet smoke, and when the smoke was finished it was time to get the evening meal. Rayton and Dick Goodine went to the kitchen, and set to work. They were interrupted by Timothy Fletcher, the captain's reserved and disagreeable old servant. Timothy's wrinkled face wore an expression of intense anxiety and marks of fatigue.

"Cap'n here?" he asked, looking in at the kitchen door.

"Yes, he's here," replied Rayton, with a note of sharpness in his voice. The soul of politeness himself, he could not stand intentional rudeness in others.

"Glad to hear it. I've been huntin' over the hull damn country for him," remarked Timothy.

"Do you want to speak to him?" asked Rayton.

Before the other could answer, Wigmore himself darted into the kitchen.

"What the devil do you want?" he cried, going close up to his servant, and shaking a thin but knotty fist in his face. "Go home, I tell you."

His frail body trembled, and his very beard seemed to bristle with wrath.

"But — but I thought you was lost," stammered the old servant.

"Get out!" screamed Wigmore. "Go home and mind your own business."

Timothy Fletcher stood his ground for a few seconds, staring keenly into the captain's face. Then, without another word, he turned and walked out of the kitchen. Old Wigmore glared around, swore a little, mumbled an excuse, and followed his servant.

"That old captain is a character," said Mr. Banks. "He's worth watching."

"He's a queer cuss, and no mistake," agreed Dick Goodine.

"Not a bad sort at heart," said Rayton, dishing the fried potatoes. "He has had his troubles, I

## Mr. Banks Takes a Hand 105

imagine, but when he is feeling right he is a very agreeable companion."

"I like his room better nor his company," said the trapper.

A couple of hours later, when the three were smoking lazily by the sitting-room fire, they were startled by the sounds of a vehicle and horse tearing up to the house at top speed. Rayton and Turk got quickly to their feet. The front door flew open and heavy boots banged along the uncarpeted hall. Then the door of the room was flung wide, and David Marsh burst in. His right arm was bandaged and slung, but in his left hand he held a heavy stick.

"Have you seen that skunk, Dick Goodine?" he cried. "My camp on Teakettle Brook's burnt to the ground! Oh, there you are!"

By this time Mr. Banks and Goodine were also on their feet. Marsh started forward, with murder in his eyes, and his mouth twisted. Rayton stepped in front of him.

"Kindly remember that you are in my house," said the Englishman quietly. "Just stop where you are, please, and explain yourself."

"Get to hell out of my way!" cried David. "I ain't talkin' to you. There's the sneak I'm after — the dirty coward who cut halfway through my canoe pole, and then set my camp afire, stores and all! Let me at him, you pie-faced Englishman!"

## CHAPTER VIII

### RAYTON GOES TO BORROW A SAUCEPAN

"WHAT do you want of me, Davy Marsh?" demanded the trapper. "If you think I cut your canoe pole, yer a fool, and if you say so, yer a liar!"

"And what is all this about your camp?" asked Rayton, wrenching the club from David's hand. "Keep cool, and tell us about it."

"By ——!" cried the guide, "I'd knock the stuffin' out of the two o' ye if I had the use o' my arm! You call me a liar, Dick Goodine? That's easy — now — with my right arm in splints. And as you are so damn smart, Rayton, can you tell me who burnt down my camp? And can you tell me who cut that pole? There's a piece of it standin' in the corner — proof enough to send a man to jail on!"

"This is the first I have heard of the camp," replied Rayton, "and I am very sorry to hear of it now. When did it happen?"

"Happen?" cried Marsh bitterly. "It happened this very day. Peter Griggs was out that way with a load of grub for one o' Harley's camps, this very afternoon, and it was just burnin' good when he come to it. Hadn't bin set more'n an hour, he cal'lated, but it was too far gone for him to stop it. So he unhitched one of his horses and rode in to tell me, hopin' I'd be able to catch the damn skunk who done it. And here he is, by hell!"

"You are wrong there, Marsh," said Mr. Banks. "Goodine has been with us since early yesterday morning, way over in the Long Barrens country — and we didn't get home till this afternoon."

"We made camp near the Barrens last night," said Rayton.

"Is that the truth?" asked Marsh. "Cross your heart! So help you God!"

"It is the truth," said Rayton.

"Damn your cheek, Marsh, of course it is the truth," roared Banks.

Dick Goodine nodded. "Cross my heart. So help me God," he said.

The flush of rage slipped down from David's brow and face like a red curtain. He moistened his lips with his tongue.

"Then it's the curse of them two marks on the

## Rayton Goes to Borrow a Saucepan

card!" he whispered. "It's the curse of them two red crosses!"

"Rot!" exclaimed Mr. Banks. "Just because Goodine didn't fire your camp, you jump to the conclusion that the devil did it. Rot!"

"There's nobody else would do it but Dick Goodine," returned David sullenly, "and if you say he didn't, well then — but lookee here! Who cut half through that pole? Goodine did that, anyhow! Molly Canadian told me where she found it. You can't git out of that, Dick Goodine!"

"That's so?" replied Dick. "You'd best go home and take a pill, Davy."

"Molly told us where she found it, too," said Rayton. "I call it a mighty clever piece of spruce, to crawl out of the eddy at the tail of the rapid, and lie down on top of a flat rock. How does it look to you, Marsh?"

David frowned, and glanced uncertainly at Mr. Banks.

"That's queer," he admitted, "but I guess it don't alter the fact that the pole had bin cut. Look at it! It was cut halfway through! And there's the man who cut it, say what you please! He was the last but myself to take it in his hands."

"I was the last, but you, to handle it afore it

was broke," replied Dick Goodine calmly, "but somebody else has bin at it *since it broke*. Who fished it out o' the river and laid it on the rock, high and dry, for Molly Canadian to find? When you know that, David Marsh, you'll know who made the cut in it. But one thing I'll tell you — I didn't do it. If I'd wanted to smash yer durned silly arm, or yer neck, I'd have done it with my hands. So don't call me any more names or maybe I'll get so mad as to forget yer not in shape to take a lickin'. That's all — except I'm sorry yer havin' a run o' bad luck."

"Keep yer sorrow for them as wants it," replied Marsh, and left the house.

"That young man shows up very badly when things go wrong with him," remarked Mr. Banks mildly. "Trouble seems to rattle him hopelessly. Suppose we turn in."

"Guess I'll be steppin' home, gentlemen, if you don't mean to hunt to-morrow," said the trapper.

"Better stay the night, Dick. It is late — and a long walk to your place — and we want you to help us skin and clean Mr. Banks' moose head in the morning," said Rayton.

So Goodine remained.

On the following morning, while the New York

## Rayton Goes to Borrow a Saucepan 111

sportsman and the trapper were busy over the intricate job of removing the hide from the moose head, and cleaning the skull, Rayton invented an excuse for going over to the Harley place. Since Jim Harley's pressing invitation he had made three visits and had talked with Nell Harley three times. Never before had he ventured to show himself in the morning. Those three visits, however, had fired him with recklessness. Clocks stop for lovers — and Reginald Baynes Rayton was a lover. He was not aware of it, but the fact remains. He did not know what was the matter with him. He felt a mighty friendship for Jim Harley. So, having told Banks and Goodine that he wanted to borrow a saucepan of a very particular size, he made his way across the settlement by road and field, wood and pasture. He was within sight of the big farmhouse when old Captain Wigmore stepped from a thicket of spruces and confronted him.

"Good morning, Reginald," said the captain. "Where are you bound for so early?"

"Good morning," returned the Englishman. "I'm out to borrow a saucepan."

"So. Who from?"

"I think Mrs. Harley has just what I want."

"I haven't a doubt of it, Reginald. As I'm going that way myself, I'll step along with you. But it's a long walk, my boy, every time you want to use a saucepan. You had better buy one for yourself."

Rayton laughed, and the two advanced elbow to elbow.

"I hear," said the captain, "that poor young Marsh is up to his neck in the waters of tribulation. His luck, in the past, has always been of the best. It's a remarkably queer thing, don't you think so?"

"His luck was too good to last, that is all," replied Rayton. "One cannot expect to have everything work out right forever — especially a chap like Marsh, who has a way with him that is not attractive. I think he has an enemy."

"I saw him this morning," said Wigmore, "and what do you think he is worrying about now?"

"Heaven knows!"

"He has given up the idea that young Goodine is persecuting him, and now lays all his troubles to the score of the devil. He broods over those two little marks on that card that was dealt to him during our game of poker. I don't believe he slept a wink last night. Jim's story concerning the past

## Rayton Goes to Borrow a Saucepan

history of those crosses has done its work. The poor fellow is so badly shaken, that when he is out he's afraid the sky may fall upon him, and when he's indoors, he is anxious about the room. He is a coward at heart, you know — and it does not do for a coward to consider himself in love with Nell Harley."

Rayton blushed quickly, and laughed his polite but meaningless laugh.

"I suppose not," he said. "None but the brave, you know."

"Exactly, Reginald. You are not such a fool as you — well, we'll say sound, for you don't look like a fool. No offense is meant, my dear boy. Fact is, I'm your very sincere admirer, and I should like to hear what you think of that marked card, that turned up the other night at your little party."

"I think it was nothing more than a queer chance."

"You believe Jim's story? You believe all that about his mother and grandmother?"

"Yes, of course; but I think what happened the other night was just chance."

"But you must admit, Reginald, that David Marsh, who received the marked card, has had a peck of trouble served to him since that night."

"Yes. That is more queer chance — a very strange coincidence."

"You are a firm believer in chance, evidently. Or is it that you call everything chance that you can't explain?"

Reginald sighed profoundly. "Chance," he said — "why, chance is chance. It was chance that you and I met this morning. It was just chance that David's luck should turn, or that some one with a grudge against him should get busy, just after that marked card turned up."

Old Wigmore smiled and nodded.

"I, too, am a great believer in what you call chance," he said. "But here we are, my boy. I see Miss Harley on the veranda, in a very becoming and seasonable jacket of red wool. No doubt she'll be able to find you a saucepan. Good morning, Reginald."

Captain Wigmore lifted his hat to the young woman on the veranda, and then turned aside and moved briskly away. Rayton also lifted his hat, but he continued to advance. Upon reaching the steps leading up to the veranda he uttered a choking sound of embarrassment and concern, for it was quite evident that Nell Harley had been weeping recently. But the right to refer to this lamentable

## Rayton Goes to Borrow a Saucepan 115

fact was not his. He must hide his pity and tender curiosity.

"Good morning, Miss Harley. Isn't it a ripping morning for the time of year?" he said.

"I am afraid it is going to rain," she replied.

"Of course," agreed Rayton, somewhat abashed, and glancing up at the gray sky. "That's what I meant, you know. Rain's just what we need. It will keep the frost off for a while longer, don't you think so?"

"Oh, *please* don't talk about the weather, Mr. Rayton. I feel too — too worried to talk about the weather."

"Worried!" exclaimed the young man. "I am sorry. Is there anything I can do, Miss Harley? If so, just name it, please. I'd be delighted, you know. May — may I ask what is the trouble?"

"Please come in. There is a fire in the sitting room. Come in, if you can spare the time, for I want to tell you all about it — though I suppose you know already."

Reginald followed her into the sitting room and took a seat across the glowing hearth from her. He felt torn by her undisclosed trouble, and bewildered by his own good fortune. He forgot to inquire after Jim and Mrs. Harley, and the saucepan of very particular dimensions fled from his mind. He sat in a low chair and gazed anxiously and expectantly at Nell Harley. She sat with her elbow on her knee, her round chin on the heel of her hand, and the shadow of retrospection over her bright, pale face. Her eyes were lowered, but presently, and it seemed to him as suddenly as a flash of lightning, she raised them to his glance.

"It is about that card I am worrying so," she said. "I have heard all about it — about the card that was dealt to David Marsh with the two little red crosses drawn upon the face of it. Already he has broken his arm, lost his canoe, and had his camp burned down. It is terrible — and I am frightened. I know the tradition, and believe it fully. Jim does not like to talk about it, and Kate thinks it is all nonsense, though she is too kind to actually say so. But I *know* that every word of the old story is true. It frightens me. Do you believe that — that the curse is still following us — or does it all seem utterly ridiculous to you?"

Reginald turned his eyes away from her face with a visible effort, gazed into the heart of the fire for a moment or two, studied the pattern of the rug at his feet, and inspected the ceiling. His glance returned to her face, held for a moment, then veered in panic to the window.

"Of course I believe the story that Jim told to me," he said, "and I consider it a — a very remarkable story — and terribly sad, too; but it was the work of man, or men, of course. There was nothing supernatural about it. An enemy — a rival — used those red marks on a card in each case, as a warning. First it was the Spanish count, and next it was that Mr. Jackson. But now, in Samson's Mill Settlement — why, I feel quite sure it is nothing but chance. Nobody but Jim knew of that family story, and he certainly did not mark the card. And — and the conditions are not right. At least, that's how it looks to me."

"The conditions?" she queried softly.

Rayton shot a brief, but imploring glance at her.

"What I mean is — ah — why should David Marsh get the card? I hope — I mean I can't see — ah — I can't see any association between a chap like David and ——"

He fell silent, became very red, and blinked at the fire.

"Please go on," she whispered. "*Please* tell me what you think, for I know you are honest, fearless and sane, Mr. Rayton. You must forgive me for speaking so frankly — but that is what Jim says of you. You were saying that you cannot see any connection between David Marsh and — and what?"

Reginald took a deep breath and squared his shoulders.

"Between Marsh and those others who received the marked cards," he said. "First, it was the young sailor, the chap in the navy — the Spaniard's winning rival. Next it was your father — a man of character and — and breeding. Now David Marsh gets the card! That seems absurd to me. It seems like a man going out to kill a partridge with an elephant gun. It — it does not look to me like a continuation of the — the same idea at all."

"Why not? Please be quite frank with me. Why does it seem different?"

"But really, Miss Harley, I — I have no right to air my — my opinions."

"I want you to. I beg you to. I am sure your opinions will help me."

"If anything I can say will make you feel easier, then I'll — I'll go ahead. What I'm driving at is, that the navy chap was the kind of chap your grandmother might have become — ah, very fond of. Perhaps she was. He was a serious proposi-

## Rayton Goes to Borrow a Saucepan 119

tion. So with your father. The others who were fond of your mother saw in him a real rival — a dangerous man. But — it is not so with Marsh. He is not big. He is not strong. The truth is, if you forgive me for saying so, there is no danger of — of your caring for a chap like David Marsh. There! So the case is not like the others, and the old idea is not carried out. Fate, or the rival, or whatever it is, has made a stupid mistake."

He glanced at the girl as he ceased speaking. Her clear face was flushed to a tender pink, and her eyes were lowered.

"There is a good deal of truth in what you say, Mr. Rayton," she murmured. "It sounds like very clear reasoning to me. And you are right in — in believing that I do not care at all for David Marsh, in the way you mean. But may we not go even farther in disproving any connection between this case and the other two?"

For the fraction of a second her glance lifted and encountered his.

"Even if David happened to correspond with that young sailor of long ago, or with my dear father, the rival is missing," she said uncertainly. "The rivals were the most terrible features of the other cases."

Rayton got nervously to his feet, then sank down again.

"There would be plenty of rivals — of a kind," he said. "That is the truth, as you must know. But like poor Marsh, none is — would be — worth considering. So, you see, fate, or whatever it is that plays this game, is playing stupidly. That is why I think it nothing but chance, in this case — the whole thing nothing but the maddest chance."

"You have eased my mind very greatly," she said.

The Englishman bowed and rose from his chair. "I am glad," he said simply. "Now I must be starting for home. I left Banks and Goodine working over a moose head that Banks got yesterday."

"You do not think Dick Goodine set fire to David's camp, do you? There is bad blood between them, you know," she said anxiously.

"He was with us all yesterday and the day before," he answered, "so I knew he had nothing to do with it."

At the door the young woman said, "I am very glad you came over this morning." And then, with an air of sudden awakening to the commonplaces of life, "Did you come for anything in particular? To see Jim, perhaps?" she asked.

"No. Oh, no," he answered, hat in hand. "I just came — that is, I just happened along."

He was halfway home when he remembered the saucepan.

## CHAPTER IX

### RAYTON CONFESSES

OLD Timothy Fletcher, Captain Wigmore's servant and companion, was more of a mystery to the people of Samson's Mill Settlement than the captain himself. He was not as sociable as his master, kept to the house a great deal, and moved with a furtive air whenever he ventured abroad. In speech he was reserved to such an extent that he seldom addressed a word to anybody but Wigmore, and in manner he was decidedly unpleasant. He was neither liked nor understood by his neighbors. He did not care a rap what the people thought of him, and yet, with all his queerness and unsociability, he possessed many common human traits. He served the captain faithfully, had a weakness for rye whisky and Turkish cigarettes — weaknesses which he indulged on the sly — and spent much of his time in the perusal of sentimental fiction.

The afternoon of the day on which Mr. Rayton

went across the fields to borrow a saucepan was bright and warm. The morning had promised rain, but a change of wind had given to late autumn a few more hours of magic, unseasonable warmth and glow. Timothy Fletcher, shod with felt, went to the door of the captain's bedroom and assured himself that the worthy gentleman was deep in his after-luncheon nap. Then he tiptoed to his own chamber, produced a paper-covered novel and a box of cigarettes from a locked trunk, and crept downstairs again. In the kitchen he changed his felt-soled slippers for a pair of boots. He crossed the garden, the little pasture beyond, and entered a patch of young firs and spruces. He walked swiftly and furtively, until he came to a little sun-filled clearing, on a gently sloping hillside. Here he found his favorite seat, which was a dry log lying near a big poplar. He seated himself on the log, leaned back against the poplar, lit a fat cigarette, and opened the book.

For a whole hour Timothy read steadily, chapter after chapter, and smoked four cigarettes. Then he placed the book face down upon his knee. The sun was warm and the air soft and fragrant. He closed his eyes, opened them with an effort, closed them again. His head sank back and settled slightly to the left. The book slid from his knee. But he gave it no heed.

He awoke, struggling violently, but impotently. He opened his eyes upon darkness. He cried out furiously, and his voice was beaten thunderously back into his own ears by an enveloping blanket. He knew it for a blanket by the weight and feeling of it. His back was still against the familiar poplar tree, but now it was pressed to the trunk by something that crossed his chest. His hands were bound to his sides. His ankles were gripped together.

Now it happened that a large widow, named Mrs. Beesley, came to the little hillside clearing just before sunset. She had been hunting through the woods all the afternoon for an herb that enjoys the reputation, in this country, of being a panacea for all ailments of the stomach. Now she was on her way home.

Rounding the big poplar, she beheld a shapeless, blanket-swathed, rope-bound form lumped against the trunk. She did not see the ropes clearly, nor fully comprehend the blanket; in fact she received only a general impression of something monstrous, bulky, terrific. She uttered a shrill scream, and, for a few seconds, stood spellbound. A choking sound, muffled and terrible, came from the shapeless bulk, and one end of it began to sway and the other to twist and wag. Mrs. Beesley turned and ran for her very life.

Instinct, rather than reason, directed Mrs. Beesley's fleeing feet toward the clearings and farmsteads of the settlement. She left the haunted woods behind her, crossed a lumpy pasture at an amazing pace, sprang into the middle of a brush fence, and fought through without a halt, sighted a house with a male figure in the foreground, and kicked her way toward these signs of protection with such high action that her elastic-sided boots acknowledged themselves frankly, and Captain Wigmore's suspicions of white stockings were confirmed. She arrived with such force as to send the frail old captain reeling backward across an empty flower bed. Following him, she reclined upon the mold.

"Bless my soul!" cried the captain. "Why, it is Mrs. Beesley! My dear Mrs. Beesley, what the devil is the matter with you? Allow me to help you to your feet. You'll ruin your gown in that bed, I'm sure. Did you see a bear?"

She had no breath for words, just then, and her legs felt as if they had melted. Wigmore possessed himself of her fat hands, set his heels in the edge of the flower bed, and pulled. He suggested a small terrier worrying a large and sleepy pig. Presently he desisted from his efforts, retreated a few paces, and wiped his face with his handkerchief.

"Collect yourself, my dear Mrs. Beesley," he pleaded. "I'm afraid you'll catch your death sitting there. Come now, try to tell me all about the bear — and try to rise."

The widow found her voice, though she did not move.

"It weren't a b'ar, captain," she cried. "Sakes alive! No b'ar 'u'd scare me like that. Don't know what to call it, captain. The devil, I reckon — or a ghost, maybe — or a annerchrist. You better git yer gun, captain, and go back and take a look. Oh, lor'! Oh, sakes alive! I never thought to see the day Mary Beesley 'u'd jump fences like a breechy steer!"

"Calm yourself, Mrs. Beesley," returned old Wigmore, "and tell me where you saw this creature. Did it chase you?"

"It was in the little clearin' where the spring is," replied the widow. "No, it didn't chase me, captain, as far's I know. I didn't look 'round to

## Rayton Confesses

see. It jes' growled and wiggled — and then I lit out, captain, and made no more to-do about a fence than I would about crossin' a hooked mat on the kitchen floor."

"Come in and sit down, Mrs. Beesley," said Wigmore. "I'll get my man Timothy and go up to the spring and look 'round. I haven't a doubt about it being a bear."

Wigmore went through the house shouting vainly for Timothy Fletcher. Then he went out to the road and caught sight of Benjamin Samson in the distance. He whistled on his fingers and waved a hand violently to the miller. Benjamin came to him as fast as his weight allowed.

"What's bitin' you, cap'n?" he asked.

"There is something by the spring up in the little clearing," said Wigmore — "something that frightened Mrs. Beesley, and growled and wagged itself. She is in the house, recovering from her fright. She ran like a deer."

"Then I'll bet it wasn't a man up by the spring," said Benjamin.

The captain let this mild attempt at humor pass without notice.

"I want to go up and take a look 'round," he said, "but I can't find Timothy anywhere. It may be a bear — and I am an old man. Will you come along with me, Benjamin?"

"Sure. If you can lend me a gun," replied Mr. Samson.

They found a shotgun, slipped two cartridges loaded with buckshot into the breech, bade Mrs. Beesley sit quiet and be of good heart, and set out to investigate the little hillside clearing. It was now dusk. The sun had slipped from sight, and the shadows were deep in the woods. The captain carried a lighted lantern, and Benjamin the ready fowling piece.

They soon reached the poplar tree and the blanket-swathed figure bound against it. By lantern light it looked more grotesque and monstrous than by day, and Mr. Samson came within an ace of taking a snap shot at it, and then beating a hasty retreat. The captain was too quick for him, however, noticed the twitch of the miller's arm, and gripped him by the wrist.

"It's tied fast, whatever it is," he said.

"Don't you see the ropes? Come on, Benjamin, and keep a grip on your nerve. Here, let me take the gun!"

"I ain't scart," replied Samson thickly. "It gave me a start for a second, that's all."

## Rayton Confesses 129

They approached the shapeless figure cautiously.
"Who are you?" cried Wigmore.

The thing twisted and squirmed, and a muffled, choking, bestial sound came from it.

"I'll bet a dollar it's a man," said Benjamin. "Now what kind o' trick is this, I'd like to know? Maybe there's bin murder done. There's bin too many queer tricks 'round here lately to suit me."

"It is tied up in a blanket," said the captain. "Feel it, Benjamin, and find out what it is."

"Not me," returned Samson. "I guess it's only a man, but I ain't particular about feelin' of it. You go ahead, cap'n. I'll hold the light for you."

Old Wigmore stepped closer to the blanketed form and touched it gingerly with his left hand. It squirmed beneath his fingers, and again gave utterance to that amazing sound.

"Yes, it's a human being," said the captain. And then, "Bless my soul, look at his feet! It's poor Timothy Fletcher, by Heaven! Quick, Benjamin, lend a hand here! Cut that rope, man!"

In less than half a minute old Timothy was free. Lacking the support of the rope that had circled his chest and the tree, he tipped forward and slid heavily to the ground. The captain knelt beside him.

"Run to the house and get some brandy," he ordered. "You'll find some in my bedroom, behind the wardrobe. Make haste, Benjamin!"

"Well," replied Benjamin Samson, "I reckon I don't have to, cap'n. Queer thing, cap'n, but I happen to have a drop o' rye whisky in my pocket. Ain't carried sech a thing for years and years — but I've had a spell o' toothache lately and t' only thing does it any good's rye whisky. I hold some in my mouth now and again — and always spit it out, of course. Here you are, cap'n, and welcome."

Wigmore twisted out the cork and held the bottle to Timothy's lips. Timothy's eyes were shut, but his lips were open. His throat seemed to be in working order.

"He takes it like a baby takes its milk," said Benjamin. "I guess he ain't bin murdered, after all. There! I reckon he's had about all that's good for him. Wake up, Mr. Fletcher, and tell us all about it."

"Tell me who did this, my good Timothy, and

I'll make it hot for him," said Wigmore. "When did it happen, my worthy friend?"

"This here country's gettin' that lawless it ain't fit fer honest men like us to live in no longer," said Mr. Samson.

Timothy growled and sat up. He glared at Benjamin, then turned his gaze upon his master.

"Ah! You feel better!" exclaimed the captain. "I am glad of it, my trusty friend. Tell me, now, when and how did this outrageous thing happen?"

"I'll trouble ye for another drop of that tonic, Mr. Samson," said Timothy.

"I reckon not," returned the miller. "Doctor Nash says as how too much is a long sight worse nor too little."

"Then where's my book?" demanded Timothy. "And my cigarettes?"

"You have not answered my questions, my dear fellow," said the captain.

"Chuck it!" returned the old servant. "I ain't in the mood for answerin' fool questions."

"I fear his nerves are badly shaken," whispered the captain to the miller. "We must get him home and put him to bed."

"But you ain't intendin' to leave the ropes and

blanket behind, surely!" exclaimed Benjamin. He stooped, picked up the blanket, and held it to the light of the lantern. "Hah!" he cried. "It's my blanket! It's my new hoss blanket, by gosh! I missed it fust, last Sunday. And the rope's mine, too — my new hay rope, all cut to bits. I'll have the law on whoever done this, sure's my name's Benjamin Samson."

"*Your* blanket?" queried Captain Wigmore. "*Your* blanket and rope? But no, Benjamin. I don't suspect you, my friend, for I know you to be an honest man. But others — people who don't know you as I do — might think you were the person who tied Timothy to the tree."

"Chuck it!" growled Mr. Fletcher, picking up the lantern and limping away.

Thanks to Mrs. Beesley and Benjamin Samson, the story of the mysterious attack upon old Timothy Fletcher soon spread to the farthest outskirts of the settlement. Some inspired person connected this with the burning of David Marsh's camp, and it became a general belief that some desperate character was at work in the country. Samson suggested an escaped convict, but where escaped from he could not say. Timothy looked more unpleasant than ever, and kept his jaws together like the jaws of a spring fox trap. He did not seem to enjoy his position in the limelight. Mrs. Beesley found herself a heroine for a little while, but this did not make amends for the speedy ruination of her dreams concerning Captain Wigmore.

She had expected a warm continuation and a quick and romantic development of the friendly — aye, more than friendly — relations commenced by that adventure. But, alas, it had all ended as suddenly as it had commenced. The poor woman sometimes wondered if she had made a mistake in sitting for so long in the captain's flower bed.

"Men are queer critters," she said. "The late Mr. Beesley was touchy as a cat about them little things, and maybe the captain's the same. But he was that friendly and perlite, I really did think his intentions was serious."

Mr. Banks was keenly interested in Timothy's adventure. He talked to Captain Wigmore about it for fully an hour.

Two days after the mysterious, and apparently meaningless attack upon Wigmore's servant, the first snow of the coming winter descended upon the wilderness. Jim Harley had two full crews of lumbermen in the woods by now, but was himself spending half his time in the settlement. David Marsh's arm was still in splints, and Dick Goodine had not yet gone out to his bleak hunting grounds, beyond the fringes of the made roads and buckwheat-stubble belt.

Dick spent much of his time with Mr. Banks and Reginald Rayton. As for Mr. Harvey P. Banks, he seemed to have forgotten both his business and his distant home. He had still one hundred of those long cigars, and a tin box of fat cigarettes — and he knew he was welcome to his bed and board. He felt a warm friendship for his host and the Harleys, and a deep interest in all the other people of the place. Captain Wigmore and his old servant excited his curiosity like the first — or last — volume of an old-style novel. They suggested a galloping story; but Benjamin Samson, David Marsh, and the others suggested nothing more exciting than character studies. Doctor Nash did not interest the New Yorker at all, but of course the doctor could not realize this fact, and persisted in considering himself to be Mr. Banks' only congenial companion in the neighborhood.

On the day of the first snow Dick Goodine walked over to Rayton's farm to borrow a drawknife." He was making an extra pair of snow-shoes, and overhauling his outfit for the winter's trapping. Banks and Turk were afield, looking for hares and grouse; but Dick found the Englishman in his red barn, threshing buckwheat. Rayton threw his flail aside and the two shook hands.

"Have you sech a thing as a drawknife, Mr. Rayton?"

"Two of them, Dick. I use them mostly to cut my fingers with."

"Can I have the loan of one for a few days?"

"I'll give you one, Dick. You'll be doing me a kindness to take it and keep it, old chap, for I am a regular duffer with edged tools."

He found the knife and spent ten minutes in forcing it upon the trapper as a gift. At last Dick accepted it.

"But I tell you right now, Mr. Rayton," he said, "I'll git mad if you try givin' me a horse, or a cow, or your farm. You've already give me something of pretty near everything you own. It ain't right."

Rayton laughed. Then his face became suddenly very grave.

"See here, Dick, I've something serious to say

to you," he said. "Something I've been worrying over for the last day or two. You've always been honest with me — the soul of honesty — so I must be honest with you."

"What have I bin doin'?" asked the trapper uneasily.

"You? Oh, you haven't done anything that you shouldn't, old man. I am thinking of myself. You told me, a little while ago, that you were — ah — very fond of Miss Harley. But you told me in such a way, old man, as to lead me to think that — that you didn't believe yourself to have — much chance — in the quarter."

"That's right, Mr. Rayton," replied the trapper frankly. "I knew there wasn't any chance for me, and I know it still. I said that *you* was the kind of man she'd ought to marry, some day. I'm a good trapper, and I try to be an honest friend to them as act friendly to me; but I'm just a tough, ignorant bushwhacker. She ain't my kind — nor David Marsh's kind — and neither is Jim. She's more like you and Mr. Banks."

Rayton blushed deeply.

"My dear chap, you must not talk like that," he said. "You live in the bush, of course, but so do I, and so do all of us. But — but what I want to say, Dick, is this: I am — I am in love with Miss Harley!"

"Good for you!" exclaimed the trapper. He extended his hand. "Lay it there! And good luck to you!"

## CHAPTER X

### RED CROSSES AGAIN

"I am investigating the mysteries of Samson's Mill Settlement along lines of my own," said Harvey P. Banks. "My system of detection is not perfect yet, but it is good enough to go ahead with. So far I have not nailed anything down, but my little hammer is ready, I can tell you. I am full of highly colored suspicions, and there is one thing I am ready to swear to."

"What is that?" asked Reginald Baynes Rayton.

"Just this, Reginald. I'll eat my boots — and they cost me twelve plunks — if the burning of young Marsh's camp and the attack upon old Timothy Fletcher are not parts of the same game. I don't see any connection, mind you, but I'll swear it is so. I have two pieces of this picture puzzle on the table, and I am waiting for more. I know that these two pieces belong to the same picture."

"And what about the marked card?" inquired Rayton. "Is it part of your puzzle?"

"Certainly. It is the title of the picture. But

## Red Crosses Again 139

I want more pieces, and just at this stage I need another game of poker. Can you get the same bunch of players together for to-night — and Dick Goodine?"

"I'll try. If we both set to work we can make the round this afternoon. Jim Harley is home, I know. Why do you want Dick? I give you my word, H. P., that you'll not find him one of the crooked pieces of your puzzle picture."

"Right you are, son! But he has sharp eyes, and as he is our friend it would not be polite to give a party and leave him out. He needn't play. Somebody must sit out, anyway, or we'll have too many for a good game, but he can talk, and look on, and help burn tobacco."

"Good! Then we must get Goodine, Nash, Wigmore, Marsh, Jim Harley, and Benjamin Samson."

"Never mind Samson. We don't need him. He is harmless and hopeless — and one too many. Also, he has promised Mrs. Samson never to stay out again after ten o'clock at night."

"All serene. We'd better start out with our invites right after grub. And as the roads are bad we may as well ride. You can have Buller and I'll take Bobs. Who do you want to call on?"

"I'll see Nash and Wigmore, and leave the others to you."

So, after the midday meal, they saddled the two farm horses and set out. Mr. Banks rode straight to Captain Wigmore's house. The air was still mild and the sky was clouded. About four inches of slushy snow lay upon the half-frozen ruts of the roads. The New Yorker hitched Buller in an open carriage shed, and hammered with the butt of his whip upon the front door. He waited patiently for nearly ten minutes, then hammered again. This time the summons brought old Timothy Fletcher, looking even more sullen than usual and with his gray-streaked hair standing up like the crest of some grotesque fowl. His eyes had the appearance of being both sharp and dull at the same time. They showed inner points, glinting like ice, and an outer, blinking film like the shadow of recent sleep. For several seconds he stood with the door no more than six inches ajar, staring and blinking at the caller, his wind-tanned brow forbidding, but his lower face as expressionless as a panel of the door.

"Who d'ye want, sir?" he inquired at last, in a grudging voice.

"Good!" exclaimed Mr. Banks. "I really

thought you were asleep, Timothy. I want to speak to the captain for a few minutes. Is he at home?"

Timothy Fletcher lowered his staring eyes for an instant, then raised them again, blinking owlishly. The glint in their depths brightened, and took on sharper edges.

"What d'ye want to speak to him about?" he asked suspiciously.

"I'll tell that to your master," replied Mr. Banks blandly.

"He ain't at home."

"Not at home? Guess again, my good man."

"I tell ye, he ain't at home!"

"Not so fast," said the sportsman coolly, and with astonishing swiftness he advanced his heavily booted right foot, and thrust it across the threshold. The door nipped it instantly.

"It is not polite to slam doors in the faces of your master's friends," he said.

Then he threw all his weight against the door, flinging it wide open and hurling Timothy Fletcher against the wall.

"I don't like your manners," he said. "I intend to keep my eye on you. I give you fair warning, Timothy Fletcher."

The old fellow stood against the wall, breathing heavily, but in no wise abashed. He grinned sardonically.

"Warning?" he gasped. "Ye warn *me!* Chuck it!"

Mr. Banks halted and gazed at him, noting the narrow, heaving chest and gray face.

"I hope I have not hurt you. I opened the door a trifle more violently than I intended," he said.

Fletcher did not answer. Banks glanced up the stairs and beheld Captain Wigmore standing at the top and smiling down at him. He turned sharply to the servant. "There!" he whispered. "Just as I suspected! You were lying."

The old fellow twisted his gray face savagely. That was his only answer.

Timothy retired to the back of the house as Captain Wigmore descended the stairs. The captain was in fine spirits. He clasped his visitor's hand and patted his shoulder.

"Come into my den," he cried. "What'll you have? Tea, whisky, sherry? Give it a name, my boy."

"A drop of Scotch, if you have it handy," replied the caller. "But I came over just for a moment, captain, to see if you can join us to-night in a little game of poker."

"Delighted! Nothing I'd like better. We've been dull as ditch water lately," answered the captain, as he placed a glass and decanter before his visitor. "Just a moment," he added. "There is no water — and there is no bell in this room. Timothy has a strong objection to bells."

Wigmore left the room, returning in a minute with a jug of water. He closed the door behind him.

"Same crowd, I suppose," he said, "and the cards cut at eight o'clock."

Banks nodded, and sipped his whisky and water. "Yes, about eight," he answered. "We don't keep city hours."

"Do you expect the marked card to turn up again?" asked Captain Wigmore, fixing him with a keen glance.

The New Yorker looked slightly disconcerted, but only for a fraction of a second.

"Yes, I am hoping so," he admitted. "I want to see those marks. Do you think there is any chance of the thing working to-night?"

"That is just what I want to know," returned the captain. "If the devil is at the bottom of that trick, as Jim Harley would have us all believe, I see no reason why he should neglect us to-night. But, seriously, I am convinced that we might play a thousand games and never see those two red crosses on the face of a card again. It was chance, of course, and that the Harleys should have that family tradition all ready was a still more remarkable chance."

Mr. Banks nodded. "We'll look for you about eight o'clock," he said, and then, very swiftly for a man of his weight, he sprang from his chair and yanked open the door. There, with his feet at the very threshold, stood Timothy Fletcher. Banks turned to the captain with a gesture that drew the old man's attention to the old servant's position.

"I'd keep my eye on this man, if I were you," he said. "I have caught him both at lying and eavesdropping to-day."

"Timothy, what the devil do you mean by such behavior?" cried Wigmore furiously.

Timothy leered, turned, and walked slowly away.

Mr. Banks mounted his horse and set out for Doctor Nash's at a bone-wrenching trot.

"I'll bet a dollar old Fletcher is at the bottom of the whole business," he murmured. "I wonder where Wigmore picked him up. He looks like something lifted from the bottom of the sea." During the ride to the doctor's, and throughout the homeward journey, his mind was busy with Timothy Fletcher. When he reached home he told something of his new suspicion to Rayton.

"How could that poor old chap have got at that card?" asked Rayton. "He has never been inside my sitting room in his life."

"That is just what you think, Reginald," replied Mr. Banks. "But we'll soon know all about it, you take my word. I am on a hot scent!"

Jim Harley was the first of the company to arrive. He looked worried, but said nothing about his anxieties. Next came young Marsh, with his right arm in a sling and a swagger in his stride. Dick Goodine and Captain Wigmore appeared together, having met at the gate. The captain wore a cutaway coat, a fancy waistcoat, and a white silk cravat fastened with a pearl pin. His whiskers were combed and parted to a wish, his gray hair was slick as the floor of a roller-skating rink, and his smiling lips disclosed his flashing "store" teeth. He was much merrier and smarter than on the night of the last game.

Doctor Nash was still to come.

"We'll give him fifteen minutes' grace," said

Rayton, "and if he does not turn up by then we'll sit in to the game without him."

"He is trying to be fashionable," said Captain Wigmore. "Poor fellow!"

Banks produced his cigars and cigarettes. David Marsh drew his chair close up to Dick Goodine's and began to talk in guarded tones.

"D'ye know, Dick, I'm mighty upset," he whispered. "I'd feel easier if I knew you'd done me dirt than the way I do now. I can stand up to a man — but this here mysterious business ain't the kind o' thing nobody can stand up to."

"Scart?" inquired Dick.

"No, I ain't scart. Just oneasy. D'ye reckon them little crosses will turn up to-night?"

"Guess not. That sort o' thing don't happen more'n once."

"Will you swear you didn't cut my canoe pole, Dick — so help you God!"

"So help me God, I didn't cut it nor harm it in any way. And I don't know who did."

"I believe you — now. I guess there's something worse nor you on my trail. If that marked card turns up to-night, and comes to me, I'll git out o' the country. That'll be the cheapest thing to do, I guess."

"I wouldn't if I was you. I'd just lay low and keep my eyes skinned."

Then Doctor Nash arrived, and all pulled their chairs to the table except Dick Goodine. They drew for cards and Mr. Banks produced an ace. The pack was swiftly shuffled, cut, and dealt. David Marsh put his left hand on the table, touched his cards, hesitated for a moment, and then sprang to his feet. His face was twisted with a foolish grin.

"I guess not!" he exclaimed. "It ain't good enough for me."

The captain, having settled down to business, had lost his sweet and playful temper.

"What's that?" he snapped. "Not good enough! What's not good enough?"

"The risk ain't good enough," replied Marsh, sullenly and yet with an attempt at lightness. "I don't like them red crosses. I've had enough of 'em, whoever works 'em — man or devil — he's cured me!"

"Cured you?" queried Jim Harley, glancing up from his hand.

"Yes, *cured* me!" cried Marsh forcibly, "and I don't care who knows it. I ain't 'shamed to say it, neither. I've broke my arm, lost a canoe, and a camp — and a good job! Ain't that enough? I quit! I quit right now."

"Do you mean you'll quit playing cards?" asked Rayton.

"I guess you know what I mean," retorted David. "And I guess Jim Harley knows, too."

"Oh, shut up!" snapped old Wigmore. "We came here to play poker, not to listen to you. Who sits in and takes this heroic gentleman's place? Goodine, it's up to you."

"Don't care if I do," said the trapper; so he and David Marsh changed seats.

The game went on for half an hour without any fuss. Doctor Nash was winning. Then, after a throwdown, Rayton gathered up the old pack and replaced them with a new.

"You are growing extravagant, Reginald," said the captain, glancing at him keenly.

Rayton laughed.

"I hear Turk scratching," he said. "Excuse me for half a minute."

He went into the kitchen, and threw the old pack of cards into the stove. He returned immediately to his place at the table and the game went on. Nash's pile of blue chips dwindled steadily and Dick Goodine began to stack up the red, white, and blue. Mr. Banks seemed to be playing a slack game. Captain Wigmore played keenly and snapped at every one. Rayton left his chair for a few seconds and placed glasses, a decanter, and cold water on the table.

"Help yourselves," he said. "We'll have coffee, and something to eat, later."

Captain Wigmore waved the liquor aside, but the others charged their glasses. Goodine displayed three aces and scooped in a jack pot that had stood secure and accumulating for several rounds.

"Hah, Davy, you dropped out too soon," said Nash. "You got cold feet at the wrong time of day. Don't you wish, now, that you'd stayed in the game?"

"Wouldn't risk it, doc — not even for a ten-dollar pot," replied Marsh.

"Bah!" exclaimed old Wigmore, as he cut the deck for Jim Harley. Jim dealt. Rayton looked steadily at his five cards, then slipped them together between thumb and finger, and tilted his chair well back from the table.

"You look as if you'd been given something pretty good," said Captain Wigmore.

"Not half bad," answered the Englishman quietly.

"On the side," said Nash, "I bet you a dollar, even, that I hold the best hand — pat."

Rayton shook his head. "Not this time, Nash, if you don't mind," he replied quietly. "I want to take cards."

"That's easily managed," persisted the doctor. "I want cards, too; but we can lay our discards aside and show them later. Come, be a sport! Thought all Englishmen were sports."

Rayton hesitated, flushing.

"Right-o!" he said. "But I'll not be what you call a sport on one dollar! Twenty-five is my bet, Nash — even money. Come! How does that suit you?"

"It doesn't suit me at all — thanks just the same," returned the doctor sullenly.

"Perhaps you'll leave the English sporting instinct alone, after this," said Mr. Banks.

"For Heaven's sake, get on with the game!" cried old Wigmore.

All "came in" and took cards. Rayton asked for two, and though he did not bet, he kept the five cards in his hand. Wigmore took the money, this time.

"Supper," said the Englishman quickly, and gathered up all the cards with swift hands, his own included. He entered the kitchen quickly, and they heard him clattering about the stove.

After supper the game went on, with another fresh pack of cards. They had been playing for about a quarter of an hour when Captain Wigmore suddenly began to chuckle.

"What's the matter with you? Have you laid an egg?" asked Nash insolently.

For a second the old man's face was twisted with white-hot rage and his eyes fairly flamed upon the doctor. He trembled — then smiled calmly.

"Some one has, evidently," he said, and spread his five cards face-up upon the table. He pointed at the ace of clubs with a lean finger. It was marked with two little red crosses!

"You!" cried Jim Harley, staring incredulously from the card to the old man and back again to the card.

Nash and David Marsh began to laugh uproariously. Goodine and Rayton looked bewildered, and Banks scratched his head reflectively.

"That beats the band!" cried Nash, at last. "Jim, the spook who works that family curse of yours must be going daffy. Good for you, captain! There's life in the old dog yet! No wonder you are dressed up so stylish."

He leaned halfway across the table, guffawing in the old man's face.

Wigmore's hands darted forward. One gripped Nash's necktie, and the other darted into an inner pocket of his coat.

"Here! Drop it, you old devil!" cried the doctor.

Captain Wigmore sat back in his chair, laughing softly. He held something in his hand — something that they had all seen him draw from Nash's pocket.

"Gentlemen," he said, "look at this. It is another card marked with the two red crosses. I took it from the pocket of our worthy young pill roller. Who'd ever have thought that he was the mysterious indicator of trouble — the warning of the gods — the instrument of fate?"

"You darned old fool!" cried Nash, "that is the same card that was dealt to Davy Marsh last time we played. You know it as well as I do, you old ape! Look at it. Look at the back of it. Here, Rayton, you take a look at it."

"It is the same old card," said Rayton. "Nash took it away with him that night."

"Ah! My mistake," said the captain mildly.

When the company left the house, Rayton called Jim Harley back.

"I can't make it out," he said, looking from Banks to Harley, "but I want you chaps to know that two marked cards were dealt to me before supper. I kept quiet and changed the pack each time."

Harley clutched the Englishman's shoulder.

"You!" he exclaimed, with colorless lips. "Twice! Is that true?"

"Yes, it's true; but it is nonsense, of course," returned the Englishman.

"Don't worry, Jim," said Mr. Banks calmly. "The thing is all a fake — and I mean to catch the faker before I leave Samson's Mill Settlement!"

## CHAPTER XI

### AN UNFORTUNATE MOMENT FOR THE DOCTOR

The morning after the second card party found Banks and Rayton eating an early breakfast with good appetites. If Rayton felt uneasy, face and manner showed nothing of it. The big New Yorker was in the highest spirits. He had found an unfamiliar sport — a new form of hunting — a twisted, mysterious trail, with the Lord knows what at the far end of it. He was alert, quiet, smiling to himself. He ate five rashers of bacon, drank three cups of coffee, and then lit a cigar.

"I'll have my finger on him within the week," he said, leaning back in his chair.

The Englishman glanced up at him, and smiled.

"I do not think we should encourage the idiot by paying any further attention to his silly tricks," he said. "Whoever he is, let him see that he does not amuse or interest any one but himself. Then he'll get tired and drop it. The whole thing is absolute foolishness, and the man at the bottom of it is a fool."

## An Unfortunate Moment 155

"I mean to trail him, and pin him down, fool or no fool," replied Banks. "I'll make him pay dear for his fooling, by thunder! He is having his fun — and I mean to have mine."

Rayton laughed. "Go ahead and have your fun, old chap; but I tell you that the more notice you pay his silly tricks, the more you tickle his vanity."

"I'll tickle more than his vanity before I'm done with him," promised Banks.

The two were washing the dishes, when the kitchen door opened, and Dick Goodine stepped into the room.

"We're in for another spell o' soft weather," he said. "It's mild as milk this mornin'. This little lick o' snow'll be all gone by noon. It don't look as if I'll ever get into the woods with my traps."

He sat down, filled and lit his pipe, and put his feet on the hearth of the cookstove.

"That was an all-fired queer thing about old Wigmore," he said. "All the fools ain't dead yet, I reckon. Since the captain got that there card, the thing don't look as serious to me as it did. Not by a long shot! What d'you say, Mr. Banks?"

"You are right, Dick, according to your lights," replied the New Yorker.

The trapper looked puzzled.

"He means that you don't know all the particulars of what happened last night," said Rayton. "Captain Wigmore got the marked card, right enough, after supper — but I got it twice, before supper. That is the puzzling part of it, Dick."

The care-free smile fled from Goodine's handsome and honest countenance. His dark cheeks paled, and a shadow, starting far down, came up to the surface of his eyes.

"You!" he exclaimed. "Twice — before supper! That — that looks bad to me. That's the worst yet."

"My dear chap, if the silly thing was dealt to me every night, and chucked into my bedroom window every morning, it wouldn't be a jot less silly," replied Rayton. "Some idiot, who has heard Jim Harley's story, is trying to have some fun out of it. That is all. It amuses him evidently, and doesn't hurt us."

Dick Goodine shook his head. "I guess it hurt David Marsh," he said — "whatever it may be. It smashed his arm, an' pretty near drownded him, an' burned his camp, an' about fifty dollars' worth o' gear an' grub. That don't look much like fun to me — not like fun for the man who gets the card, anyhow. I'll tell you right now, if ever it comes to me I'll light out within the hour, an' hit the trail for my trappin' grounds over beyond the back o' nowhere."

"Don't believe it, Dick."

"But that's just what I'd do all the same. It ain't natural. It's more nor a game, I tell you — it's like something I've read about, somewheres or other."

"You're wrong there, Dick," said Mr. Banks. "It is a game — a dangerous one, maybe, but a game, for all that. I'll show you the player, one of these days, as sure as my name is Harvey P. Banks! In the meantime, Dick, I'll bet you five dollars that if you happened to be picked out to receive those red marks, as Reginald has been picked out — for the same reason, I mean, according to the family tradition — you'd not budge an inch or back water half a stroke. You'd just put your finger to your nose at the warning, as Reginald does, even if you thought Fate, family curses, Spanish ghosts, old Jackson, and the devil were all on your trail."

The color came back to the trapper's cheeks. He lowered his glance to the toes of his steaming boots on the hearth of the stove, and shifted uneasily in his chair.

"I guess yer right," he said huskily. "I guess I'd be brave enough to face it, devil an' all, if I had that reason to be brave. But I ain't got that reason, an' never will have — so I'm scart. I'm a durned ignorant bushwhacker, I reckon. Anyhow, I'm scart."

Rayton placed a hand on the other's shoulder for a second.

"That is like you," he said. "You are more frightened about your friend than you'll ever be about yourself. But cheer up, old man! I don't think Fate will break any canoe poles on me."

"Fate!" repeated Mr. Banks, laughing merrily. "Oh, you are safe enough from Fate, Reginald!"

But Dick Goodine shook his head.

During the morning, Rayton went over to the Harley place. The sun was glowing with a heat as of September, and the snow was already a mixture of slush and mud. Dick Goodine went about his business; and Mr. Banks sat by the kitchen stove, smoking and struggling with his puzzle. Rayton found Jim Harley in the barnyard. Jim's greeting was emotional. He gripped the English-

## An Unfortunate Moment 159

man's hand, and looked steadily into his face with troubled eyes.

"I was just going over to see you," he said. "I'm glad you're here. I — I feel pretty bad about you, Reginald — mighty bad, I can tell you!"

"For Heaven's sake, Jim, what's the trouble?" asked Rayton. "What have I done — or what d'you think I've done?"

Harley flushed. "You know what the trouble is — what is worrying me," he said. "You have not done anything. I am thinking of the marked card, as you know very well."

Rayton laughed, and slapped the other on the back.

"Laugh, if you choose," returned Harley; "but I tell you it is no laughing matter. Have you forgotten what I told you about those red crosses? Have you forgotten the manner of my father's death? Great heavens, man, it is nothing to laugh about! Those marks have brought two men to their death. And there's Marsh! He came within an inch of being drowned that day his pole broke. Of course, you think I am a fool. You may call me one if you want to. But, for God's sake, get out of here until the danger passes! That's all I ask,

Rayton. Get out! Get away from this settlement for a little while!"

The smile left the Englishman's face, and he gaped at his friend in utter astonishment.

"Get out?" he repeated, in a dazed voice. "Get out? What for? What good would that do to any one? What — in the name of all that's sensible — are you driving at?"

"Get away from here — away from me — and save yourself," replied Harley. "Don't you understand? This trouble is all *our* fault — all due to my sister. Don't you see that? Then get away from us! Drop us, and clear out!"

"To save myself from the curse of the little red marks on the card, I suppose?"

"Yes, yes. Go away and save yourself. That is what I ask you, Rayton."

"You really believe, then, in the power of those crosses? You really believe that my life is in danger — that I have been marked by Fate?"

"I only know what those crosses have done in the past. The evil is not in the marks, though. Don't think I'm quite a fool! But they are sent as a warning — by some unknown enemy of ours. Can't you see that, Rayton? My father was mur-

## An Unfortunate Moment 161

dered after receiving a card marked with those crosses. David Marsh's life was attempted! Don't you see? We have a bitter, hidden enemy!"

"No, I don't!" retorted Rayton, with spirit. "I don't think Marsh's life was attempted. Great heavens, Jim, didn't a canoe pole ever break in this country before? And didn't a shack ever burn down before? Buck up and look at the thing like a sensible man! What happened to that young bounder Marsh was nothing but chance. You make me angry, 'pon my word you do! But don't think for a minute that you can make me angry enough to run away — or that you can scare me away. I stand pat; but if my house catches fire, or anything of that kind happens, then I'll set to work and dig up the fool who hands out those marked cards, and land him in jail."

"I have asked you to go, for your own sake. I can't do anything more," returned Harley.

Rayton gazed at him earnestly, eye to eye; but Harley kept his eyes steady.

"Jim, that sounds queer," he said. "It sounds like some rot that Nash was talking, not long ago. Perhaps you know what I mean. Nash's idea was that you dealt the marked card to Marsh, and then invented the story, just to scare Marsh away from your sister. Now he will say that you are trying to frighten me away."

"He is a liar!" cried Harley.

"I know your story is true," said the Englishman, "and I know you are just as much in the dark about those cards as I am; but if you go on like this, old chap, other people will think as Nash thinks. Nash is not the only fool in these woods.

"And I want to tell you that even if you were trying to frighten me away from here you couldn't do it! That's my position, Jim. I am here — and here I stay! Whoever marks those cards is a harmless idiot. I love your sister — though she doesn't know it, yet — and the only thing that can chase me away from her is her own word. So save your anxiety for me, old chap, and keep your wind to cool your porridge. Also, think the thing over quietly; and, if it continues to worry you, go hunting for the man who makes a fool of you by marking those cards. Good morning."

Reginald Rayton turned and strode away without waiting for an answer to his last long speech. He was angry — hot and cold with it, from his head to his feet. He had been excited into a premature disclosure of his sentiments toward Nell Harley. He had been talked to like a fool — and

## An Unfortunate Moment 163

he had talked like a fool. He was furious. He felt the need of some one to punch and kick. It was years since he had last been in such a wax. And this was his mood when Doctor Nash appeared over the brow of a hill in front, driving toward him in a mud-splashed buggy. Nash drew rein within a yard of the Englishman. The Englishman halted. Nash leaned forward, and grinned.

"That was a good one, last night," he remarked. "A good joke on old Wigmore; but I don't quite see the point of it. Do you?"

"No. Is there supposed to be any point?" returned Rayton.

"Sure! What d'ye think it's all about if there isn't a point to it? You fellows are lobsters, I must say, if you are still cloudy on that business. Those marks are warnings — oh, yes! But they are not sent by Fate. They are sort of 'keep off the grass' signs issued and posted by a very dear friend of yours. Last night he felt my eye on him, and so threw the bluff. It worked pretty well, too. It had me guessing for about an hour; and then I thought it over after I went to bed, and got it all straight and clear."

"I am glad that some one has it straight and clear," said Rayton. "I am in the dark, myself;

but I agree with you that the deal to Wigmore was a bluff. I am positive about this because a marked card came to me twice before supper."

Nash uttered a derisive whistle, then slapped his knee with an open hand.

"I might have guessed it!" he cried. "So it's your turn, is it? Keep off the grass, Reginald. Good old Jim! He knows what he's about."

"What are you driving at?" demanded the Englishman. "What has Jim to do with it?"

He had heard the doctor's theory before, but wanted first-hand proof of it — and he was looking for an excuse for letting loose.

"What has Jim to do with it?" repeated Nash sneeringly. "Why, you lobster, he has everything to do with it. He's *it!* What's your head made of, anyway? A block out of the oak walls of old England, I suppose."

Rayton averted his face.

"Do you mean that Jim has anything to do with the marks on those cards?" he asked, in a faint and unsteady voice.

"You lobster! He marks them, and he deals them!" cried Nash.

Rayton faced him.

"You are a liar," he said quietly. "Not only

*"Plunged at Rayton, with his fists flying"*

## An Unfortunate Moment 165

that, but you are a bounder. Better whip up your nag and drive away, or I'll be tempted to pull you out onto the road and give you what you need. You are a disgrace to this settlement." He stepped back to the edge of the road. "Drive along, fat head," he commanded.

But Nash did not drive along. He had a great opinion of himself — of his physical as well as his mental powers. He hung the reins on the dashboard.

"Do you mean that?" he asked. "Are you trying to insult me? Or are you drunk?"

"I am not drunk. Yes, I am trying to insult you. It is rather a difficult thing to do, I know."

"Steady, Champion!" cried Nash to his nodding horse. Then he jumped over the wheel, threw aside his hat and overcoat, and plunged at Rayton, with his fists flying. He smote the air. He flailed the sunlight. He punched holes in the out of doors. At last he encountered something hard — not with his fist, however, but with an angle of his face. With a futile sprawl, he measured his considerable length in the mud and slush of the highway. So he lay for a little while, one leg flapping, then scrambled slowly to his feet. He gazed around in a dazed way, and at last rested his glance upon Rayton.

"See here!" he exclaimed; "that — that's no way to do! Can't you fight fair? What did you hit me with?"

The Englishman lifted his right fist, and pointed at it with the index finger of his left hand.

"That is what I hit you with," he said in matter-of-fact tones. "But if you don't think that fair, I'll land my left next time."

"Don't trouble," replied Nash. "I'm no match for a professional prize fighter. That's not my line."

"Oh, cheer up! We've just begun."

"I've finished."

"In that case you can take back what you said about Jim Harley."

"What did I say?" asked the doctor, making a furtive step toward his trap.

Rayton advanced. "Quick!" he cried. "Call yourself a liar, or I'll try another prod at you!"

"Leave me alone. D——n you! I'll have the law on you for this. Keep off! Mind what you're about. Keep your distance, I say. Yes, yes! You're right. I'm a liar. *I'm a liar!*"

He jumped into his buggy, wakened Champion

with a cut of the whip, and drove away at a gallop, leaving his hat and overcoat on the side of the road. For a minute Rayton stood and gazed after the bouncing vehicle. Then he picked up the hat and coat, and placed them on the top rail of the fence.

"That is the worst thing I ever saw in the way of a doctor," he said. "Most of them are mighty good fellows — and I didn't know before that any of them were quitters. But that chap? Why, he's a disgrace to a pill box. Hope he'll come back for his duds, though."

Mr. Reginald Baynes Rayton turned, and continued on his homeward way, swinging his feet well in front of him, and expanding his chest. But presently he lost the air of the conquering hero. Misgivings assailed him. He had picked a fight simply because he was in a bad temper. He had called a more or less harmless individual names, and then punched him in the jaw and forced him to call himself a liar.

"I'm ashamed of myself," he murmured. "What has become of my manners?"

He reached his house, and found Mr. Banks in the kitchen, still reflectively consuming tobacco.

"What's the matter with you, Reginald?" inquired the New Yorker. "You look excited."

"I am," replied Rayton, and told frankly but briefly of his talk with Jim Harley and of his fight with Nash.

"I am glad you punched Nash, for I don't like the animal," said Banks. "But why in thunder didn't you trim Harley first? He insulted you."

"He didn't mean to insult me. He believes in the potency of those red crosses. It is a matter of family pride with him," answered Rayton.

## CHAPTER XII

RAYTON IS REMINDED OF THE RED CROSSES

THE snow vanished during the day, under the unseasonable glow of the sun; but with evening came a biting frost and a choking, quiet wind out of a clear sky. The next morning lifted bright and cold, with a glint of ice over all the wilderness, but not so much as a patch or tatter of snow anywhere.

Banks and Rayton breakfasted by lamplight, for they had planned a morning after ruffled grouse. The sun was just over the eastern forests when they stepped out from the warm kitchen to the frosted open, buttoned their fur-lined gloves, and turned up the collars of their blanket "jumpers." They separated at a spur of spruces and firs that thrust itself, like a green buttress, into the yellow-brown of a back pasture.

"You can have Turk. He may find you a belated woodcock or two," said Rayton.

So Banks swung to the left, and entered the

forest, with the obedient, eager dog at his heels, and a trail of fragrant smoke drifting over his shoulder, pure blue in the sunshine.

Rayton entered the woods to the right. He walked carelessly through the underbrush, heedless of everything about him, and of the gun in the hollow of his arm, grieving over his conversation the day before with the brother of the woman he loved. Had Jim really expected him to behave like a coward — to run away from the marked cards? Had Jim no better opinion of him than that? He wondered if Nell knew that the cards had been dealt to him? And if so, how she felt about it? Had Jim told her of their heated argument, and of his — Rayton's — childish exhibition of temper? That would not strengthen his chances with her. And what would she think of him when she heard of his crude outbreak against Doctor Nash? He trembled at the question.

"Those red crosses may be my undoing, after all, in a sneaking roundabout way," he reflected.

A bird went whirring up from close in front of his trampling feet, and got safely away. He halted, leaned his gun against a tree, and lit his pipe.

"I must keep my wits about me," he said, "and stop worrying about those silly cards, or every-

## Rayton is Reminded of the Crosses 171

thing will get away from me — birds and everything."

He sat for about half an hour on a convenient stump in a patch of sunshine, smoking, and working himself into his usual happy state of mind. He dreamed of Nell Harley. He had visions of her — and he discovered a golden trail of thought, and followed it into a golden magical future. The cards, the argument with Jim, and the fight with Nash were all forgotten. At the end of the half hour he continued on his aimless way.

The lanes and little clearings of the forest were comfortably warm, for the sunlight filled them, and the wind was walled away from them. The peace of the frost-nipped, sun-steeped wilderness soothed and healed his spirit. He moved slowly, and halted frequently to spy out some twittering chickadee or flitting blue jay, to gaze up at the purple spires of the spruces, or down at some flaming, grotesquely shaped toadstool. He loved it all — every stump, shadow, sound, and soaring wall of it, every flickering wing and furtive call, every scent, tone, and silence.

He tramped onward, comforted, following his whim. At noon he halted beside a brown brook, twisting among cedars here, alders there. He had several thick slices of bread and butter in his pocket. He built a small fire at the edge of the stream, skinned, in woodman's style, a plump partridge that he had shot an hour before, broiled it to a turn, and dined to a wish. After his meal, he spent a dozing hour between the red fire and the brown stream, with the stem of his pipe between his teeth, and great dreams behind his eyes.

"This suits me," he murmured. "I'll make a day of it."

He got to his feet at last, picked up his gun, and followed the course of the stream downward, taking his time, and avoiding all tangles of underbrush and difficult places. He waked up several grouse, and got one clean shot. But he was not keen about making a bag. He was enjoying himself in quite another way. Had there been paper and pencil in his pocket, instead of feathers, crumbs of bread, and shreds of tobacco, it is more than likely he would have tried to write a poem; for Mr. Reginald Baynes Rayton was in love with a woman, and in love with nature on one and the same golden day. Everything was forgotten but the quiet, magical joy that steeped him to the soul.

It was about mid-afternoon when Rayton altered his course for home. He studied the sky and his

## Rayton is Reminded of the Crosses 173

compass, and then turned his back to the brown brook. He calculated that this line would take him out to Samson's Mill Settlement shortly after sunset.

An hour later Rayton was still far from home, and among tall timber and heavy underbrush. Red rays of sun flooded from the west, low and level, and became tangled and lost among the black screens of the forest. Rayton moved slowly, pushing his way through moosewood saplings. He halted, drew his compass from an inner pocket, and reassured himself as to his position.

And then, on the left, a rifle shot rang out, sharp and vicious. Rayton jumped, spun round on his heels, then dashed forward, shouting strongly and angrily. He heard the swishing and crackling of flight ahead of him. He halted, raised his fowling piece, and let fly both barrels. He bellowed murderous threats after the retreating, unseen sniper.

Then, quick as lightning, the strength went out of him. Voice and knees failed together, and he sank silently to the forest loam. So he lay for a minute, dizzy and faint, and stunned with wonder. In a dazed way he set all his senses on a vague inquiry, searching for pain. But he felt no pain — only a quick, strong pulsing in his left shoulder. He took note of this cloudily. Then, of a sudden, his brain cleared, and anxiety sprang alive in his heart.

He sat up, and put his right hand across his body. His shoulder — the thick blanket stuff that covered it — was wet and hot. He held his hand close to his eyes in the waning light, and saw that it was reeking red from finger tips to wrist. A gasp of dismay escaped him. Again he felt all about the wet place with his right hand. Now the blood was streaming down his arm. He discovered the wound — a tender spot, high up.

"I must stop it," he muttered. "It's working like a pump. If I don't plug it up, or tie it up, mighty quick, I'll be drained dry."

A vision of his bloodless corpse prone on the forest moss flashed across his mind. Then he set swiftly and cleverly to work to check the flow of blood. First, he made a thick pad of dry moss and a handkerchief, and bound it tightly over the wound with a silk scarf from his neck. Then he removed his elastic suspenders, and twisted them over his shoulder and under his armpit four times. The pulsing became fainter and fainter, and at last could not be felt at all.

"Thank God!" he exclaimed. "I do believe

I've done the trick. Fine thing, these patent Yankee suspenders."

He got to his feet, swayed, and sat down again.

"I must have lost a quart or two," he muttered. "No head — no knees — no insides."

He sat very stiff for a little while in deep but meaningless thought. His mind felt like a feather — a puff of smoke — drifting dust. An impish wind was blowing it, and would not allow it to settle.

"This is queer," he said. "Is it loss of blood — or shock? Must do something."

He scrambled to his feet again, picked up his gun, and pressed forward a distance of about twenty yards. He felt a tickling in his shoulder again. It strengthened to a faint throbbing. The horror of bleeding to death returned to him with a grip on his heart. Pain he could struggle against, and perhaps dominate; but this was not pain. This was tender and warm — this flowing out of life.

He sat down again, and again the pulsing quieted and ceased. He saw that he must make a night of it in the woods, unless help came to him. He could not go forward in search of help. He must keep still — or bleed to death. He saw this very clearly, as if written in great white letters on a wall of blackness. And, more dimly, he saw the danger of freezing during the long, cold night. Though warmly clothed, he had no blanket or wrap of any kind.

Fire was the only thing at his command that could keep the frost away. Reaching about with his right hand, he pulled up a great quantity of dry moss. Then he shifted his position a little, and repeated the operation. His arm was feeling numb now, and he could not detect any hint of the pulsing sensation.

Twilight had deepened to night in the forest, and a still cold was creeping in from the vast overhead and the wide, empty portals of the north. Rayton felt about in the underbrush, and discovered plenty of dry fuel, some of it even lying detached upon the ground. He piled his brush and moss to one side of the irregular circle which he had cleared down to the rock and soil, working with the least possible effort. With his sheath knife he cut some living brush, some young spruces, and a few small saplings.

By this time, his left arm and side were aching dully, but his head felt steadier. He placed a bunch of moss, twigs, and larger sticks in the cleared

## Rayton is Reminded of the Crosses 177

space, and struck a match. The flame curled up, grew, crowned the dry heap, and painted the crowding walls of the forest with red, dancing shadows. There was no wind — nothing astir in the air but the drifting frost. The smoke of the fire went straight up toward the high, aching stars, and the heat spread around in a narrow circle. Rayton squatted close to the fire, and fed it with more dry sticks, and soon with some of the green wood.

A sudden drowsiness came to him with the soothing glow of the fire. He fought against it for a few minutes, and even nerved himself to crawl away and drag in a large half-rotted stump. He placed this valuable addition to his store of fuel fairly on the top of the fire, banked more dry stuff beneath and around it, and then lay down on his couch of moss. He felt comfortably warm, deliciously sleepy, and absolutely care free. The pain in his arm was almost as numb as the arm itself. He scarcely noticed it.

"This isn't so very bad, after all," he murmured. "So long as that pumping doesn't begin again, I really don't care."

He lay on his right side, deep in the dry moss, and gazed into the fire. He saw the red and yellow flames crawl up the flanks of the shattered and hollow stump.

"It will catch," he murmured. "It will be all right. That's — a good — fire. I'll just lie — here — and watch it — burn. Don't think I'd — better — go to sleep. Not sleepy — any — way."

And then his lids slid down; and in his dreams he continued to watch the red and yellow flames rise and fall, creep up, bring down, and mount again. He dreamed that he did not sleep, but lay and watched the fire crown the shattered stump and gnaw a dozen passages into its hollow heart. That was all of his dream. It was no more than a picture, as far as progress and action were concerned. It seemed to him that he lay deep in the dry moss, on his right side, with his eyes wide open. So, for a few minutes — and then the fire died down suddenly to blackness — so suddenly that he sat bolt upright, and uttered a cry of dismay.

It had been a dream. Rayton had dreamed the long night away, thinking himself awake; and now the cheerless gray of a November dawn was sifting through the forest. The fire was a patch of dead ashes. The air was bitterly cold. Rayton felt stiff and sore. His hands and feet were like

## Rayton is Reminded of the Crosses

ice. As he sank back upon his right elbow, a sharp pain stabbed him in the side. He groaned pitifully.

"This is worse than the bullet wound," he muttered. "And this is all my own fault for going to sleep."

His shoulder, fortunately, neither bled nor pained him. The blood in the pad of moss was dry. The arm was stiff, owing largely to the grip of the elastic suspenders and the bandages; but that was only to be expected. This hot pain in the side, however, leaping inward with every breath and movement, told him of a serious danger.

"I'll just warm myself a bit, and then get out," he said. "I *must* get out, this time!"

He managed to heap up an armful of moss and twigs, and set it alight. He crawled close to the quick flames, almost embracing the mound of smoke and fire. Little sparks flew out, and fell upon his heavy, frosted clothing, scorched for a little while, and then blinked to nothingness, unheeded. He piled on more fuel, and fairly breathed the heat into his lungs.

A shout rang strongly and hopefully through the silent forest. Rayton sat up weakly, and gazed around him. The light was dim, and he saw nothing but the soaring trees and crowding underbrush. He tried to shout — but his voice was no more than a whisper. He tried again, with desperate effort, and groaned with the hot agony that stabbed his lungs. He put more dry fuel on the fire, for here was a signal more sure to guide help to him that any outcry. Not content with this, however, he crawled to his gun, inserted a loaded cartridge, and discharged it into the ground; then crawled close to the fire again, lay prone, and made no struggle against waves of flashing color and gigantic sound that flowed over him, trampling him down, down fathoms deep.

When Rayton returned to the surface of that mighty tide, he discovered his head to be supported by a human shoulder and arm. A flask, gripped by a big, familiar hand, was against his lips. On the other side of the fire stood Dick Goodine, gazing across at him with haggard eyes. Among the trees, the daylight was stronger, and held a hint of sunshine. He sighed, and parted his lips, and the potent liquor from the tilting flask trickled down his throat and glowed within him.

"Thanks, you chaps," he muttered. "I'm mighty glad you found me."

"Drink some more," said Banks tenderly.

## Rayton is Reminded of the Crosses 181

"You feel like a block of ice. Swig away, there's a good fellow. Better be drunk than dead!"

Rayton took another big swallow of the stinging brandy. Then, reviving swiftly, he pushed the flask away.

"That's better," he said. "But I'm afraid I've caught a whacker of a cold. Let my fire go out, you know. Got shot — and built a fire — and went to sleep. Very foolish. How'd you happen to find me so soon? Good thing. My side feels like the devil!"

"You just keep quiet for a while longer," said Banks. "We're going to roll you up in this blanket, now, and feed you with hot beef tea."

Dick Goodine, who had not moved or spoken before, now passed around the fire, stooped, and took the Englishman's right hand in both of his.

"I'm almighty glad you — you are awake, Reginald," he said huskily.

Then he straightened himself quickly, and turned away.

They rolled Rayton in two blankets, and placed him on a deep couch of moss, close to the fire. They bared his feet, and rubbed them to a glow. They filled him to the neck with scalding beef tea, strongly laced with brandy. They built up the fire, until it roared like a burning hay barn. Banks cut away the left sleeve of the blanket jumper, removed some of the dry blood, and examined the wound.

"Clean as a whistle!" he exclaimed. "In here and out there. That is nothing to worry about, I guess — now that it has stopped bleeding."

Goodine examined the shoulder in silence, and looked tremendously relieved to see so clean a wound. Banks loosened the pinch of the elastic suspenders over and under the shoulder. Then he put on fresh bandages.

"How is the side feeling now?" he asked.

The Englishman smiled and nodded, mumbled some ghosts of words, and then, under the spell of the beef tea and brandy inside him, and the heat of the fire on his body, sank again to sleep. For a few minutes his two friends sat and watched him in silence. Dick Goodine was the first to speak.

"D'ye think he'll pull 'round all right?" he whispered.

"Of course he'll pull 'round," replied the New Yorker. "He is as strong as a horse, and the bullet wound is not serious. His blood is clean, thank Heaven! — as clean as his heart. He has

## Rayton is Reminded of the Crosses 183

got cold right into his bones; but if the heat will drive out cold, I guess we'll thaw him, Dick. Now is the time to try, anyway, before it gets set. We'll keep the fire roaring. And in half an hour we'll wad more hot drinks into him. We'll drive that pain out of his side, or bust!"

The trapper nodded, his dark eyes fixed upon Rayton's quiet face with a haunted and mournful regard.

"We'll take him home before night," continued Mr. Banks; "and then we'll go gunning for the skunk who tried to murder him!"

"You bet we will!" replied Goodine huskily.

## CHAPTER XIII

CAPTAIN WIGMORE SUGGESTS AN AMAZING THING

Rayton's chest and side felt much better when he awoke from his second deep sleep by the fire. It was noon; and though the air was frosty, the sun was shining. Mr. Banks administered more beef tea to him, piping hot.

"How did you happen to find me so soon?" asked the Englishman.

"Thank Dick for that," said Banks. "He dragged me out of bed before dawn. He heard the shooting last night; but didn't think much about it then. But when he learned that you had been out all day he began to worry."

Dick Goodine nodded.

"That's right," he said. "The more I thought over them two shots, an' the yellin' I heard, the queerer it all seemed to me."

"Did you see any one, Reginald?" asked Banks. "Do you know who plugged you — or can you make a guess?"

## An Amazing Thing 185

Rayton shook his head. "I didn't see anything," he replied — "not even the flash of the rifle. No, I can't guess. It was all so sudden! — and I was so dashed angry and surprised, you know! I let fly with both barrels — and then I fell down. Blood was just spurting, you know. I felt very weak — and mad enough to chew somebody."

"So *you* fired the second shot, did you?" queried Banks.

"Yes. I only hope I peppered the dirty cad. Of course, it may not have been intentional. I haven't thought it out yet. Whoever fired the shot may have mistaken me for a moose or deer. But it is pretty hard lines, I think, if a chap can't walk through the woods without being sniped at by some fool with a rifle."

"That's what set me wonderin' — that second shot," said the trapper. "I was a durned idjit, though! I might er known there wasn't any strangers shootin' 'round this country now — any of the kind that hollers like all git-out every time they hit something — or think they do. But I was a good ways off, an' late, so I just kept hikin' along for home."

"That's all right, old boy," said Rayton. "No harm done, I think. But are you sure there are no strangers in the woods now? Who do you think shot me, then?"

"Certainly not a stranger!" exclaimed the New Yorker. "You may bet on that, Reginald. The murderous, sneaking, white-livered skunk who shot you is the same animal who set fire to young Marsh's camp — the same vicious fool who is at the bottom of all this marked-card business."

"Great heavens!" exclaimed the Englishman. "Do you really believe that? Then the card trick is getting pretty serious. What do you think about it, Dick?"

"It beats me!" said Dick, in a flat voice. "I don't know — an' I can't guess. It's a mighty nasty-lookin' business, that's all I can say. Looks to me like a job for the police."

"Not yet!" cried Rayton. "I can look after myself. Promise me to keep quiet about it, will you? That will give us a chance to look 'round a bit for ourselves. We don't want to start the whole country fussing about."

"But what about Nash?" asked Mr. Banks. "He is bound to know. You'll have to tell him how you came by the puncture in your shoulder."

"That is all right. It is only a flesh wound, and clean as a whistle. I don't need Nash."

"We'll not argue about that, Reginald," returned Banks. "Here, drink this brandy, and then we'll start for home with you. I am bossing this show."

Two hours and twenty minutes later they had Rayton comfortably tucked away between the warm sheets of his own bed. His two stalwart friends had carried him every yard of the way, in a blanket, and he had not suffered from the journey. Banks unbandaged his shoulder, and examined the wound. He washed it in warm water, and moved the arm gently. The blood began to flow freely. He bound the shoulder tightly, and nodded to the trapper.

"Where are you going?" asked Rayton, as Dick opened the door.

"For Doctor Nash," answered Dick, and the door slammed behind him.

Dick saddled one of the horses, and rode off at a gallop. He was lucky to find the doctor at home in the farm-house where he boarded. He delivered his message briefly, but clearly. Nash rubbed his hands together, and informed the trapper that there was another doctor at Bird Portage, twenty miles away. When asked to explain this remark, he blustered and swore, and at last said frankly that Rayton could bleed to death for all he cared.

"If you don't come peaceful an' quiet," said Goodine slowly, "then — by hell! — you'll come the other way!"

Their eyes met, and flared for a second or two. Then Nash wavered.

"I'll come," he said.

"I'll wait for you," said the trapper. "Git a move on."

When they reached Rayton's house they found old Captain Wigmore in the sitting room, smoking a cigar and smiling sardonically. Nash went upstairs, but Wigmore beckoned the trapper to him.

"I've wormed it out of them," he said. "I know all about it; and that means that I know a good deal more about it than you do."

"What? More about what?" asked Goodine anxiously.

"Just this, my good trapper of foolish beasts! Nash is the man who put the hole through the Englishman's shoulder!"

Dick stared. At last he regained the use of his tongue.

"You're cracked!" he exclaimed. "Nash didn't do it!"

## An Amazing Thing

"What do you know about it?"

"Well, I guess I know that much, anyhow."

"Then who did it?"

"Don't know."

"But I do. You keep your eye on Nash when I tackle him. Then you'll know."

Dick shook his head.

"I guess not," he murmured, and went upstairs, leaving the captain alone with his thin smile and long cigar.

"I do believe that old crow has a slat loose," reflected the trapper. "I'd give a good lot to know what he's truly thinking about, anyhow."

Doctor Nash, after brief greetings, set to work on Rayton's wounded shoulder. He made a close examination, but asked no questions. He worked swiftly for about half an hour.

"That's done," he said. "All you have to do now is to keep still for a while." He paused and turned to Banks. "Has he been insulting and assaulting somebody else lately?" he asked.

"Don't know," returned the New Yorker. "Why?"

"Just an idea of mine," replied Nash. "Some men are not as good-natured as I am, you know. Somebody took a shot at him — and I was just wondering why. It does not often happen 'round here."

"You are the only person I have behaved like that to," said Rayton, "and — and — well, I am dashed sorry I lost my temper. I beg your pardon, Nash. I am very sorry, honestly. I behaved like a cad."

"You should have thought of that before," sneered Nash.

At that moment old Captain Wigmore entered the room on the tips of his neat little toes, smiling behind his whiskers.

"I see you've brought your company manners with you," said Nash. "I thought you saved them up for the ladies." He had the old fellow on his black list.

"Is that you, doctor?" returned the captain pleasantly. "So you have been patching up this young man, I see. What do you think of your work?"

"Of my work? Oh, I guess my work is good enough. Have you anything to say about it?"

"Why, yes, now that you ask me. Five or six inches to the side would have done the job. Why didn't you do it when you were at it?"

Dick Goodine guessed what was coming; but

## An Amazing Thing

the other three stared at the old man in frank amazement. Nash looked bewildered.

"Six inches?" he queried. "Done the job? What the devil are you talking about?"

"There are none so blind as those who won't see," replied Wigmore, leering.

"What d'you mean? What are you grinning at?"

"Don't get excited, doctor. Bluster and bluff don't frighten me." He stepped close to Rayton. "Who d'you think put that hole through your shoulder, Reginald?" he asked.

"Haven't the least idea. Wish I had," replied the invalid.

"Dear me! What a dull young man you are," jeered Wigmore.

"Don't follow you," said the Englishman.

"Same here," said Banks.

Captain Wigmore chuckled. "I don't suppose you have an enemy anywhere within five hundred miles of here?" he queried.

"Not to my knowledge," said Rayton.

"Then why did you and Nash fly at each other day before yesterday, in the middle of the road? Why did you knock your dear friend flat in the mud?"

"Oh, give us a rest!" exclaimed Nash, flushing darkly, and scowling at the old man.

"That was nothing more than — than a sudden explosion of bad temper," said Rayton.

Wigmore nodded his head briskly, and turned to the doctor.

"And I noticed," he said, "that you did not wait to be knocked down a second time. You hopped into your rig, and drove away at top speed. He who fights and runs away — ah?"

"Really, captain, what is the necessity of all this?" protested Mr. Banks.

Wigmore waved his hand toward the big New Yorker, as if at a fly that had buzzed in his ear. His keen, glinting eyes were fixed with a terrible, rejoicing intentness upon Doctor Nash.

"What were you doing in the woods yesterday afternoon?" he asked.

"Confound you!" cried Nash furiously. "What are you talking about? What do you mean to imply? You skinny little runt, you must be mad!"

Wigmore laughed with a sound like the clattering together of dry bones. Mr. Banks gripped him roughly by a thin, hard arm.

"Enough of this!" cried the big sportsman. "Either speak out like a man, or shut up!"

## An Amazing Thing

"Very good," returned the captain, with another mirthless laugh. "All I want to know is what Doctor Nash was doing in the woods to the west of here yesterday afternoon, with a rifle. What game were you after, doctor? I have always heard that you were not very keen on that kind of sport."

"I wasn't in the woods!" cried Nash. "You are a liar!"

"Don't call *me* a liar, *please*," protested the old man. "It is Benjamin Samson who is the liar, in this case. He told me that you borrowed his rifle yesterday, just before noon, and struck into the woods."

Nash gasped, and his face faded to the sickly tint of a tallow candle. He stared wildly at Wigmore, then wildly around at the others. He opened and closed his mouth several times noiselessly, like a big fish newly landed on the bank. But at last his voice returned to him suddenly and shrilly.

"I forgot!" he cried. "I was out yesterday — with Samson's rifle — after all. But what about it? Why shouldn't I go shooting if I want to? This is a free country! But I know what you are — trying to make Rayton think — you dirty little gray badger! You are hinting that I shot him! I'll have the law on you for this, you — you ——"

"I'll not wait to hear the rest of it, though it is sure to be apt and picturesque," said the captain, flashing his dazzling "store" teeth. "Good-by, Reginald, Good-by, all. See you to-morrow."

He bowed, skipped from the room, and hurried downstairs, and out of the house. Doctor Nash sprang after him to the top of the stairs, trembling and stuttering with rage; but he did not go any farther. He turned, after a moment or two, and re-entered the room. He strode up to the bed.

"Do you believe that?" he cried. "Do you believe that I shot you, Reginald Rayton?"

"Certainly not," replied Rayton promptly. "You wouldn't be such a fool as to borrow a rifle to do it with, even if you wanted to kill me."

Nash turned upon Banks and Dick Goodine.

"And you two?" he cried. "Do you think that I tried to murder Rayton? That I fired that shot?"

Dick Goodine, who stood by the window, with his face averted, answered with a silent shake of the head. Mr. Banks did not let the question pass so lightly, however. For several seconds he gazed steadily, keenly, inquiringly into Nash's angry eyes. He was very cool and ponderous. The scene suggested to Reginald Rayton the judgment of a mortal by a just but inexorable god. Only his ever-ready sense of politeness kept him from smiling broadly. Nash glared, and began to mutter uneasily. At last the big New Yorker spoke.

"Circumstances are against you, Nash," he said slowly. "Nobody can deny that. There is bad blood between you and Reginald. Reginald loses his temper, and gives you a trimming. On the following day you borrow a rifle, and go into the woods, and that evening the man who punched you in the jaw is shot through the shoulder. It looks bad, Nash — mighty bad! But — keep quiet! — but, in spite of appearances, I don't think you are the guilty person."

"Then why the devil didn't you say so before?" cried the doctor, trembling.

"Calm yourself," replied Mr. Banks, "and I'll try to explain to you my reasons for naming you guiltless. In the first place, I believe you to be a touch above shooting a man in the dark. Whatever you may be in yourself, your profession would make you better than that. In the second place, I don't think that you have any hand in the game of the marked cards — and I am quite sure that the person who marks those cards knows who put the hole through Reginald's shoulder."

Nash looked startled.

"I forgot about that!" he exclaimed. "Rayton told me that the card was dealt to him — and then the — the subsequent argument we had kind of put it out of my head."

Banks smiled. "Quite so. I don't wonder at it," he said. "But tell me, do you still believe Jim Harley to be at the bottom of the card trick?"

Nash shot a glance at the bandaged man in the bed. "I do," he replied. "I stick to that until some one proves it untrue, though every man in this room gives me a punch in the jaw. It is a free country, and I have a right to my opinion."

"Of course you have," agreed the New Yorker; "but I'll show you the real trickster within two days from now. In the meantime, I shall keep my suspicions and plans to myself."

Early that evening the snow began to fall, and by breakfast the next morning it lay a foot deep over the frozen wilderness. Mr. Banks prepared his own breakfast and Rayton's, and they ate to-

## An Amazing Thing

gether in Rayton's room. Banks was washing the dishes in the kitchen when Dick Goodine opened the door, and stepped inside.

"I'm off," said the trapper. "If I don't get busy pretty quick, I won't have one fox skin to show, come spring."

He went upstairs, treading noiselessly as a bobcat, in his snowy moccasins, shook hands with Rayton, asked considerately about the shoulder, and then went out into the white world.

"I like that man," said Banks. "He's true blue."

"Right you are," replied the Englishman.

The last pan was cleaned and put away, when Banks was aroused from deep thought by a faint knocking on the front door. He pulled down the sleeves of his shirt, wriggled into his coat, made a hurried pass at the thin hair on top of his head, with a crumb brush, then took his way decorously along the hall, wondering who the formal caller might be. He opened the door, and found Nell Harley in the little porch. Her clear face was flushed vividly, and her clear eyes were wide with anxiety.

Mr. Banks mastered his astonishment before it reached his eyes.

"Come in! Come in!" he exclaimed. "This is delightful of you, Miss Harley."

He seized one of her gloved hands, drew her into the narrow hall, and closed the door.

"Jim started for one of his camps — early this morning — before we heard," she said. "So I have come to — to see Mr. Rayton. Is — he very — ill?"

"Ill!" repeated Mr. Banks cheerfully. "My dear young lady, he is fit as a fiddle. We broke up his cold yesterday, you know, and the scratch on his shoulder is nothing. Please come in here. I'll just touch a match to the fire."

"Where is Mr. Rayton?" she asked, as he stooped to light the fire in the sitting-room stove.

"Oh, he's at home. I'll tell him you are here."

"I'm sure he is in bed."

"Well, so he is. It is the safest place to keep him, you know, for he is always getting into trouble."

"I — I want to see him — to speak to him," she whispered.

"Then wait a minute, please. I'll run upstairs and try to make him look pretty," said Mr. Banks.

When Miss Harley entered Rayton's bedroom, she found the invalid sitting up against a stack of pillows, smiling cheerfully, slightly flushed, his shoulders draped with a scarlet blanket. He extended his hand. She drew off her gloves, and took it firmly. Neither spoke for fully half a minute. Mr. Banks left the room, light on his feet as a prowling cat.

"It is the curse," she said, at last, unsteadily. "When you are strong again you — you must go away."

"Am I really in danger?" he asked very softly. "Under the old conditions of the curse, you know?"

Her eyes wavered.

"Your life has been attempted," she whispered.

"I mean to stay," he replied, somewhat breathlessly, "until that curse has done its worst on me — or until you love me!"

## CHAPTER XIV

#### FEAR FORGOTTEN — AND RECALLED

The color slipped away, then flooded back to Nell Harley's cheeks and brow. Her fine eyes brightened, then dimmed sweetly. She withdrew her hand from his, and turned away.

"Until you love me," repeated Rayton, in a dry voice that strove to be both commonplace and courageous. "If — if that is not to be," he continued, "then I will go away."

She whispered something; but because of her averted face he did not catch the words.

"I beg your pardon?" he queried fearfully. "I did not hear."

Now she stood with her back to him; but not far from his one capable hand hanging empty and hungry over the edge of the bed.

"Can't you — pretend?" she asked very faintly.

"Pretend?" he repeated, in wonder; for, after all, he was rather a simple soul in some things. "Pretend? I am not pretending. I don't think

I am much of a hand at pretending. What — do you mean?"

"If — you — care for me — please pretend that you do not like me at all. Keep away from our place — you know, and — and when we meet by accident — don't — don't look at me as — you do."

Rayton did not answer immediately.

"I couldn't do that," he said, after a brief but electrical silence. "Of course I *could* — but it would be harder for me than — than being shot every day of my life. I am rather a fool at pretending, I'm afraid. But if you say so, if you say I — I have no chance, then I'll clear out — at the double — without a kick!"

"It is because — because I care so for you — that I ask you to do these things," she whispered.

The Englishman gasped, then trembled. He gazed at the young woman's straight, fur-clad back with an untranslatable illumination in his wide eyes. His lips moved, but uttered no sound. Then a brief, wondering smile beautified his thin face. He moved his shoulders on the pillow furtively. He leaned sideways, and stretched forth his hand. The strong, brown fingers touched a fold of the long fur coat, and closed upon it tenderly, but firmly. She neither turned nor moved.

"That curse is only a bad dream," he said, his voice gruff with the effort of speaking in a tone below a joyous shout. "There is no curse! Some misguided person is trying to make fools of us all. His game will be spoiled in a day or two. Why should we fear him? — whoever he is! I do not want to go away from you — even for a minute! I cannot hide my love for you. You would think me a poor sort of man if I could. I love you! I love you! I love you! Dearest — say that again!"

He pulled gently, half fearfully, on the fur coat. Nell turned slowly, and faced him. Her lips trembled, and her white throat fluttered. Two bright tears glinted on her cheeks, all unheeded — by her. He took note of them, however, and was enraptured with their beauty, as no fire and gleam of diamonds could have enraptured him. She smiled slowly, with parted, tremulous lips and shining eyes. She smiled at his illuminated, awe-stricken, yearning face. She looked down at the hand clasping the skirt of her coat so desperately.

"Do you care — so much?" she asked.

"I love you," he said gravely.

"I wonder why you love me! I am not — beautiful."

## Fear Forgotten — and Recalled

He pulled again, with a spasmodic jerk, on the fur coat.

"Beautiful!" he cried. "You? You are the most beautiful thing God ever made!"

"Reginald!" she protested, in a whisper, gazing down at his hand so as to hide her face from him.

He was full of courage now. Even love could not frighten him. Daring blazed in him.

"Kiss me — quick!" he whispered. "I hear Banks on the stairs! Quick!" He pulled at the coat, with fearless determination. For a fraction of a second she resisted; and then, sudden, impetuous, whole-hearted, she stepped forward, sank to her knees beside the bed, pressed her young breast to his unwounded shoulder, and her lips to his. He felt the moisture of her tears. The ascending Banks was forgotten.

"Hem! Ah — I *beg* your pardon!" exclaimed the New Yorker.

The girl was on her feet, and two yards away from the bed in a flash. Her cheeks and brow were crimson; but she faced the big sportsman with something of defiance in her attitude. Reginald Rayton neither moved nor spoke. He lay with his eyes closed, breathing quickly. Mr. Banks looked the most guilty of the three. He shuffled his feet. His glance fell before the glory and daring of the girl's face. He saw that it was beautiful, now absolutely beautiful, and he knew love to be the beautifier. He was abashed. For a few seconds he was utterly bereft of his usual aplomb. Had he been the inspiration of that light on her face and in her eyes, it is probable that he would have known exactly what to do. At last he advanced, bowed ponderously, and lifted one of her hands to his lips. Then he stepped over to the bed.

"Reginald, you have all the luck," he said. "I congratulate you from the bottom of my heart. I'd take on the risks myself for — well, for one-tenth part of the reward."

Nell came back to earth — to the lower levels where lives are lived out, and fear stalks through sun and shadow.

"The risks! I had forgotten them," she whispered.

Mr. Banks completed his recovery at that. He turned to her, smiling, his capable, bland self again.

"If you are thinking of the card trick," he said, "I beg you to put it out of your mind forever. There is a fool working that card trick — and that

## Fear Forgotten — and Recalled

is all it has to do with a curse. A fool is always a curse. So don't worry! Reginald is as safe as I am, for I'll have the mask off that fool, and the claws out of him before he can try any more of his mad games. All you have to do, my dear, is trust Harvey P. Banks — and love this calf, Reginald, I suppose."

"You are very, very kind," she answered gently, "and I hope and pray that you are right. I must go home now, or Kate will be anxious. Good-by, Mr. Banks. Good-by, Reginald."

When the New Yorker returned from letting Miss Harley out of the house, he sat down in a chair beside his friend's bed, lit a cigar, tilted his head far back, and smiled at the ceiling. For several minutes neither of the men spoke. Then Rayton said, in a nervous voice: "You don't think she'll catch cold going home, do you?"

"No, my soft and addled lover," replied Mr. Banks. "She is not at all likely to catch cold. She is wearing a long coat of mink skins, with other things inside it, no doubt. Her boots are thick; her gloves are lined with fur; her hat — ah, I am not sure of her hat. There is danger, of course, that the sky may fall down on her, or that a rail may fly off a fence and hit her on the head.

But the chances are that she'll win home safely, and live until to-morrow."

"Those are not things to joke about," said Rayton reprovingly.

The other laughed long and hard. Then: "Right you are," he said. "Seriously, Reginald, I am sore with envy of you. I have lived a long time, in many cities of the world, and have known many women — but I give first prize to this girl of yours. I have loved many; but here, again, Nell Harley takes first honors."

"What? D'ye mean that *you* love her, too, H. P.?" asked the Englishman anxiously.

"Sure thing," replied the New Yorker. "What d'you think I am made of, anyway? D'you think I am blind, deaf, and heartless? Of course, I love her! — but you needn't glare at me, Reginald. I'm not running. I know when to sit down and do the delighted uncle act. That girl loves you; and, if I have learned anything in my varied career, she'll keep on loving you till the end of the game. You are a lucky dog, Reginald, and I give you my blessing."

"Thanks very much, H. P.," returned Rayton, with emotion. "I am a lucky chap, and no mistake!"

In the meantime, Nell Harley made a swift and glowing passage across the field. She found Kate in the sitting room.

"Is Mr. Rayton in a serious condition?" asked Kate. "Dear me, what a splendid color you have! You look really beautiful. What has happened?"

Nell began to laugh excitedly. She threw aside her gloves and mink-skin coat. She cut several unclassified dancing steps on the rug in front of the fire.

"What on earth is the matter with you?" demanded the young matron anxiously.

"Nothing," said Nell. "I kissed him — that is all."

"You kissed him? Good gracious! What for?"

"He told me to."

"*Told* you to?"

"Yes. Well, he asked me to. He — he said he would rather be shot through the shoulder every day of his life than go away from — me. He said he loved me — he said it over and over and over again. He says it is nonsense — all about that curse. So it is. Then, all of a sudden, I just ——"

"Fell into his arms," interrupted the young matron.

"No, indeed! That would have hurt his shoulder. Anyway, he was in bed, and bandaged. I just didn't care about anything or anybody in the world except him — and then I kissed him. Then Mr. Banks came in — and caught us!"

"Nell!"

"And as soon as he recovered himself he kissed my hand, and congratulated Reginald, and promised to catch the man who shot him before he has a chance to shoot him again."

"Nell, you talk like — like a — I don't know what! You went away almost frightened to death about that marked card and the old family curse — and now you — you are absolutely brazen. I never heard you talk like this before. I never saw you act or look like this before. What will Jim say when he hears of it?"

"I don't care what Jim says," replied Nell. "He can keep on believing in that old curse if he chooses. Reginald is not afraid of it — so neither am I — now. It is wonderful to be loved like that, Kate!"

"Pooh! Teach your grandmother!" retorted Kate.

## Fear Forgotten — and Recalled

Nell's excitement soon passed, and fear stole back into her heart — fear that some new danger threatened the man she loved. And just as her love was greater now than it had been before that first kiss, so was the fear greater now. And her belief in the curse — the supernatural curse — of the marked card, returned to her. She remembered her father's adventure and tragic death. She went up to her own room, and knelt by the head of her own bed, as she had knelt at the head of Reginald Rayton's. But now she knelt to pray.

Things continued to happen at Rayton's house during the remainder of the day. Doctor Nash called just about noon, examined the wound, detected and treated a slight cold in the chest, and stayed to dinner. He helped Banks get dinner, and even made a show of drying the dishes afterward. He was evidently doing his best to forget his quarrel with the Englishman. Old Wigmore's accusation seemed to be worrying him considerably. He referred to it frequently, and even accounted for himself minutely during the season of his possession of the borrowed rifle. Rayton laughed at him.

"I know you didn't shoot me, so why explain?" said the Englishman.

"It is just as well to explain the thing. Old Wigmore has a poisonous tongue and a poisonous mind," returned the doctor. "I believe he is cracked."

Nash had not been gone more than an hour when Captain Wigmore himself appeared.

"I am lonely," said the old man, "and I am getting rather sick of doing my own cooking."

"Thought Fletcher did the cooking," said Mr. Banks.

"So he did; but he has gone away," replied Wigmore. "He cleared out some time or other night before last — the night you were shot, Reginald."

"Where for — and what for?" asked Banks, getting interested.

"He said, in a letter that he was good enough to leave behind him, that he is tired of me and of the backwoods, and can do better for himself in New York. I suppose he has set out for New York. He is a queer fish, you know, is old Timothy Fletcher. He has been with me for years, and has always been more trouble to me than comfort. But he was a handy man and a good cook. I am sorry he took it into his head to go just now. It makes it very awkward for me."

"Did he take anything with him?" asked the would-be detective.

"Only his own duds — and a little rye whisky."

"Where was he the afternoon and evening before his departure?"

"Where was he? Let me think. I am sure I can't say, Banks. Why?"

"Oh, I don't know. He seemed to me rather an interesting old codger. His manners were the worst I ever saw. I wonder what struck him to leave you so suddenly."

Captain Wigmore shrugged his neat shoulders and laughed harshly.

"Perhaps the poor old chap thought he would be suspected and accused of potting our young friend here," he suggested. "He is a prowler, you know. He frequently wanders 'round in the woods for hours at a time, and he usually carries firearms of some kind or other."

Mr. Banks leaned forward in his chair. "I never heard of Fletcher as a sportsman," he said. "But even so, how could he have heard of Reginald's accident? You say he was gone by morning — and it was not until morning that Goodine and I found Reginald. So there can't be anything in that suggestion of yours, captain."

"Very likely not," replied Wigmore. "I am not a detective and have no ambitions that way. All I know is that Timothy went away in a hurry, leaving a letter behind him in which he addressed me in very disrespectful terms."

"Is that all you know, captain?"

"Not quite, after all. I had a rifle — and it has vanished."

"Great heavens! You knew all this, and yet you accused Nash of having wounded Reginald!"

"Well, why not? Some one must have done it — and the circumstances are more against Nash than Fletcher. Nash had a score to settle with Reginald; but I do not think there was any bad blood between our friend and Timothy."

"But you say Timothy is queer?"

"Oh, yes, he is queer. Always has been. He is mad as a hatter — if you know how mad that is. I don't."

"What about the marked card?" asked Rayton. "Don't you think it is potent enough to pull a trigger without the help of either Nash or Fletcher?"

The old man laughed. "I am getting a bit

weary of that card," he said. "Whoever is playing that trick is working it to death. And now that I come to think of it, it strikes me that I was the last person to receive those red marks. So why hasn't the curse, or whatever it is, struck me?"

"You were the last," replied Rayton, "but it was dealt to me that same evening."

"Bless my soul! D'you mean to say so?" exclaimed Wigmore. "That is interesting. It looks as if there is something in Jim's story, after all. Let me see! The marks were handed to Jim's father several times, weren't they? And he came to a sudden and violent death, didn't he? Of course it must be all chance, combined by somebody's idea of a joke — but it looks very strange to me. I don't like it. But why do you get the marks, Reginald? Are you sweet on Miss Harley?"

Rayton laughed — and his laughter was his only answer.

Banks and the captain played chess, and said nothing more about the marked cards or Timothy Fletcher. Captain Wigmore won all the games easily. Then he went home. Banks put the chessmen away, fixed the fires downstairs, and then returned to his seat by Rayton's bed. He sat for a long time in silence, with puckered brows.

"Queer thing about old Fletcher," said the Englishman.

"I believe you, my son," answered Mr. Banks. "It is so darned queer I guess it calls for investigation. Fletcher is an exceedingly rude old man — and his master is an exceedingly *uneven* old man."

"Yes. I don't understand either of them," admitted Rayton.

Banks raised his heels to the edge of the bed, leaned well back in his chair, and lit a cigar.

"Who tied old Fletcher to the poplar tree, d'you suppose?" he queried.

"Haven't the faintest idea."

"But I have," said the would-be detective. "I'm on a double track now. I'll have something to show you coming and going."

## CHAPTER XV

### MR. BANKS IS STUNG

MR. BANKS went over to the Harley place early on the morning after Nell's visit, with a note from Reginald Rayton. The contents of the note seemed to delight and comfort the girl. Banks saw violets on the sitting-room table. He stared at them in astonishment. Mrs. Jim Harley caught the look and laughed.

"They belong to Nell," she said. "Captain Wigmore brought them last night. I am sure he sent all the way to Boston for them."

"Wigmore, too," remarked Banks reflectively. "Well, we are all in the same boat."

He remained for half an hour, and then went home with a fat missive for Reginald, from Nell, in his pocket. The letter threw the Englishman into a foolish glow. For a whole hour after reading it he lay without a word and grinned.

Banks went for a walk in the afternoon, and

met Captain Wigmore. The captain wore a new, fur-lined overcoat. His whiskers were brushed to the last hair, and his manner was as dazzlingly polished as his false teeth. He walked jauntily. The two exchanged a few commonplaces very agreeably. Then Banks, prompted by a sudden inspiration, went to the house of one Silas Long and engaged the eldest son of the family, Billy Long, aged sixteen, to live at Rayton's for a month and attend to the wood and the stock. He made the arrangements in Rayton's name. He told the lad to put in an appearance before sunset, and then went home. He explained this move to Reginald by saying frankly that he wanted to be absolutely free to solve the mysteries upon which he was engaged. The Englishman had no objections.

Mr. Banks left the house again right after the evening meal. It was a clear, starlit night. He walked slowly toward Captain Wigmore's dwelling, and within a few yards of the gate came face to face with the captain.

"Hello!" exclaimed Wigmore. "Is that you, Banks? Are you coming to see me?"

"No, I was just strolling 'round for a bit of fresh air," replied Banks.

"Well, I am glad of that. I have an engagement for the evening."

"An engagement — in Samson's Mill Settlement! You seem to lead a gay life, captain."

Wigmore chuckled. The New Yorker turned, and the two walked side by side along the snowy road for a short distance. Then Banks said: "I'll leave you now, captain, and cut home through the woods. Hope you'll have a pleasant evening."

"I look forward to a very entertaining one," replied the old man, chuckling.

Banks left the road, climbed a fence, and strode along through dry snow that reached halfway to his knees. He was in a pasture dotted with clumps of young spruce.

"The conceited old idiot!" he muttered. "I see his game. I'll fix him!"

He halted, behind a thicket, and stood motionless for a few minutes, listening intently. Then he made a wide half circle to the right, and soon came out again upon the beaten road but now about a quarter of a mile beyond the captain's house. His feet were cold and he stamped vigorously on the road to warm them. The night was windless, but bitter.

Mr. Banks advanced stealthily toward the dark

house. Not a glimmer of light showed in any window. He opened the front gate cautiously, closed it cautiously behind him, and went furtively up the narrow path between the snow-banked lawns. On the step of the little front porch he paused and listened. Then he grasped the knob of the outer door and turned it. The door opened noiselessly.

He entered the narrow porch and stood with his ear against the inner door. He could not hear anything. He fumbled for the knob, found it, and learned that the inner door was locked. He hunted under the mat and in every corner of the porch for the key, having heard somewhere that keys were sometimes hidden away in just such foolish places. He did not find it. Again he listened at the door, this time with his ear against the keyhole. The house was silent as a tomb.

He left the porch, closed the outer door, and made his way to the left along the front of the house and around the corner to the woodshed. Knowing that he could not possibly avoid leaving a trail in the snow, he shuffled his feet so as to make it an unreadable one. He did this so artfully that not one clear impression of his big New York hunting boots was left in his path. He opened the door of the shed without a check and felt his

## Mr. Banks Is Stung 219

way between piles of stove wood to the door of the kitchen.

"I don't feel respectable," he murmured. "But I'll feel a darned sight worse if any one finds me sneaking 'round like this. I must get in, though, and have a look 'round."

The kitchen door was fastened tight. Banks twisted the knob this way and that, all in vain. In spite of his coonskin coat and fur cap he was beginning to feel extremely chilly. He promised himself a husky pull at a bottle of some kind or other should he ever manage to break into the house. He left the shed and tried a back window. He could not get a hold on the sash, however. He drew a heavy clasp knife from his pocket and forced the strong blade between the sill and the bottom of the sash. In this way he pried the sash up almost half an inch. The window had not been fastened. He returned to the shed, and after a few minutes of fumbling about in the darkness he found an axe. By using the thick blade of the axe in place of the knife he soon had the window on the move. He propped up the sash, put the axe back in its place, and returned to the window. With a shove of his right hand he forced it up to the top. This done, he paused for a moment and stood with every sense and nerve on the alert. He heard nothing, saw nothing, felt nothing.

"I wonder if my little idea is the right one," he murmured. "I wonder what I shall find."

He put his gloved hands on the sill, hoisted himself, tipped forward, and wriggled through the window into the dark and silent room. His hands touched the floor first. He pulled his legs across the ledge and was about to stand straight when his knife slipped from the pocket of his coat and clattered on the floor. Still crouched low, he groped forward, found the knife — and then!

It seemed to Harvey P. Banks that he had been asleep a long, long time on a very uncomfortable bed in a very stuffy room. The greatest trouble with the bed must be in the arrangement of the pillows, he reflected, for his neck was terribly stiff and sore. He did not open his eyes right away. There was a feeling in his head and eyes — yes, and in his mouth — suggestive of other awakenings, in the years of his gay youth. So he lay with his eyes closed, remembering that a too sudden opening of the lids under certain once familiar conditions was decidedly unpleasant. He tried to get his wits into line. Where was he? Where had he been

## Mr. Banks Is Stung

last night? What had he been drinking? His poor head only throbbed in answer. So, at last, very cautiously, he raised his heavy lids. He gazed upon darkness — against utter darkness on every side. No. Directly above his head was a faint sheen of gray. That was a window, no doubt; but what was a window doing above his head? That beat him, and he closed his eyes again and tried hard to remember things. The far-away past came clearly to him; but that did not help him. He knew that the things he remembered were of months — even of years — ago.

He was surprised to find that he wore heavy, fur-lined gloves, a fur cap pulled low over his ears and forehead, and a coonskin coat. He put out his right hand and touched a wall of ice-cold dusty floor. He judged that the floor was not more than six inches below the level of his body. He put out his left hand and touched a wall of ice-cold plaster. With a grunt of dawning dismay he sat up, and though his neck ached, and his head spun and throbbed with the effort, he leaned forward and touched his feet with his gloved hands. He felt his heavy shooting boots and a flake or two of pressed snow on their soles — and at that his brain awoke and the memory of his informal entrance into Captain Wigmore's house flashed clear. He uttered a low cry of wonder and consternation.

"What happened?" he whispered. "Did I fall and stun myself as I climbed over the window sill?"

His head behaved so badly at this point that he lay prone again on his hard couch. But now his brain was working clearly, though painfully. Every incident of his attempt to enter the house, with a view to reading the mystery which he was sure it contained, was now as plain as a picture before his inner vision. He reviewed the whole adventure minutely, from the meeting with Wigmore to the opening of the window and the dropping of the knife upon the floor of the pitch-black room. But what had happened after that? Something sudden — and hard! Yes, there could be no doubt of the suddenness and hardness of the next occurrence. But what was it? Had he toppled forward and struck his head against a piece of furniture? Or had something possessed of individual initiative hit him over the head? He sat up again, removed his gloves and cap, and felt all over his head with chilly, inquiring fingers. He could not find any lump or cut; but the back and

## Mr. Banks Is Stung

top of the head were agonizingly tender to the touch.

"A sandbag — whatever that is," he muttered. "I have heard that they effect one somewhat in this way, if properly applied."

He laughed shortly and painfully. His head seemed to have recovered something of its normal position and balance. It felt more solid and steady, and the ache in it was duller. He fumbled through the pockets of his fur coat and found a pipe, tobacco pouch, and box of matches. His clasp knife was not there. Evidently he had not succeeded in picking it up, that time.

"Sorry for that," he muttered. "I could carve my way out of any place with that knife."

He opened the fur coat, and found the contents of his inner pockets intact — his watch, cigar case, three rifle cartridges, the stub of a pencil, a few pocket-worn letters, and a railway timetable. He knew each article by the feel of it. He opened the match box, and was glad to discover that it was full. Then he took out his watch and lit a match. The hands of the watch marked the time as half-past two — and the fact that the watch had not run down proved to him that the hour was of the early morning. He had lain unconscious more than five hours. He wound the watch and returned it to his pocket. Then he struck another match, held it high, and gazed inquiringly around him. The match was of wax, and held its flame for nearly half a minute. He saw a small room, white and bare of walls, bare of floor, with a sloping ceiling, broken by the square of a little skylight. The only article of furniture in the place was a narrow couch upon which he sat. A door of unpainted spruce divided the wall at that end of the room where the ceiling reached its greatest height.

Harvey P. Banks dropped the butt of the match to the floor and rubbed the spark out of it with his foot. He knew that he was in some one's attic; and he felt almost equally sure that it was the attic of Captain Wigmore's house. But who had hit him over the head and then carried him up and deposited him in this place? He had his suspicions, of course. Perhaps the captain had sandbagged him. The old man might easily have returned to the house immediately after parting with him on the road. Or Timothy Fletcher? Why not Timothy Fletcher? Wigmore had been lying when he said that Fletcher had run away to New York. Banks had felt sure of that at the

## Mr. Banks Is Stung

time the statement was made — and now he felt doubly sure of it. Very likely they had both taken a hand in the game. Neither one of them by himself could have carried Harvey P. Banks up to the garret.

Mr. Banks felt cold and sleepy and sore. The soreness was of spirit as well as of body and head. He had certainly made a mess of things. And he felt anxious — decidedly anxious. Who was to make the next move? And what was the next move to be? He would have paid high to find himself snug and safe in his own bed in Reginald Rayton's house. What was Reginald thinking? But he had proved one thing! He had proved, beyond a doubt, that the inmates of Captain Wigmore's house were mysterious and undesirable persons.

He lit a cigar, lay back on his hard couch, and smoked reflectively. His head was not yet steady enough to allow of action. After an inch or two of the cigar had turned to ash, he sat up and got noiselessly to his feet. He had not heard a sound since recovering consciousness. Perhaps the house was empty? He lit a match and tiptoed to the door. He turned the knob cautiously. The door was locked.

"I guess it's not my turn yet," he murmured, and went back to the couch. He drew his cap down about his ears, fastened his fur coat up to the chin, and lay flat on his broad back. But before the cigar was finished he was on his feet again. He lifted the couch and placed it with his head against the door. Then he extinguished the butt of the cigar, lay down, and went to sleep.

Mr. Banks awoke suddenly. He was stiff and cold, but every sense was on the alert. His head felt much better than it had before his sleep. The room was full of gray light that filtered down from the snow-veiled window in the roof. He looked at his watch. It was seven o'clock. He listened intently, but could not hear a sound.

"I can see well enough now to take a hand in the game," he said. "So I guess it is my turn to play."

He lifted the cot away from the door and set it down at one side without a sound. Then he raised his right leg, drew his knee well back, presented the heel of his big boot at the lock of the door, and drove it forward with all the strength of his great hip and thigh. The lock burst, and fell in fragments; and the door, having been constructed so as to open inward, split, and tore itself

## Mr. Banks Is Stung

from its hinges and flapped wide. Thick muscles had bested thin iron in a single effort.

"There! Confound you!" exclaimed Mr. Banks, staggering a little to recover the balance of his big body. He saw, beyond the gaping and twisted door, by the feeble light from his own room, a dark, bare hall and the unpainted rails around the top of a narrow staircase. He advanced one foot across the threshold, stooped forward, and listened, intently. His big body, in its big coat of coonskins, filled the width of the doorway and shut out much of the feeble illumination that descended from the skylight behind and above him. So he stood for a minute or two before he heard a sound save that of his own breathing. And then! What is that? A single, furtive tap, as of something hard on a thin edge of wood, close in front of him. He turned sideways on the threshold so as to let the light from behind him reach the floor in front.

What was that, thin and black, slanting up at him between the rounds of the railing? It had a sinister look. It did not move. Behind it was the black gulf of the stairway. Mr. Banks hesitated for a moment, then began to edge forward.

"Stop where you are!" commanded a voice —

the voice of old Captain Wigmore. "This thing is the barrel of a rifle. I am behind the rifle. If I press on the trigger, my dear Banks, I am sure to hit you somewhere, you are so unnecessarily large. In the belly, most likely. That's right! Stand still."

"You, Wigmore!" exclaimed the New Yorker. "What is the meaning of this? What are you talking about? You must be stark mad!"

The other laughed. It was a most discomforting sound. The laugh of a land crab — if the beast *could* laugh — would doubtless resemble Captain Wigmore's expression of mirth.

"You seem to be indignant, my dear fellow," he said, with exasperating calm. "But what do you expect? I caught you breaking into my house when you were under the impression that I was not at home. Do you think I should have put you in my own bed, with a hot-water bottle at your feet, and carried your breakfast up to you this morning? No, no, my dear Banks! It is my duty to this country, and to society in general, to keep a firm hand on you until the officers of the law relieve me of the charge."

"You old hypocrite!" cried Banks. "You scheming, lying, old devil! Bring the officers of the

## Mr. Banks Is Stung

law! The sooner they get here the better I'll be pleased. I have something to say to them."

Wigmore chuckled. "I haven't sent for them yet," he said. "I rather enjoy the prospect of looking after *you* myself for a little while. I can stand it — if you can."

Mr. Banks watched the barrel of the rifle out of the corner of his eye; but the menacing thing did not waver.

"Where is Timothy Fletcher?" he asked.

"So that is your bright suspicion, is it?" returned Wigmore cheerfully. "He went to New York, I told you. Where do you think he is?"

"In this house, you old ape!" cried Banks.

Wigmore hooted.

## CHAPTER XVI

#### THE LITTLE CAT AND THE BIG MOUSE

The light was stronger, though still gray and thin. It was the light of an unsunlit November day filtered through a small square of snowdrifted glass into a chilly garret. The light alone was enough to drop a man's heart to the depths; but it was not the only thing that depressed Harvey P. Banks. He was anxious, cold, and hungry. He was sickened with disgust of himself and hate of Captain Wigmore. His head ached, his neck and shoulders were sore. To add to all this he could now see the face and eyes of his jailer by the cheerless light. The sight was not one calculated to dispel his anxiety or warm his blood. The eyes gleamed balefully up from the gloom of the stairway, with a green gleam in them like the eyes of a cat watching its helpless prey. In front of the eyes showed the black barrel of the rifle.

"How long do you intend to keep up this farce?" inquired Banks.

## The Little Cat and the Big Mouse 231

"I can stand it as long as you can," was the crisp reply.

"Very likely; but I don't see that I have any say in the matter just now."

"You are wrong, my big friend. You can have your liberty — qualified liberty — this minute if you wish. All you have to do is swear to me, on your honor as a Christian and a gentleman, that you will never mention this little adventure to a living person. You must invent some story for Rayton and set out for New York to-night. You must drop this feeble idea of yours of playing the detective. In short, you must swear to mind your own business in the future and leave me and mine alone."

"I'll see you in hell first!" cried the sportsman. "I am on your trail, and I'll stick to it. You'll pay heavily for this."

Wigmore chuckled. "Pay?" he said. "Pay? You forget, you big slob, that I am banker in this game — and I am not the kind of banker that pays."

"What do you think you are going to do with me?" asked Banks, with outward calm.

"Lots of things," replied Wigmore. "I will reduce your flesh, for one thing; and your fat pride for another. I'll make you whimper and crawl 'round on your knees. But just now I'll request you to come downstairs. Since you have broken the door of that room, I must give you another."

"I hope the other room will be an improvement on this."

"Yes. A very comfortable room."

"And what about breakfast?"

"You will have a cup of tea in half an hour — if you behave yourself in the meantime."

Banks laughed uncertainly.

"See here, captain, don't you think this joke has gone far enough?" he asked.

"Not at all," replied Wigmore. "My joke has just begun. Yours ended very quickly, on the floor of my sitting room — but that was your own fault. You are a blundering joker, Banks. You should have made sure that I was not at home before you went round shaking all the doors, and then crawled through the window. But that is a thing of the past, now, and so beyond mending. I hope you will derive more entertainment from my joke than you did from your own."

Banks had no answer to make to that. He fisted his big hands and breathed heavily.

*"Then he halted and recoiled, clutching at the cold walls!"*

## The Little Cat and the Big Mouse 233

"I must ask you now to step back to the farther wall of your room," said Wigmore.

Banks hesitated for a moment, then backed across the threshold and across the little room until his shoulders touched the farther wall.

"Stay there until I give you the word," said the old man.

Then face and rifle barrel vanished, and, at the same instant, Banks moved forward noiselessly and swiftly, lifted the couch in his strong hands, and dropped it down the dark well of the staircase. It crashed and banged against the wooden steps and the plaster walls; and before its clattering had ceased the big sportsman himself was halfway down the stairs. Halfway — and then he halted and recoiled, clutching at the cold walls! The couch had been a second too slow in following Wigmore, and Banks a second too slow in following the couch. The captain stood at the bottom of the stairs, a foot beyond the wreckage of the couch, laughing sardonically and presenting the muzzle of the rifle fair at his captive's waist.

"That was a false start," he said. "But I was expecting it, fortunately."

Banks sat down on a dusty step, trembling violently. He felt sick — actually sick at his stomach

— with rage, chagrin, and terror of that ready rifle and the sinister face behind it. The eyes of the old man were more terrifying than the menacing black eye of the weapon. The gleam at their depths was scarcely human.

"Well?" asked Banks, at last, weakly. He passed a gloved hand across his forehead. "Well? What are you going to do?"

"That depends on you," said the captain. "If you throw furniture at me every time I turn my back, I'll be forced to knock you out again and tie you up. I can't risk being killed by you, for my life is valuable."

"Do you intend to hit me again with the sandbag?" asked the New Yorker thickly.

"No, I don't mean to take that risk again," replied the other. "Another crack like that might kill you — and I don't want to kill you just yet, unless I have to. Perhaps I won't kill you at all, my dear fellow. I may — of course; but I don't think so at the moment. I am whimsical, however — a man of quick and innumerable moods. However, I do not expect to thump you again with the sandbag. I have this rifle — for serious work — and this queer-looking little pistol for the joking. It is a chemical pistol — quite a new invention. I

## The Little Cat and the Big Mouse 235

have tested it, and found it to be all the manufacturers claim for it. Don't move! You can see and hear perfectly well where you are! If I discharge it in your face, at a range of twenty feet, or under, it will stun you, and leave you stunned for an hour or more, without tearing the flesh or breaking any bones. The thing that hits you is gas — I forget just what kind. It is pretty potent, anyway — and I don't suppose you are particular as to what variety of gas you are shot with. It is a fine invention, and works like a charm. I am quite eager to test it again."

"Don't! Don't! Great heavens, man, have you gone mad?" cried Mr. Banks.

Old Wigmore raised the odd, sinister-looking pistol in his left hand.

"I don't think it hurts very much," he said. "Feels like being smothered, I believe. Of course the shock may be quite severe at such close range as this."

Banks closed his eyes. He was less of a coward than most men; but to sit there on the narrow stairs, chilled and helpless, and wait for the discharge of an unknown weapon in his face was more than courage and nerves could stand.

"Shoot!" he screamed. "Shoot, and be done with it!"

He cut a queer figure, humped there bulkily, in his great fur coat, with the fur cap pulled low about his ears, his eyes shut tight, and his big face colorless with fatigue and apprehension — a queer, pathetic, tragic figure. He waited for the explosion, every sense and every nerve stretched till his very skin ached. His mind was in a whirl. The thumping of his heart sounded in his ears like the roaring and pounding of surf.

"Shoot! Shoot!" he whispered, with dry lips and leathern tongue.

And still he waited — waited. At last he could bear the strain no longer. He uttered a harsh cry, stumbled to his feet, and opened his eyes, leaning one shoulder heavily against a wall of the staircase. A gasp of relief escaped him. Wigmore had retreated, and now stood several yards away from the bottom step. The muzzle of the rifle was still toward his victim, but his left hand, gripping that terrible, mysterious, little weapon, was lowered to his side. He chuckled. His face looked like that of a very old, very unhuman, and very goatish satyr.

"Wipe your eyes, my dear Banks," he said. "I

won't hurt you, you poor little thing. Dry your eyes, and come down the rest of the way. I'll stand here, at the head of these stairs, while you toddle into that room. Then I'll lock the door, which is very strong, and get you your cup of tea. Come along! Come along! I haven't the heart to hurt such a white-livered whimperer."

For a moment the big sportsman glared at him, contemplating a mad rush, at the risk of a bullet through his breast — but only for a moment. Something in the old man's leer told him that the finger on the trigger would not hesitate, the muzzle would not waver. To attack now would be suicide. He realized that he was at the mercy of a madman.

"I'm coming. I'll be mightily glad of the tea," he said, with a painful attempt at a smile.

He made his way falteringly to the bottom of the steps, across the hall, and into the room indicated by the old man. All the fight and all the strength had gone out of him — for the time being, at least. The terrible play on the stairs had taken more stamina out of him than a day's march through a tangled wilderness, with a seventy-pound pack on his shoulders. He staggered to the bed, and sat down dizzily on the edge of it. Old Wigmore stood on the threshold, leering.

"I hope you like the room," he said. "I spent most of the night in fixing it up for you."

"Thanks. It looks fine," replied Banks. And it really was fine, he noticed, gazing around with reviving hope. There was a window — a real window — in the wall. He could soon attract attention from that window, or let himself out of it by a rope made of bedclothes. He had read of that dodge a dozen times. The old fellow was mad certainly; but there did not seem to be much method in his madness, after all. Banks turned his face away so as to hide a wan smile.

"Sit where you are, my boy, and I'll bring your tea in a minute," said the old man.

Then he stepped back and closed the door. Banks continued to sit on the bed and gaze around the room, uncertain whether to go to the window now or wait until Wigmore had brought the tea and again retired. He did not want to bungle things by being in too great a hurry. With a little patience and cunning on his part, his mad old jailer would soon be in his power. He decided to wait where he was. The bed was soft, and he was woefully tired. He turned sideways, threw his feet up, and sank head and shoulders back upon the tempting pillows.

## The Little Cat and the Big Mouse

With a sharp click, followed by a soft thud, the middle of the bed sank to the floor, and the bulging sides folded inward upon the astonished Mr. Banks. He shouted and struggled; but his head was lower than his heels, and his arms were pinned firmly against his sides. At last he twisted over until he lay on his left shoulder, and his right arm was clear. In another minute he would have been out of the ridiculous trap; but suddenly Captain Wigmore appeared, slipped a rope around the imbedded ankles, and bound them tight; and another around the free arm, and made it fast to the head of the bed. Then the old man stood and leered down at him.

"You are a terrible fellow for smashing furniture," he said. "You have a very violent temper. Out you come! Out you come!"

With incredible strength, the old man gripped the big, floundering sportsman, and yanked him from the bed, where he lay helpless, with his feet tied together, and his right wrist fast to the bed.

"There you are!" remarked Wigmore briskly. "Now, will you be good? Sit up, while I fix the bed. Sit up, do you hear? Then I'll give you your breakfast. You don't deserve it — but I have a tender heart."

He prodded Banks with the toe of his boot. Banks sat up without a word. His rage clouded his mind and deadened his tongue. Wigmore dragged the heavy bedding to the floor, and gazed with admiration at the bedstead. All the slats, save a few at the foot, were hinged in the middle.

"My own invention," said the old man. "Very ingenious, don't you think? But it has done its work, so let it lie. Here are some blankets for you, Banks. Hope you don't object to sleeping on the floor."

He tossed an armful of blankets into his prisoner's lap, and walked briskly from the room. He was back in half a minute, carrying a tray, which he placed on the floor within reach of Bank's free hand.

"Help yourself," he said. Then he went out, shutting the door behind him.

Mr. Banks sat motionless for a full minute, staring at the tray. A small teapot stood there, with steam rising from its spout. It was flanked on the right by a small jug of cream, and on the left by an empty cup. In front squatted a round dish under a cover. At last Banks pulled off his fur cap, and wiped the cold perspiration from his brow with the palm of a grimy hand.

## The Little Cat and the Big Mouse 241

"I suppose the old devil has doped it," he whispered, with a sigh. "Of course he has! What's the good of supposing?"

With an effort, he turned his face away from the teapot and the covered dish. He shifted back a little, so that the rope did not pull on his right arm. He gazed intently at the window, door, walls, and ceiling.

"I must plan a way to get out," he muttered. "I must plan a way to fool this old fiend."

But he could not concentrate his thoughts, for most of them were with his heart — yearning toward the teapot and the covered dish. At last he gave way, and allowed his gaze to rest again upon the silent tempters. His left hand went out to them, then came slowly back. He sighed, unfastened his coonskin coat, and cursed old Wigmore huskily, but heartily. Again the hand advanced. He lifted the teapot and poured some of the steaming amber liquid into the cup.

"It looks all right," he murmured. "But what's the use of looking at it? Of course the old beast has doped it! Heaven help him when I get hold of him!"

He set the teapot down, and groaned. He told

himself to turn away; to forget the craving in his stomach; that he was not really hungry. He assured himself that it is beneficial to go without food now and then — for a day, or even for two days. Then he remembered having read somewhere that smoking allays the gnawing of hunger. He produced a cigar from the case in his pocket, and lit it fumblingly. While he smoked he kept his eyes fixed upon the tray. Suddenly he leaned forward and lifted the cover from the dish.

"Buttered toast!" he exclaimed, in so tragic a voice that the sound of it brought a smile to his dry lips. He replaced the cover with such violence as to crack the dish. After smoking gloomily for another minute or two, he again allowed his attentions to dwell upon the tea, toast, and cream. He lifted the half-filled cup and sniffed it. Did he detect a bitterness in the clean, faint fragrance of it, or was the bitterness only in his imagination? He tilted the cup this way and that, searching the clear liquid for some cloudy sign of danger. He was unsuccessful. He sniffed it again, and this time could not detect the least suggestion of bitterness.

"I am a fool!" he muttered. "My nerves have gone to pieces!"

With a quick hand, he slopped a little of the cream into the tea, and raised the cup swiftly to his lips. But he did not part his lips. For a moment he sat motionless, with the cup raised and tilted — and then, with an oath, he replaced it on the tray, untasted. The momentary gratification of thirst and hunger was not worth the risk. He turned his back upon the tray, and puffed away resolutely at his cigar. He would show the old devil that he was not entirely a fool!

Banks finished the cigar; and still old Wigmore had not returned. The tray still remained on the floor. Banks hitched himself to the head of the bed, and set to work with his left hand to unfasten the knots in the rope which bound him to that cursed, ingenious bedstead. The rope was small, and the knots were hard; but at last the outer knot began to loosen. He paused frequently in his work to glance over his shoulder at the door, and to hearken intently. At last he was free from the bed, but with the length of line still hanging from his wrist. Now he crawled across the room to the door, stood up on his bound feet, and tried the handle. The door was locked, as he had expected. Seated with his broad back against it, he worried the cord at his ankles with both hands until its three stubborn knots were undone. Then, moving on tiptoe, he carried the heavy bedstead across the room, and stood it solidly against the door.

## CHAPTER XVII

### AN ASTONISHING DISCOVERY

THE room was not elaborately furnished, but every piece was good of its kind. Mr. Banks worked busily, moving about stealthily on the toes of his great boots. He had shed his coat, by this time, and rid his right arm of the dangling length of rope. Atop the hinged slats of the bed he placed a substantial chest of drawers, thus reënforcing the barricade and squaring himself with the ingenious slats by one and the same move.

"It will take a bigger man than Wigmore to get in at me now," murmured the sportsman.

He was tremendously pleased with his job, but did not waste much time in admiring it. Now that he was secure from interruption for a while, at least, was the time to develop the possibilities of the window. He would try to attract the attention of some passer-by. If there did not happen to be any passer-by, which was frequently the case, in Samson's Mill Settlement, for hours at a time —

then he would join the pieces of rope with which he had been bound, lengthen the result with a blanket, and lower himself into the free outside world. Old Wigmore might shoot at him through the panels of the door, but he was more than willing to take the risk of being hit by such blind shooting. Once outside, he felt that he would be safe. Not even the mad captain was mad enough to murder him in open sight of the road and fields. These reflections occupied his mind during the seconds in which he turned from his contemplation of the barricade. He made one step toward the window, and then ——

"Halt!" exclaimed the voice of Captain Wigmore, shrill, clear and menacing. Banks halted, with a gasp, and turned his face toward the hateful sound. To his dismay, he beheld the devilish face of the old man leering horribly within seven feet of him, through a square and unsuspected aperture in the door. With a low cry of defiance and nervous fright, he tried to set his limbs in motion again. Would his feet never move? He seemed to pass through a whole minute of terrific but futile exertion. It was like a grotesque nightmare of childhood days — grotesque, but horrible. He saw the old man's hand appear beside the leer-

## An Astonishing Discovery

ing face. In the hand was that queerly shaped pistol. And still his feet clung to the floor as if they were lead! A dull, feeble, popping report came to his aching ears. And then something gripped his windpipe with huge, hard fingers; some one struck him to earth with a gigantic balloon; a blank wave curled about him, fell upon him, pounded the life from his battling lungs, and dragged him, limp and dead, to the unsounded depths.

Captain Wigmore had discharged his chemical pistol in the big sportsman's face. That is all. He had slipped the panel, cried halt, raised his hand, and pulled the trigger, all within two seconds of time.

When Mr. Banks recovered consciousness for the second time since crawling into Wigmore's house, he felt much worse than he had on the first occasion. He felt very, very sick at the very pit of his stomach. His poor head was in a terrible way. At one moment his brains seemed to be floating far above him, light and thin as smoke, and at the next they lay heavily, but loosely, in his sore skull, like a fragment of iron, sliding from side to side. He lay flat, and groaned. Half an hour passed before he ventured to sit up and open his eyes. Absolute darkness surrounded him. He felt about with his hands, and found that he was lying on a folded blanket. He inquired further, and discovered that his new lodging was nothing but a tiny closet, about seven feet deep, and four feet wide, with a steeply sloping roof. The roof was made of a series of sharp-cornered humps. He bumped his head against one of them — and that enlightened him. He was in a closet under a staircase. His fur coat had been left in the bedroom; but, fortunately, the closet was not very cold. After another and briefer rest upon the flat of his back, he decided to try a smoke. He thrust a hand slowly into one pocket, less slowly into another, then swiftly and desperately into pocket after pocket. All were empty! Not so much as a match had been left to him; not so much as a crumb of tobacco.

The rage which this discovery inspired in the breast of Mr. Banks was out of all proportion to the seriousness of his loss. The effect upon him was stupendous. Sandbagging, binding, and pistoling had all failed to lift him to such a height of resentment at this. Why, even he could not have explained. His big boots were left to him — and his voice, such as it was. He began to shout and

## An Astonishing Discovery 249

stamp his feet on the floor. His voice limbered up, and grew in strength, until the dry-tongued cry became a gigantic bellow. The feet pounded up and down until they encountered the door; and then they began to swing back and forth. The door winced and shook at every blow. It was a strong door, however, hung on massive hinges, fastened with a big lock, and barred in three places with rods of iron. Wigmore had taken no chances with this door. He had fixed things this time so that his prisoner was put to stay. That was his idea, anyway.

At last, reeling and breathless from his exertions, Banks sank to the floor, and lay still and silent. For a little while his head span sickeningly, and his mind and senses lay torpid; but only for a little while. This outbreak had done him good — had revived him to the finger tips. He sat up presently and listened for the approach of his enemy. Surely all that bellowing and thumping would bring him.

"If he opens that door, pistol or no pistol, it'll be the end of him," remarked the New Yorker. And he meant it. He was ready for murder. He raised himself to his knees, ascertained the position of the door with his hand, and faced it, waiting in savage expectancy.

At last his straining ears caught a sound. It was a very faint sound, and it came from the left instead of from the door. It was repeated — a faint, furtive tapping, like the tapping of a flipped finger against plaster. He moved cautiously toward the sound. It came again. He put out his hand, and touched the rough lath and plaster of the wall. How frail the barrier felt! He stood up very cautiously. "It may be a mouse — and it may be Wigmore — but it is worth trying," he whispered. Then he swung his right foot backward slowly, and brought it forward with all the force that lay in that long and muscular shank. A sound of cracking plaster and splintered laths rewarded and encouraged him. He steadied himself, with one hand on the door and one on the slope of the staircase, and settled down to kicking. His boot was thick, his leg strong, and his heart in the job. Things cracked and smashed and splintered. At last he knelt and advanced an inquiring hand. The blackness was full of the dust of powdered plaster. He found a ragged-edged break in the wall, and thrust his hand into it.

Mr. Banks snatched his hand back to his own side of the pierced partition, at the same time uttering a sharp cry of dismay. Nothing had hurt

## An Astonishing Discovery

him; but in the blackness beyond his own narrow blackness his fingers had encountered flesh — the flesh of a human nose and eyebrow. He sagged back on his haunches, limp and trembling. Whatever he had expected to find, this was not it.

"Who is there? Speak! Who is there?" he whispered.

No voice answered him; but again he heard that thin rapping, like the flipping of a finger against a hard, dry surface. It was a trifle louder this time, but in exactly the same position.

"Can't you speak? Speak, for Heaven's sake!" cried Banks.

This time he was answered by a low, muffled, strangled groan. He searched his pockets again, with shaking fingers; and, at last, in a little roll of woolen dust in the corner of his match pocket, he found one wax match. This first seemed such a great and joyful thing to him that he had difficulty in restraining his laughter.

"Wigmore, you old devil, here's where I have you at last!" he exclaimed. "You're a fool! You should have picked my pockets thoroughly while you were about it. This little match will prove your undoing — as sure as my name is Harvey P. Banks!"

He began to chuckle — and the sound of his chuckling quieted and steadied him in a flash. "That won't do," he said. "That sounds downright idiotic. I must keep a grip on myself."

With his left hand he found a safe and suitable spot on the wall for the striking of the precious match; and then, with his trembling right hand, he struck it. The little flame hissed into existence, then caught the wax, and burned clear and quiet. He crouched low, and thrust the burning match through the hole in the lath and plaster, and into the chamber beyond, by the length of his arm. The hole was about three feet long and twelve or fifteen inches wide. He shuffled forward and thrust his head between the jaws of ragged plaster and splintered laths.

The match lit a closet even smaller than the one in which Banks lay. Banks beheld rough walls, a sloping roof, a door, and, directly under his hand, a small human figure, bound and gagged.

"Timothy Fletcher!" he exclaimed. "So this is New York — for you!"

The old man's bright eyes blinked like an owl's. He lay close against the wall, and now Banks saw one finger — one free finger — dart out and tap the plaster.

## An Astonishing Discovery

"Roll away from the hole," said Banks. Then the match scorched him, and he withdrew his hand and head. He sat back for a second or two, considering the situation.

"The old fiend!" he muttered. "He must be mad — or the devil himself. This explains the other thing that happened to poor Fletcher — the attack in the woods. Oh, the cunning old beast!"

Now he set to work with his hands, tearing away the light materials of the wall in strips and lumps. He put his hand through, found that Fletcher had rolled away, and then wriggled through himself. It was a tight passage, but at last it was safely accomplished. To remove the gag from Fletcher's stiff jaws was the work of a few seconds. To untie and unwind the complicated knots and cords that bound the old fellow's body and limbs took fully half an hour. During that time, Fletcher did not say one word.

For a little while after the freeing of Timothy Fletcher, Banks sagged weakly against the floor. His head was spinning again. He closed his eyes against the blackness, and began to drift off into a delightful, restful dream. He was all done — all in — down and out! What was the good of worrying? What was the good of anything? He had escaped from his cell. He had found Fletcher and set him free. He had earned his rest.

Timothy Fletcher dragged himself over to where Mr. Banks sagged against the door like a big, half-empty sack. Having spent half an hour in moving his tongue up and down, and round and round in his mouth, he now found himself in possession of a fragment of voice. Also, the blood was beginning to move in his arms and legs again. His mind was as clear as glass. He fastened his thin fingers in his rescuer's collar, and shook that careless head until it flopped and knocked against the door.

"Wake up!" he croaked. "Wake up! We got to get out of here."

Banks opened his eyes, and, in the dark, grabbed Fletcher with his big hands. For a moment he mistook the servant for the master, and, with a sudden, furious surge of strength, he shook him as a terrier shakes a rat. Fletcher yelled, and clawed the sportsman in the face. Then Banks realized what he was doing.

"Sorry," he gasped. "I was half asleep. How are we to get out?"

Fletcher did not answer immediately, but lay panting in the dust. At last he raised himself to his hands and knees. "This door," he whispered.

## An Astonishing Discovery

"It is locked — that is all. You are strong. We must get out! Quick! Smash it!"

Mr. Banks got to his feet, and found the position of the door. He moved slowly. He laughed softly.

"Stand out of the way — out of the danger zone," he cautioned. "I'm going to kick. I can kick like an army mule."

"Kick! Kick!" croaked Timothy Fletcher, crouching off to one side. "There's drink downstairs. Food an' drink."

Banks balanced himself, lifted his right knee high against his waistcoat, and shot forward his right heel. With a rending of wood and ripping of dislodged screws, the door flew open, letting a flood of faint moonlight into the black closet. Banks staggered forward, fell flat on the floor outside, then nipped to his feet again as nimble as a cat. Weariness and sickness were forgotten. He felt superior to anything old Wigmore might try to do.

Fletcher staggered up, and reeled against the New Yorker.

"He'll shoot — if he's home," he gabbled. "Get hold of a chair — to let fly at him. Kill him if you see him! He's mad! Kill him like a rat!"

"You bet," replied Banks. "If I see him — then God pity him! Ah!"

He saw a heavy chair standing by the moonlit window. He ran forward, seized it by the back, and lifted it. He whirled it around his head. He felt strong enough to annihilate a score of maniacs.

"This will do. Come on," he whispered.

They went down a flight of heavily carpeted stairs to the lower hall. The winter moonshine lit the place faintly. Banks went ahead, with the big chair ready in front of him, and poor old Timothy crawling at his heels. The house was quiet as death. They reached the hall. Banks' anxious eye caught sight of the shadow of a curtain at the door of the dining room. The big chair hurtled through the air, and burst against the casing of the door.

"My mistake!" he cried, and the next moment had armed himself with another chair. They entered the dining room, found it empty, and closed and fastened the door. They rifled the sideboard of apples, soda biscuits, bread, butter, and a half bottle of sherry. Timothy Fletcher wet his insides with a dozen great gulps of the wine, direct from the bottle, and then crammed fragments of dry bread into his mouth.

## An Astonishing Discovery

"Go easy," cautioned Banks, between mouthfuls. "Dangerous. Chew your food."

At last he got possession of the bottle. The wonder is that the meal did not kill them. As it was, Timothy Fletcher lay down on the carpet, and swore that he would not move another step until he was dashed well ready, and felt a good deal better. Mr. Banks became indignant.

"I save your life, and then you go and eat yourself to death!" he cried. "It's enough to make any one angry. If you don't get up and come along out of this cursed house, I'll go without you."

Timothy rolled and twisted on the carpet.

"Don't," he whined, changing his tune. "I feel terrible bad, Mr. Banks. Don't leave me. He may come home soon. What time is it?"

Banks had forgotten that such a thing as time existed. He heard a clock ticking, tracked it to the chimneypiece, and carried it to the window. The moonlight was strong enough to read the hands by.

"Half-past nine," he said. "Half-past nine at night, of course — but of what night? Can it be only twenty-four hours since I crawled into this infernal house through a back window? I can't believe it! I've been sandbagged, and shot, and starved! Twenty-four hours!"

"I got an awful cramp," groaned Fletcher. "Get me some whisky! Quick! Cupboard in the corner."

"I told you not to make a pig of yourself," said Banks. But he found the cupboard, brought the whisky, and held the decanter to the old man's lips. He soon withdrew it, in spite of the other's expostulations.

"Half-past nine," he said. "Do you get that? When does Wigmore usually come home?"

"When do he come home?" repeated Timothy. "Blast him! Just when you don't expect him! That's when he comes home. After nine, you say? Then he must be out for the evening. We'd better go — soon. Let's have another drop of that whisky first."

"No more whisky for you. How are the cramps?"

"Bad! Bad! The soda crackers lay on my insides like bits of flint. I was near gone, Mr. Banks. He left me days and days without bite nor sup — may hell's flames scorch him!"

"But we must get away! He may be back at any moment. Once outside the house, we're safe."

"He has that pistol in his pocket. We'd soon be back again, if he met us."

"Rot!" exclaimed Banks. "Come along! Buck up!"

"Can't do it, sir. Not just now — anyhow. I feel that bad — I'd like to die."

The New Yorker relented, knelt beside him, and let him drink a little more of the whisky.

"Now, lie quiet until you feel better," he said. "I'll keep a watch out for Wigmore — and if I see him coming, I'll meet him at the door — with a chair. But you let me know as soon as you feel fit to move."

He took his stand at a window beside the front door. The night was almost as bright as day, and he could see clearly for hundreds of yards up the white road. So he stood for fifteen minutes, and nobody came in sight.

"Never before in all my life did I put in such a day as this," he reflected.

Then he heard Timothy's husky voice.

"I feel a mite better now. Maybe we'd best get out, Mr. Banks."

## CHAPTER XVIII

### DICK GOODINE RETURNS UNEXPECTEDLY

To hark back! After Mr. Banks' departure on his secret mission, Reginald Rayton climbed out of bed and dressed himself as well as he could. As it was hopeless to attempt a coat, he folded several blankets about his shoulders, the red one outside. Then he went down to the sitting room, where a good fire was burning, and shouted for his new stableboy. Bill Long entered from the kitchen and sat down, when requested, on the outer edge of an armchair. He answered a dozen questions concerning the horses and cattle fluently; but when his employer asked him suddenly if he knew of any one who held a grudge against him — Rayton — the youth rubbed one gray-socked foot across the other and scratched the back of his head uneasily.

"You will be helping me out if you say what you think, Bill," encouraged Rayton.

"Well," replied Bill, "they do say as how you an' Doc Nash ain't any too friendly."

"That was nothing, Bill. Just a fit of bad temper. We are on very good terms now. Who else, d'you think?"

"There's Davy Marsh. He's got a mighty sore head. I hear him talkin' pretty wicked about ye, one day."

"But he don't mean it, you may be sure. It was just his trouble made him talk like that. He and I are on a very friendly footing. He has nothing to be sore at me about."

"I guess he thinks he has, Mr. Rayton. You've cut him out — or he thinks so. But he weren't never in to be cut out."

"Oh, come now, Bill! I don't think you should talk that way about Marsh. He means well enough. Who else?"

"Well, Mr. Rayton, what about old Cap'n Wigmore? He be mighty sweet on Miss Nell Harley — an' he's an all-fired wicked-lookin' old cuss. I guess if you knowed his heart you'd find him yer enemy."

Rayton laughed. "Poor old chap! I am sorry for him. But come now, Bill, you are not serious?"

"Yep. He be soft as mush on that girl. Father, he says so, too — an' so does ma."

"But you don't think he'd shoot me, do you?"

"Guess he would — if he got a good chance. Guess he'd as lief kill a feller as eat his supper — judgin' by the looks of him. Tell you what, Mr. Rayton, if I was you I wouldn't trust that old gent no farther'n I could chuck him over my shoulder. He's got a bad eye, he has, jist like Jim Wiggins' old hoss had — an' it ended by chawin' off two of his fingers when he wasn't lookin'."

"Whose fingers, Bill?"

"Jim's, in course."

"Oh! Of course. But, see here, Bill; you surely don't think old Captain Wigmore shot me in the shoulder?"

"That's what I think, Mr. Rayton. It be jist the kinder skunk trick he'd do. *I've* watched him, many's the time — when he didn't know it. He talks to himself — an' sometimes he laughs, an' dances 'round on his toes. That's gospel, Mr. Rayton. An' he makes faces — lor'! I'll bet ye a dollar, Mr. Rayton, that 'twas him shot you. He's bin a pirate, I guess — an' 'u'd jist as soon kill a man as Jack Swim 'u'd kill a pig. He's got a anchor thing inked in on his arm, anyhow — all red an' blue. I seen it one day when he didn't know I was lookin'."

"You seem to be greatly interested in him, Bill. You seem to have watched him pretty closely."

"That's right. First time I seen him and heard his name was Cap'n Wigmore, I began to spy on him. He brought to my mind some other cap's I've read about — Cap'n Kidd, an' Cap'n Flint. Yes, Mr. Rayton, I've watched him, you bet — 'cept when he was lookin' at me. I'd jist as lief have a b'ar look at me as that old cuss!"

"For all that," replied Rayton, smiling, "I don't think Captain Wigmore is the man who shot me. He has an uncertain temper, I know, but I don't believe he would try to kill a man in cold blood. I can't think of any one who would try, deliberately, to kill me. It must have been an accident, Bill. That's what I think, anyway."

"Accident nothin'," returned Bill. "Pirates kill folks, don't they? You bet they do! Mr. Banks ain't so soft as you, Mr. Rayton. He's nosin' round, I kin see that. I'll bet he's spyin' on Cap'n Wigmore this very minute. Smart gent, Mr. Banks. Most Yanks be smarter nor Englishmen, anyhow, I guess."

Rayton's laughter was interrupted by Turk. The dog jumped up from the rug before the fire, stood for a moment, then ran into the kitchen, with his plume waving. The kitchen door opened and closed, Turk yelped a welcome, and next moment Dick Goodine entered the sitting room. The trapper carried his snowshoes under one arm and his blanket-cased rifle under the other.

"You, Dick!" exclaimed Rayton. "Has anything gone wrong? What's brought you back, old chap?"

"Yes, it's me," answered the trapper, with an uneasy laugh. "Didn't make much of a start, did I? But nothing's gone wrong. I made camp twenty miles out, on Dorker Crick — an' then I lit out on the back trail — just to tell you something that's on my mind."

He leaned in the doorway, smiling at the Englishman and swinging his fur cap in his hand. Snowshoes and rifle lay on the floor. Rayton gazed at him with a puzzled shadow in his clear, kindly eyes.

"Why, Dick, that's too bad," he said. "But pull off your togs and get something to eat — and then let me hear what you have on your mind. If I can help you, I'll do it. If it's money for more traps, I'm your man, Dick."

"It isn't money," said the trapper quietly. He threw off his mittens and outer coat, and drew a chair close to Rayton. "It is something pretty private," he said, "*and* important. It brought me all the way out of the woods, to see you."

Rayton was more deeply puzzled than ever, and a sharp anxiety awoke in him. Had this fate that had struck others also struck Dick Goodine? He inspected his friend anxiously, and was relieved to find that he had suffered no physical injury, at any rate.

"Bill," he said, "skip out and make a pot of coffee, there's a good chap. Shut the door after you."

Bill Long obeyed with dragging feet. He took half a minute to cross the threshold and shut the door.

"Now, Dick, fire away," said Rayton. "Get it off your chest. I'm your man, whatever your trouble may be."

The trapper leaned forward. Though his lips smiled, there were tears in his dark eyes.

"Is the shoulder gettin' along all right?" he asked huskily. "And the cold? How's it, Reginald?"

Rayton laughed with a note of astonishment and relief. "Did you come all the way out to ask about my shoulder and my cold?" he cried. "Well, you are a considerate chap, I must say! But it was foolish of you, Dick. I'm right as wheat; but it is mighty good of you to feel so anxious, my dear old chap — and you may be sure I'll never forget it."

Still the trapper smiled, and still the moisture gleamed in his dark eyes.

"I — I felt anxious — oh, yes," he said slowly. "I couldn't think o' nothin' else all the time I was trailin' along through the woods an' all last night in camp. That's right. So I just up an' lit out to tell you — to tell you the truth. I was a fool an' a coward not to tell it before. I'm the man who shot you!"

"What?" cried Rayton, staring. "You? For Heaven's sake, Dick, don't be a fool! Have you been hitting the jug again?"

"It's the truth," said the trapper quietly. "I shot you — an' I was scart to own up to it. I didn't know it was you until — until I *guessed* it. I thought I had come pretty near hittin' somebody — but not you. I didn't know who. I heard the yells — an' they sounded strong enough. I'll tell you just how it was, Reginald."

He paused, breathing quickly, and brushed his

hand across his face. Rayton went to the door and turned the key.

"Buck up, Dick," he said. "If you shot me — well, that's all right. No harm done; but tell me all about it if it will make you feel any better."

"It was this way," began the trapper. "I was trailin' 'round, lookin' for a buck deer or anything that might happen along — and after a while I seen what I took to be the neck an' shoulders of a buck. The light was bad, you know. The thing moved a little. I was sure I could see its horns. So I let fly. Down he went — an' then I heard the durndest hollerin' an' cussin' — an' I knew I'd made a mistake. But the cussin' was that strong I thought I'd missed. I cal'lated the best thing I could do was just to get away quietly an' keep my mouth shut; and just then came a bang like a cannon an' half a peck of pa'tridge shot peppered the bushes all round me. Then I was more'n sure I didn't hit the man, whoever he was, so I just lit out fer home, runnin' as quiet as I could.

"I got home all right, thinkin' it was all a mighty good joke on me, an' turned in soon after supper. But I couldn't get to sleep. I began to wonder if I'd missed the mark, after all. The light was bad, of course; but I don't often miss a shot like that at two hundred yards. I commenced workin' it out in my mind, an' thinkin' it over an' over every way.

"Moose an' caribou, an' even deer, run miles with these here nickled bullets in them — aye, an' right through 'em; an' I've read about soldiers fightin' for five or ten minutes after they was hit. Then why shouldn't the man I fired at by mistake holler an' cuss an' let fly at me, even if he was plugged? That's the way I figgered it out — an' pretty soon I began to think I had hit him.

"I couldn't get it out of my head. I saw him layin' out on the ground, maybe bleedin' to death. I reckoned the thing to do was hike over an' tell you an' Mr. Banks about it an' see what you thought of it. So, after studyin' on it a while longer, I got up an' dressed an' sneaked out of the house. When I got to your house there was a light in the settin'-room window. That scart me, for it was past two o'clock in the mornin' — pretty near three. I let myself in, quiet; an' there was Mr. Banks in the things he goes to bed in — the cotton pants an' little cotton jumpers — asleep in his chair by the settin'-room fire. That gave me another scare. I woke him up. He jumped like I'd stuck a pin into him.

"'Hullo, Dick,' says he. 'I thought it was Reginald. Where is Reginald, anyhow?'

"'Well, where is he?' says I, feelin' kinder faint in my stomach. 'Maybe he's gone to bed. It's three o'clock, anyhow.'

"Then he told me as how you an' him had gone out gunnin' together that mornin',' an' how you hadn't come home yet. Then I felt pretty sick; an' I up an' told him what I was afeared of — but I was too scart and rattled to tell him all I knew about it. It was only guessin', anyhow — though I felt as certain I'd shot you as if I'd seen myself do it. I made up a bit of a yarn for him.

"I told him as how I was in the woods when, about sundown, I heard a rifle shot, an' then a lot of hollerin', an' then a gun shot. I told him what I thought — that maybe somebody had plugged somebody — and how that somebody might be you. Well, he fired a few questions at me, an' then he grabs the lamp an' hits the trail for upstairs. Inside ten minutes he's down again; an' we get lanterns an' brandy an' blankets, an' out we start. It took us a long time to find you — but we did — thank God!

"That's the truth of it, Reginald; an' I couldn't rest easy till you knew of it — an' until I'd had another look at you. What with all the queer things goin' on 'round here of late — an' them cards dealt to you — an' the bad name I have, I was scart to own up to it before."

"I understand," said Rayton slowly — "and I don't blame you, Dick."

He put out his free hand, and they shook heartily.

"You're a rare one," said the trapper. "You're white, clean through."

The Englishman laughed confusedly.

"Now, we'd better let Bill Long in and try that coffee," he suggested. "About what you've just told me, Dick — well, I think we'd better keep it quiet for a few days. We'll tell Banks, of course; but nobody else. Unlock the door, will you, Dick?"

They drank coffee and smoked. Bill Long went to bed, yawning, before eleven.

"Where's Mr. Banks, anyhow?" inquired Dick Goodine. "Is he makin' a call over to the Harleys'?"

"He went out to find the man who shot me," replied Reginald, with a smile; "but, as he has missed him, no doubt he is at the Harleys'. What time is it? Eleven! He should be home by now."

Half an hour later they both began to feel anxious. Banks was not in the habit of staying out after eleven o'clock. There was nothing in Samson's Mill Settlement to keep a man out late.

"He went out lookin' fer trouble," remarked the trapper, "an' maybe he's found it. Guess I may's well go over to Harleys' an' take a look 'round."

"Perhaps he has gone to see Nash," suggested Rayton.

"Or old Wigmore."

"That's so. Better turn out Bill Long, too. He can go one way and you another, Dick. Banks went out in search of trouble, as you say — and perhaps he has found it. What sort of night is it?"

"Cloudin' over. Looks like snow — and it's milder."

Fifteen minutes later the trapper and Bill Long left the house, each carrying a stable lantern. Bill Long returned within an hour. He had been to Doctor Nash's, Samson's, and several other houses, and had failed to see or hear anything of the New York sportsman. Twenty minutes later Dick Goodine returned, accompanied by Jim Harley. Jim had come in from one of his lumber camps early that evening, having heard of Reginald Rayton's accident. He looked worn and anxious;

but expressed his relief at finding the Englishman alive.

"It is more than I expected when I first heard you had been shot," he said frankly.

Goodine told of the unsuccessful search for Banks. At the Harley house he had learned that Banks had not been there during the evening. Captain Wigmore had been there, however, for a little while, and had mentioned seeing Banks on the road. Then Jim Harley and Dick Goodine had called on the captain to make further inquiries.

By that time, it was snowing moderately. They had banged at the door for fully ten minutes; and at last the old man, yawning and draped about in a dressing gown, had let them in. No, he had seen nothing more of the New Yorker. He had persuaded them to enter and sit down for a little while, and had mixed hot toddy. He had suggested that Banks was safe home by that time. Then the two had left the yawning captain to return to his bed — and that was all.

"Well, he's not here," said Rayton. "What's to be done now? What do you suggest, Jim?"

Jim had nothing to suggest. His anxiety was written large on his face.

"Maybe he's gone into the woods an' got himself lost," said the trapper. " Anyhow, I reckon the best thing we can do is turn out an' hunt 'round again. Maybe he's hurt himself."

"That's right," returned Jim Harley. He laid his hand on Rayton's shoulder. "And the best thing you can do is to go to bed," he added solicitously.

Harley, Goodine, and Bill Long went out again with their lanterns. The snow had ceased, but the stars were still thinly veiled.

"I can't understand this," whispered Harley to the trapper. "Mr. Banks should be safe, anyway. He has never got the marked card."

"Can't a man get into trouble without the help of them danged cards? You seem to have 'em on the brain, Jim!" retorted Dick.

Jim sighed resignedly. The fate that made, dealt, and followed those little red crosses was a real and terrible thing to him.

The three took different roads after agreeing to inquire at every house they came to, and, if possible, to get others to help in the search. It was now after one o'clock.

Dick Goodine searched the sides of the road, the edges of fields, the pastures, and every clump of bushes and of timber he came to. He aroused the inmates of one house, made fruitless inquiries, and was informed that the only adult males of the family were away in the lumber woods, and so could not turn out to hunt for the missing sportsman. At last he found himself standing again before Captain Wigmore's residence. He could not say what influence or suggestion had led him back to this spot. He had followed his feet — that is all. One window on the second floor was faintly lighted.

"I'd like to know what that old cuss is doin' up this time of night," he muttered.

He banged at the knocker of the front door until the captain came downstairs.

"You again, Richard!" exclaimed the old man. "Come in. Come in. Still looking for Mr. Banks?"

"Yes. He ain't turned up yet," answered the trapper, stepping into the hall.

"I'll dress and help you hunt for him," said the captain. "He is a particular friend of mine. I can't get to sleep for worrying about him."

# CHAPTER XIX

### THE CAPTAIN'S CHARGE

CAPTAIN WIGMORE lit a lamp in the sitting room, and then went upstairs to dress. As soon as he was gone, the trapper commenced a noiseless tour of the room, of the hall, and of the rooms in the front of the house. He even searched beneath articles of furniture and behind every open door. He explored the kitchen, the pantry, and the pot closet behind the stove.

"Guess I'm on the wrong track this time," he admitted at last, and when Wigmore came down he was sitting patiently on the edge of his chair, with his toes turned demurely inward and his hands on his knees. The captain eyed him keenly for a moment.

"Want anything?" he asked. "A drink, or anything?"

"No; thanks all the same, captain," returned the trapper.

"I heard you wandering around," said Wigmore.

"I thought that perhaps you were looking for something. You were admiring my pictures, I suppose?"

The trapper's face flushed swiftly. "Guess again," he answered calmly. His gaze met the old man's, and did not waver. The captain was the first to look away. He sighed as he did so.

"I am afraid you do not trust me entirely," he said. "But we must go and look for poor Banks. He may be freezing to death somewhere. Come along, Richard. There is no time to lose."

As the two passed from the house, Goodine was in front, and for a moment his back was turned fairly to the captain. He heard a little gasp, and turned swiftly. The captain withdrew a hand quickly from an inner pocket, and stooped to lock the door.

"What's the trouble?" asked Dick.

"A twinge in my knee. I am growing old," answered Wigmore in pathetic tones. And to this day, the trapper has never fully realized how near he was at that moment to a sudden and choking oblivion.

The old man began to limp after half an hour of tramping the frozen roads and scrambling through underbrush and deep snow. At last he sat

## The Captain's Charge

down on a hemlock stump and confessed that he had reached the end of his endurance and must go home. He was sorry; but it was better to drag himself home now than keep at it a few minutes longer and then have to be carried. Goodine agreed with him; and after a short rest the old man set out on his homeward journey. As long as he was in range of the trapper's vision he staggered wearily; but once beyond it he scuttled along like a little dog. He was anxious to get home and assure himself that none of his neighbors were exploring his house during his absence.

Dick Goodine continued his unsuccessful searching of woods, roads, and fields until dawn. He crossed the trails of other searchers several times, but not once the trail of Mr. Banks' big and familiar hunting boots. Upon returning to Rayton's, he found Jim Harley, Benjamin Samson, Doctor Nash, and several other men drinking coffee in the kitchen. Reginald had been driven off to his bed by Nash only a few minutes before. An air of gloom and mystery pervaded the room. Doctor Nash alone showed an undaunted bearing. He talked loudly, and slammed the back of his right hand into the palm of his left continually.

"Banks is no fool!" he exclaimed, for the tenth

time. "Do you think he'd walk out of this house and lose himself on a night like this? Rot! Tell me who set fire to Davy Marsh's camp, who tied old Fletcher up in that blanket, and who shot Rayton, and I'll tell you who knows where Banks is. It may be one man, or it may be a gang doing the work; but there's one man at the back of it all. Same with the marks on the cards. At first I put it all down to you, Jim; but I couldn't see why you should tie up old Fletcher. Now, I see it pretty straight. That Fletcher business was all a bluff. He *let* somebody tie him up — and, as I've told you a dozen times, that somebody is old Wigmore. What do you say, Dick?"

The others all turned and stared at the trapper with anxious, sleep-shadowed eyes.

"I ain't sayin' yes or no yet a while, doc," replied Goodine. "What you say sounds pretty reasonable; but I wouldn't swear to it. I ain't a fancy detective, but when I see a lot of smoke I can guess at fire as well as the next man. Old Fletcher's vanished, anyhow — an' so has Mr. Banks. I don't hold that what happened to Reginald has anything to do with the other queer business. Accidents will happen! But I guess Captain Wigmore is lyin' when he says Tim Fletcher went to New

York; an' I guess he was actin' the goat when he let on as how he thought Doc Nash marked them cards. But guessin' won't find Mr. Banks!"

"Of what do you accuse Captain Wigmore?" asked Jim Harley, gripping Dick's arm. "I've heard a lot of hinting, but no straight charge. Speak up like a man and be done with it. Say what you mean. I'm sick of listening to hints against the old man behind his back."

In the silence that followed, the trapper looked steadily into Harley's eyes, and gently but firmly unfastened the grip of the fingers on his arm.

"Keep cool, Jim," he said. "Keep a tally on yer words."

"I'll keep cool enough, Dick. Don't worry about me," retorted Jim. "But answer a few questions, will you? A few straight questions?"

The trapper nodded.

"Do you think Captain Wigmore had anything to do with the marks on the cards?" asked Harley. "Give me a straight yes or no to that."

"A straight yes or no! Right you are! Yes, I do!"

"You do! Why?"

"Because I do, that's all. Ask your other questions, an' be darned quick about it. My temper's short."

"Have you any proof that he marked the cards?"

"No. And you haven't any proof that he didn't, neither."

The others crowded close around Dick Goodine and Jim Harley.

"And do you think he had anything to do with Davie Marsh's troubles?"

"Can't say. Don't know."

"Do you think he shot old Reginald Rayton?"

"No, I don't."

"Why don't you?"

"Because I shot him myself."

A gasp went up from the group of anxious and astonished men.

"You!" exclaimed Harley. "I don't believe it."

"It's the truth, anyhow. I mistook him for a buck. He knows all about it."

"Took him for a buck?"

"That's what I said; an' if any man here thinks I'm lyin' he'd better not say so, or he'll get his face pushed in."

"It's a mistake that's bin made before," said Samson.

Others nodded.

"Well, there you are!" said Harley. "If you hadn't wounded Rayton yourself, you'd say that Captain Wigmore did it. But all this talk won't help Banks. What are we to do next?"

"Have some breakfast and a nap, an' then start in huntin' him again," said Benjamin Samson. "We simply got to find him, or there'll be terrible things printed in the New York papers about this here settlement."

All left the house for their own homes except Goodine and Doctor Nash. As Goodine busied himself at the stove, preparing breakfast, Nash said: "That was a startler, Dick. Is it straight that you plugged Rayton in the shoulder?"

"Just as I said, doc," replied the trapper.

"Does Wigmore know you did it?"

"Guess not, or he would have said so before this. He put it onto you."

"He did, the old skunk. But he knew he was lyin' when he said it. If it wasn't you, Dick, I'd think Wigmore had paid some one to take a shot at Rayton. My idea is that he works the cards and then gets some one else to make the trouble."

"Maybe so. He didn't get me to do that shootin', anyhow. I guess he's the man who works the cards, all right; but I'd like to know what he does it for."

"My idea is that he had heard that story about the cards before and is trying to scare people away from Nell Harley. The old fool is soft as mush on her himself, you know."

"Well, doc, what we'd best do now is to eat a snack an' then turn in an' get a couple of hours' sleep; an' if we don't find Mr. Banks to-day we'll just up an' ask old Wigmore the reason why."

Two hours later Captain Wigmore himself arrived at Rayton's house. Nash, Goodine, and young Bill Long were in the kitchen, pulling on their moccasins and overcoats. The captain looked exceedingly tired, but very wide awake.

"I've found a clue!" he exclaimed. "Look at this knife! Did you ever see it before, any of you?"

He placed a big clasp knife on the table.

"Why, it's Banks' knife," cried Doctor Nash. "I've seen it several times. I'd swear to it."

"Yes, it's his. And there's H. P. B. cut on the handle," said Dick.

## The Captain's Charge 283

"I found it this morning, on the Blue Hill road," said the captain.

"On the Blue Hill road? How far out?"

"About three miles from my place. I've been hunting for Banks since sunrise, and this is all I've found."

"What in thunder would he be doing out there?"

"That's what we must find out," said the captain. "Perhaps he was drunk and didn't know where he was going. Or perhaps he was bound for Blue Hill station to catch a train. Heaven only knows!"

"How is the road?"

"Very fair, as far as I went."

"Then I'll hitch the horses into the sled, and we'll light out on his trail," said the trapper.

And that is what happened. Goodine and Doctor Nash set off at a brisk trot in the sled, taking Captain Wigmore along with them as far as his own gate. He gave them some exact information as to the place where he had picked up the knife. He said that he was sorry that he could not go along with them, but he was an old man and very tired. So they drove on without him. Several teams had been hauling timber and cordwood that way since the snow, so the road was in very good condition.

They reached the spot — or as near it as they could tell — where Wigmore claimed to have found the knife, and spent half an hour in searching the woods on both sides of the road. Needless to say, they found no further trace of Mr. Banks. Then they went on all the way to Blue Hill Corner and the railway station. The distance was fourteen miles — fourteen long miles. At the village and the station they made inquiries, but no one there had seen the big New Yorker. He had not left by the morning train. They remained to dinner at Blue Hill Corner, searched the surrounding country after dinner, then set out on the homeward road, making frequent stops to hunt about in the woods. It was close upon sunset when they reached Samson's Mill Settlement. Dick Goodine was depressed, and Doctor Nash was in a bad temper.

"Darn this country, anyway!" exclaimed Nash. "It's full of a lot of savages — and crooks. And what's to become of my practice if I have to spend all my time hunting round for Banks? To hell with it!"

## The Captain's Charge 285

Early in the afternoon of the same day, Nell Harley received an unexpected visit. It was from Maggie Leblanc. Jim was away, still searching for the lost New Yorker, and Kate was busy in the sewing room upstairs.

"I wanter tell'e somethin' very particular," said Maggie, in a faint voice and with a flurried manner. "Let me tell ye all by yerself. It — it be mighty particular."

"Is it about Mr. Banks? Do you know where he is?" asked Nell anxiously.

"No, it ain't about him," replied Maggie Leblanc. "I don't know nothin' about him."

Nell led the way to the sitting room, and motioned her visitor to a chair by the fire.

"Has — has anything happened to — Mr. Rayton?" she asked.

Maggie shook her head. "No! No! It is about me — an' Dick Goodine." She brushed her eyes furtively with the back of her hand. "I liked Dick," she continued unsteadily; "but he didn't seem to care. Then I — begun to feel's if I hated him. I knew him an' Davy Marsh was bad friends, so I begun to try to get Dick inter trouble with Davy — an' maybe with the law. After Davy's canoe upsot in the rapids that day, I went an' found the broken pole in the pool, an' fixed an end of it so's it looked like it had been cut halfway through. Then I put it up on a rock so's it would be found.

"I knowed folks would think Dick done it because he an' Davy wasn't good friends, an' he was the last man Davy seen afore he started upstream that day. Dick helped Davy to load the canoe. Then — then *I* sot fire to Davy's camp. But when Dick said as how he didn't fire the camp nor cut the pole, most every one seemed to believe him. I was feelin' different about Dick by that time — mighty sorry I tried to hurt him. But I was afeared to tell anybody what I done. Davy Marsh is that mean an' small, he'd have the law on me. Then Mr. Rayton, he got shot — an' then Mr. Banks, he got lost; an' this mornin' Dick Goodine up an' tells yer brother, an' Doc Nash, an' a whole bunch more, as how it was him shot Mr. Rayton."

"Yes. Jim told me of it. He mistook Mr. Rayton for a deer," said Nell.

"But some folks don't believe as how he took him for a deer," said Maggie. "It's the talk all over the settlement now — an' old Captain Wigmore, he be makin' a terrible story of it all. He has started up talk about what happened to Dave Marsh ag'in. He's makin' it look 'sif Dick done everything — an' like 'sif he done something to Mr. Banks, too. An' there be plenty of fools in this settlement to listen to him. So I'm tellin' ye the truth about who sot fire to Davy Marsh's camp. Davy don't know it himself. He says Dick done it — when Dick ain't lookin'. But I done it — an' 'twas me doctored that piece of canoe pole that broke by accident first of all — an' I'm willin' to swear to it on the book!"

"You need not swear it to me," said Nell Harley. "I believe what you have told me — every word of it — though it is a terrible thing! And I believe whatever Dick Goodine says. What can I do to help Dick?"

"I guess you like Dick pretty well," said Maggie Leblanc, with a swift, sidewise glance of her black eyes. "An' Dick likes you. That's why I got mad at him, an' Wigmore an' some other folks say that's why he shot at Mr. Rayton."

"Surely not!" cried Nell, in distress. "How can he say such things? Oh! I am growing to detest that old man — with his everlasting smile. As for Dick — why, he scarcely knows me. And he is Reginald's friend. And he knows — of course he knows — that — that Reginald and I — love each other."

Maggie Leblanc nodded her head vigorously and smiled.

"Don't you fret yerself," she said. "If he don't know it, then I'll tell him."

Her eyes clouded again instantly. "I guess ye can help Dick by just tellin' yer brother Jim what I told ye. Then he'll stand up fer Dick — him and Mr. Rayton will — an' what old Cap'n Wigmore says won't harm him much, I guess."

"I will tell him. He will be on Dick's side, of course," said Nell. And then, "But why is Captain Wigmore trying to get Dick into trouble? What has he against Dick?"

"Maybe he's just tryin' to keep folks from lookin' too close at his own doin's," said Maggie.

Nell Harley nodded, but said neither yes nor no. The thought was in her own mind. Captain Wigmore, the recent troubles and mysteries, and the marked cards had been associated in her thoughts of late.

Jim Harley got home in time for supper. He told of a fruitless search; and then Nell told of Maggie Leblanc's amazing confession. Jim sighed as if with sudden relief. After a minute of reflective silence, he said: "But, still, the accidents followed the cards — except in this last case. How are we to explain that — and the cards themselves? First, it was Davy Marsh, and then Rayton; but the card was never dealt to Mr. Banks!"

"Which shows that your foolish old curse is going all wrong," said his wife.

"Reginald does not believe in the curse — and neither do I," said Nell.

"Whoever did the injuries, and whoever dealt the cards, the injuries have followed the dealing of the cards," said Jim gloomily.

"Except in this last case," said his wife. "It looks to me as if Fate, or whatever you call it, is getting itself mixed up."

After supper, Jim, and his wife, and sister, all went over to see Reginald Rayton. A fresh force of men had taken up the hunt for Mr. Banks, and parties had started for every village and settlement within a radius of thirty miles. The Harleys found Reginald in the sitting room, in company with Dick Goodine and Doctor Nash. Rumor of old Wigmore's campaign against the trapper had already reached them, and they were talking it over. Nash was bitter.

"The old devil tried to put it on me," he said,

"and maybe he would have succeeded if Dick hadn't confessed. Just wait till I see him! Dick shot Rayton; but it was Wigmore himself who fired Marsh's camp — yes, and who's at the bottom of many more of these tricks!"

Then Nell Harley told them what Maggie Leblanc had confessed to her. The silence that followed the story was broken by Dick Goodine.

"She told you that!" he exclaimed, jumping to his feet. "She told it herself? To save me? Where is she now?"

He was about to leave the room when the door opened and he was confronted by Captain Wigmore.

## CHAPTER XX

#### THE CHOSEN INSTRUMENT OF FATE

Mr. Banks and Timothy Fletcher stood in Captain Wigmore's hall, breathing quietly and straining eyes and ears. All was silent. All seemed safe. Banks opened the door. The little porch was empty. He stepped across the threshold, followed closely by the staggering Fletcher. They pushed open the door of the porch, and stumbled out of that horrible house, into the frosty moonshine, onto the crisp snow. No lurking danger confronted them. They were free.

"Thank God!" cried Harvey P. Banks, hysterically.

The air was bitterly cold, and the two fugitives were without overcoats. They were so overjoyed to find themselves free men again, however, that they felt no discomfort from the gnawing of the frozen air. The little servant clung to the big sportsman; and so they moved down the narrow path and through the gate onto the highway.

"He's played his last dirty trick on me — or any one else," mumbled Fletcher. "I've stood 'im too long — too long! Now, he'll go back where he come from — the grinnin' snake!"

He leaned heavily on Banks' arm and laughed shrilly.

"Which way?" asked Banks.

"Don't care," replied Fletcher.

"We'll head straight for Rayton's, then," said Banks. "It seems a month since I've seen Reginald. Then we'll smoke a cigar. Then we'll hunt up our friend — and put the boots to him."

The cold, clean air strengthened them, and they were soon stepping out at quite a respectable pace. They even crawled over fences and took short cuts across snow-drifted meadows and pastures. They did not meet or see a human being, for by this time the searchers were all miles away from the settlement. They rested for a minute against Rayton's front gate, then went quickly up the long, twisting road toward the low house and glowing windows.

"There's company," said Timothy. "Maybe they're havin' another game o' poker." He grinned at Banks. "Oh, you're easy! A baby could fool the lot o' you," he added.

## The Chosen Instrument of Fate 293

"Right you are. That is the sitting-room window. The curtains are not drawn tight. Let's look in and see who's there," said Banks.

Banks took the first look.

"Reginald and Nash," he whispered. "And the girl — yes, and Jim and Dick. And who's that sitting with his back to the window?"

Old Fletcher edged himself into the place of vantage.

"It's *him!*" he whispered. "It's that snake!"

"Quiet!" cautioned the other. "Look! He's on his feet. He's wiping his eyes. There's been trouble. They have hurt his feelings, the poor, dear old saint!"

Old Timothy Fletcher trembled like a wet dog.

"I'll saint 'im!" he hissed. "Come on! Come on!"

They left the window, opened the back door noiselessly, crossed the kitchen on tiptoes, and threw open the door of the sitting room. Fletcher pushed past Banks, and darted up to within a foot of Captain Wigmore.

"You lyin', murderin', stinkin' old lunatic!" he screamed. "You thought you'd leave me to starve, did you? It's back to the madhouse for you — damn you!"

Every one in the room was standing, staring breathlessly. For a moment Wigmore gaped at his old servant, his mouth open, his eyes like stones. Then, with a choking cry, he reeled aside. Mr. Banks gripped him by the shoulder, and shook him furiously.

"You devil!" he roared. "You smirking hypocrite! You've come to the end of your deviltries!"

Wigmore made a dash for the door. Timothy Fletcher sprang in front of him, and was hurled to the floor. Then Mr. Banks jumped after Wigmore, caught the back of his coat, and at the same moment tripped over the prostrate Timothy and crashed to earth. The little room was now in tumult and confusion. Nell Harley crouched in a corner. Rayton stood guard in front of her, his sound arm extended. Jim Harley sat upon the shoulders of the big New Yorker, crying: "No murder here! No murder here! What d'ye mean by it?"

Timothy, lying flat, clung to Wigmore's right leg.

"Stop him!" he yelled. "Stop him! He's mad — a ravin' lunatic!"

Wigmore kicked his old servant in the face, and wrenched himself clear. In another second he

## The Chosen Instrument of Fate

would have been out of the room and away — but just then Dick Goodine and Doctor Nash closed with the terrible old man, crushed him to the floor, and held him there. They had their hands full, but they continued to hold him down.

There came a brief lull in the terrific tumult — but the excitement was not yet over. Mr. Harvey P. Banks was indignant. A madman had tried to starve him to death, and now a presumably sane man sat upon his back and called him a murderer. All his natural blandness was burned out — scorched to a flake of ash. The passions of fur-clad, pit-dwelling ancestors flamed within him. He arose furiously, twisted around, and flung Jim Harley aside. He gripped him by the breast with his left hand, by the right wrist with his right. He was quick as a lizard and strong as a lion. The lumberman was like a child in his hands.

"You fool!" he cried, glaring. "What d'you mean by it? So you are on Wigmore's side, are you? — on the side of the man who tried to murder his servant and me — yes, and who marked and dealt those cursed cards! You'd sit on *my* back, would you? For two pins I'd pick you up and heave you against the wall. Tell me — were you in league with this old devil? Tell me quick — or I'll finish you! Did you know Wigmore was marking those cards?"

"The cards!" cried poor Jim. "No, no! On my soul, I didn't know it! So help me God, I thought it was the family curse!"

"You fool!" exclaimed Banks, loosening his grip and turning away. His rage had also fallen to ashes, leaving his big face drawn and gray, and his great limbs trembling. His eyes were dim.

"That snake poisons the air," he muttered.

He stepped across to where Goodine and Nash held down the squirming captain.

"Let him get up. He has a good many things to explain to us," he said quietly.

Just then poor old Fletcher raised his head, showing a cut and bleeding mouth. Banks lifted him in his arms, and laid him on the couch.

"Don't stand there like a wooden image!" he said to Jim Harley. "Your inactivity has done quite enough harm already. This old man has been gagged, bound, and starved for days. Get him some brandy."

As Nash and Goodine removed their knees and hands from Captain Wigmore, that old sinner began to laugh immoderately. Still laughing, he got nimbly to his feet, bowed to right and left, and sat down in an armchair.

"Mad as a dog," mumbled Fletcher, with his bleeding lips. "He never was rightly cured, anyhow!"

"Mad?" queried the captain. "If you mean insane, my good fellow, you are very much mistaken. That's right, Jim. Give him a drink — but first wipe the blood off his lips. Don't spoil the flavor of good whisky with bad blood."

"If you are not insane," said Banks, "then you are utterly evil — a thing to crush out like a poisonous snake. But to look you in the eyes is to read the proof of your insanity."

Wigmore frowned. "Banks," he said, "you are feeble. You have the mind and outlook upon life of a boy of ten — of a backward boy of ten. But even so, I believe you have more intelligence than our friends here. However that may be, you managed to blunder across the right trail at last. That's why I took you in hand."

"You seem to forget that I have escaped you," said Banks.

Wigmore nodded. "I made the mistake of underestimating your bodily strength," he admitted. "I don't understand even now, how you managed to get out of that closet. You couldn't kick down the door — even with those boots."

"Never mind about that!" exclaimed Jim Harley, white with excitement. Tell me about the cards! What do you know about the cards?"

The old man gazed at him for a second or two with a face of derisive inquiry, and then burst again into furious laughter.

"Absolutely cracked," said Doctor Nash. "Absolutely, utterly, hopelessly off his chump!"

Wigmore ceased his wild laughter so suddenly that every one was startled.

"Jim," he said, with a bland leer, "you are so simple and unsuspecting that I hate to tell you the truth. But I have to do it, Jim, just to prove to Banks and the rest that I am not insane. Jim, my boy, *I am the chosen instrument of Fate.*"

A brief, puzzled silence followed, which was broken by the croaking voice of old Timothy Fletcher.

"Forget it!" snarled Timothy. "D'you mind the time you was the Sultan of Turkey?"

Wigmore smiled at his servant, then glanced around the room, and tapped his forehead suggestively with a finger.

## The Chosen Instrument of Fate 299

"Instrument of Fate? Sultan of Turkey?" queried Banks.

Jim Harley leaned forward, clutched the old man's shoulder, and shook it violently.

"What do you know about those cards?" he cried. "Tell me that — quick!"

"You seem to be in a terrible hurry, all of a sudden," replied the captain. "Oh, well, it does not matter; but if you really knew just who I am — if you fully realized who I am — you'd treat me with more consideration. I am the chosen husband of your sister. I am her *destiny*."

"Who *are* you?" asked Harley, scarcely above a whisper.

"I am the instrument of the Fate that haunts the steps of your mother's daughter," replied Wigmore. "I am the chosen instrument. I deal the cards — and the blow falls. I do not have to soil my hands — to strike the blows. I mark the cards, and deal them — and Fate does the rest, through such tools as come to her hand."

He leered at Dick Goodine.

"Then you admit that you marked and dealt the cards!" cried Harley.

"Certainly, my dear boy. It was my duty to do so — just as it was my duty to quiet Banks when he came blundering into my affairs. I am the keeper of the curse — the instrument of Fate — the — the ——"

He pressed both hands to his forehead, and sighed.

"The star boarder at the Fairville Insane Asylum," snarled Timothy Fletcher, "an' may the devil catch that fool doctor who said you was cured!" he added.

Wigmore lifted his face.

"I am John Edward Jackson," he said pleasantly, as if introducing himself to strangers, "Captain Jackson — the exile."

"Jackson!" cried Jim Harley. "Jackson? What do you mean? Not *the* Jackson?"

The old man nodded. "That's right, Jim. That's why I marked the cards. I came here on purpose to look after Nell, you know. It was my duty."

"He is mad," said Banks. "He is not responsible for what he says or does. He must be taken back to Fairville."

"Yes, I am Captain Jackson," continued old Wigmore. "I had to go away from my home, so I took to seafaring for a while. What was the trouble? Sometimes I remember and sometimes I forget. I got hold of a mine and made money. Then I made a voyage back to my own country, on very important business."

"That's one of the stories he used to tell me when I was his keeper in the lunatic asylum," said Timothy Fletcher. "Sometimes he was Jackson an' sometimes he was the Grand Turk."

"*You* keep your mouth shut till you are spoken to," screamed Wigmore, in sudden fury.

Harley stooped and gazed anxiously at the old man.

"Did you murder my father?" he asked, his voice shaking.

For a second the other stared at him blankly.

"Certainly not!" he cried indignantly. "All I have to do is place the card! I engaged an old sailor, or something of the kind, to dispatch your father. I indicate. Fate destroys."

Then he leaned back in his chair and laughed heartily.

## CHAPTER XXI

#### THE DEATH OF THE CURSE

JIM HARLEY'S face twisted and stiffened like a grotesque and hideous mask; his honest eyes narrowed and reddened; for a little while he stood there, motionless as a figure of wood; then his tongue flickered out and moistened his dry lips, and the fingers of his big hands opened and closed several times. The strong fingers closed so desperately that the nails furrowed the skin of his palms and came away with a stain of red.

"Damn you!" he cried, in a voice so terrible and unnatural that it startled his hearers like a gun-shot in the small room. "Damn you, you accursed murderer! You tell me that you murdered my father — and you sit there and laugh. You devil! I'll kill you where you sit — with my empty hands."

He sprang forward; but Banks threw out an arm like iron and grappled with him in the nick of time. Of the others Rayton alone moved to

## The Death of the Curse 303

help in the protection of the old man who sat laughing in the chair. Dr. Nash looked on with interest, Dick Goodine folded his arms and Fletcher snarled, " Kill the old devil. Crazy or sane, he stinks to Heaven an' cumbers the earth."

Banks and Harley staggered like drunken men within a foot of the old man's chair. Harley was blind with rage. Every drop of blood, every muscle, leapt to be at the slayer of his father. Nell, who had fled from the room a moment before, now returned and ran to her brother, crying out to him to be reasonable. Rayton followed the stumbling and reeling of the wrestlers, too weak to assist Banks but plucking constantly at a coat or shoulder. This time Harley was no child in the big sportsman's arms. He fought like a mad man, possessed and a-fire with the determination to destroy his father's murderer.

"It is a devil!" he cried. "Let me at him, I say," and twice he tripped Banks and had him down with one knee on the floor. But he could not get clear of the big fellow, nor overthrow him. And still Captain Wigmore sat in the chair and laughed as if he should die of unholy mirth.

The superior weight of Mr. Banks told at last. He crushed Jim Harley to the carpet and held him there, staring down at him with a flushed, moist face. Harley glared up at him, still squirming and wriggling.

"Lie still," said Banks, breathlessly. "Do you want to add another murder to the list of tragedies?"

"That's what I want to do," gasped Jim. "But it wouldn't be murder to clean the face of the earth of that devil. Let me up, you big slob."

"You'll thank me for this, some day," replied Mr. Banks, sitting firmly and heavily upon Jim Harley's heaving chest. By this time, Nell Harley had subsided into Reginald's anxious and ready arms.

Captain Wigmore stopped laughing suddenly and glanced from Banks and Jim on the floor to the girl and her lover.

"It's as good as a play," he said. "Banks, all this unseemly and ungentlemanly struggle is thrown away. My young friend Jim was powerless to do me any injury. I am beloved of the gods. I am the chosen instrument of fate — of the fate of the Harley family. Reginald, you silly young ass, I see you hold that lady in your arms with no other feeling than that of pity for yourself. The fates have ordained that I am to be her husband.

## The Death of the Curse 305

Timothy, you glowering old fool, bring me a drink of whisky. Don't stand there, sir! Step lively when I speak to you, or I'll send for the bosun to put you in irons."

"Forget it," snarled Timothy Fletcher. "You'll never set yer lips to another taste of whisky in this world, you old reprobate. I see death in yer eyes now — an' already the flare of hell fire. It's a drink of water ye'll be hollerin' for pretty soon."

"Let me up," said Jim Harley. "I promise you I won't touch him."

So Mr. Banks and Jim arose stiffly from the floor.

Captain Wigmore, or Captain Jackson, or the Sultan of Turkey — call him what you will — glared at Timothy in silence for several seconds, with hate and despair in his eyes. His long, slender fingers plucked at his ashen lips. Again, as suddenly as a change of thought, he burst into mad laughter; this laughter grew and thinned to shrieking, then fell presently to sobbing and muttering. He seemed to crumple and shrink; and slowly he slid from the low chair to the floor. The company looked on without moving or speaking, some in a state of helpless horror, the doctor and old Timothy

Fletcher with harsh curiosity. Nell Harley hid her face against Reginald's shoulder.

The murderer squirmed on the floor, sobbing and muttering; and by the time Doctor Nash had decided that he was really having a fit the old devil had finished having it. He was dead! Nash turned him over and felt for his heart. The heart was still.

"The ugliest death I ever saw," said Nash, glancing up at the horrified company.

"And the ugliest life," said old Timothy Fletcher.

Reginald led the girl from the room. They stumbled along the hall and sat side by side upon the bottom step of the stairs. Then the girl began to weep and the shaken young man to comfort her.

Old Wigmore's secret had not escaped with his wild and twisted spirit.

"Hoist him onto the sofa," said the doctor. "We'll sit on him here and now."

All agreed that the so called Captain Wigmore had died in a fit. Then Dick Goodine left the house, saying that a little fresh air would make him feel cleaner. Mr. Banks lit a cigar, remarking that he would fumigate this chamber of horrors. Then Dr. Nash, as coroner, and Jim Harley, who was a justice of the peace, agreed that they had the authority to search the belongings of the deceased. Timothy Fletcher said that he knew where the old devil kept all his private papers. So Rayton took Nell home, and Nash, Banks, Harley and the old servant drove over to the dead man's house, taking the shrunken and stiffened clay along with them in the back of the pung. They entered the empty house and Timothy lit a candle and led the way upstairs to the captain's bed-room. He pointed to a large, iron-bound wooden chest which stood at the foot of the bed.

"There's where he keeps his ungodly secrets," he said. "Mind the corp, gentlemen, or it'll turn over in agony when we unlock the box. Hell! how I do wish the old sinner was alive to see it. I shouldn't wonder but we'll find some bones of dead men in that box."

"Where is the key?" asked Banks, shivering at Timothy's words and puffing nervously at a freshly lit cigar.

Timothy chuckled at the big man's discomfort and borrowed a strong knife from Jim Harley. He went to a mahogany secretary which stood at the head of the bed, opened the top drawer and applied the blade of the knife to the front of a secret compartment within the drawer. He turned in a moment and tossed a bunch of keys to Mr. Banks. Nash took the keys from the New Yorker's hands and knelt down before the chest. Jim Harley held the candle. The chest had three locks and each of the three called for a separate key. At last the heavy lid was freed and lifted. The top of the trunk was full of clothing. They lifted out a tray and found more clothing. They lifted out another tray and found, in the bottom of the chest, books, nautical instruments, a chart or two, a small bag of English gold, a brace of revolvers and a small iron dispatch-box. In the dispatch-box they found many documentary proofs of the old man's claim to the style and title of Captain John Edward Jackson. They found his ship-master's certificate, an appointment to the command of a gun-boat in the Brazilian navy, title deeds to several mining properties in Brazil, a yellow clipping from a St. John newspaper recording the marriage of Captain Thomas Harley, and another reporting and commenting upon Harley's sudden and deplorable death at the hands of an unknown assassin.

"This little snake was the murderer. There can be no doubt about it," said Jim Harley.

"He is answering for it now," said Mr. Banks, quietly.

"I am afraid we must turn all these things over to the Crown," said Nash. "I don't know anything about the law; but I imagine it is the business of the Crown to take care of these things and look for heirs."

Mr. Banks nodded.

"I think the lawyers will find it a very pretty thing," he remarked. "As for Samson's Mill Settlement, it will become known to the world."

"But we'll burn these newspaper clippings," said Jim Harley, snatching them up and crushing them in his hand. "The murderer is dead and the curse is dead. We'll let the old story die, too."

"I wonder if the title-deeds are straight," murmured Nash. "Can the Crown collect, do you think? I'll make out my bill for professional services, anyway."

"Heaven only knows what the lawyers will make of it," said Banks.

Harley thrust the scraps of old newspaper into the flame of the candle, and as the blaze crawled up and threw red wavers of light around the room, Banks and Nash jumped as if they were on springs and old Timothy Fletcher let out a yell.

"I thought the old varment was a-fire already an' lookin' over my shoulder," explained Timothy, a minute later. He lit several more candles and led the way downstairs and into the dining-room. He got out a decanter of whisky, glasses and water. All four helped themselves to stiff doses. Nash took a sip, then raised his glass.

"The old bounder started all manner of mischief in this place, between friends and neighbors," he said, "but now he's dead we'll have a little peace. Here's to peace! I wish Reginald Rayton was here to shake hands with me."

"A very proper wish," said Mr. Banks. "The old rascal made fools of every mother's son of us."

"He was a wonder," said Timothy Fletcher. "This place will be dull as ditch water now. He was a great pot cracked, a great bottle busted. I hope he stays dead, that's all. What yarns he used to tell me, when I was his nurse at Fairville — afore he begun to pretend he was cured. I used to think they was all lies; but now I guess they was true — the most of them, anyhow. Of course I never stood for the Sultan of Turkey story. An' he'd talk about the sea, an' foreign ports all smelly with sugar an' rum an' spice, until I was pretty near ripe to run away an' sign on with some skipper. An' the adventures! To hear him, gentlemen, you'd swear that in all his v'yages he'd never gone ashore without savin' the life of a beautiful woman nor glanced up at a window in the narrow street without havin' a rose or a letter chucked out to him. He was a wonder. Oh, yes, I admired his brains, even after I begun to hate him. He was a good master to me for awhile after we left the mad-house — until he commenced rollin' me up in blankets every now an' agin' an' jumping on top of me when I was sound asleep, yowlin' like a moon-struck dog. I should have spoke about all them things to one of you gentlemen, I know; but I figgered as how he might grow out of them tricks some day an' maybe remember me in his will. I'll miss him; but I ain't sorry to see the last of him, damn him! I got my wages all safe — an' he paid me well."

## CHAPTER XXII

#### IN THE WAY OF HAPPINESS

CAPTAIN WIGMORE was buried in Samson's Mill Settlement, in a little graveyard on a spruce-sheltered slope behind the English church. A very young parson drove thirty miles to bury him; and as a Baptist minister had driven twenty miles for the same purpose a joint service was held.

"The old joker is safe buried, anyhow; an' I'm glad to know it," was Timothy Fletcher's comment at the side of the grave.

"I'll never dig him up, you may be sure," said Mr. Banks.

Mr. Banks returned to New York a few days after the funeral, but not before he had learned the date set by Nell Harley for her wedding. He promised to be on hand to give the groom away. Timothy Fletcher bought three big dogs for companions and continued to occupy the late captain's house as caretaker. The dogs always slept in the same room with him and he burned night lights by the score.

The Crown took charge of the late captain's properties and discovered half a dozen heirs in the persons of Brazilian ladies who had considered themselves widows for years past. The Crown had its troubles. The Brazilian government stepped in generously to share these troubles. Lawyers set to work in several languages and divers systems of bookkeeping. What they made of it I don't know; but the wives were all discredited and proven null and void — and Dr. Nash's bill remains unpaid to this day.

Nell Harley and Reginald Rayton were married in June. Mr. Banks attended in a frock coat and silk hat that surpassed everything present in novelty and glory except the head-gear and coat of the groom. It was a wonderful wedding; and to top it, the young couple set out immediately for England to visit Reginald's people.

"That's what I call style, from first to last," said Mr. Samson. "Them's the kind of folk I like to associate with, so long's they don't set in to a game of cards."

Dick Goodine married Maggie Leblanc in July.

Poker is never played now in Samson's Mill Settlement. Timothy Fletcher still lives in the house that nobody seems to own and that somehow has been overlooked by the Crown, the Brazilian Government and the lawyers in both languages. He works now and again for the Raytons or the Harleys. Reginald has bought more land and built a new house and several cottages. His farm is the largest, the best and the best-worked in the country. Mr. Banks visits the Raytons every October, for the shooting, and every June for the fishing.

Davy Marsh is guiding over on the Tobique now. He never comes home to the settlement. I have heard that he is the most expensive guide on that river — but not the best, by a long shot.

Dr. Nash is still a bachelor. He dines twice a week with the Raytons, as a regular thing, and oftener when Mr. Banks is there. He is not a bad sort, when you really know him well, and he knows you; but of course he will always be something of an ass.

THE END.

# Formac Fiction Treasures
## ALSO IN THE SERIES

## By Evelyn Eaton

### Restless are the Sails
Paul de Morpain, a prisoner-of-war in New England, overhears a plan to send an expedition against the French fortress at Louisbourg. He knows he must do whatever he can to warn the governor. It is 1744 — a dangerous time to attempt a 500-mile journey by sea and overland along dangerous forest trails. When he finally reaches Louisbourg, he is accompanied by San, his Mi'kmaq wife. While heroically risking his life to save the fortress from falling into enemy hands, he falls in love with the governor's daughter. Amidst the turmoil, he escapes on a pirate ship only to face both the tragedy of Louisbourg and his own misdeeds.
ISBN 0-88780-605-8

### Quietly My Captain Waits
This historical romance, set during the years of French-English struggle in New France, draws two lovers out of the shadows of history — Louise de Freneuse, married and widowed twice, and Pierre de Bonaventure, Fleet Captain in the French navy. Their almost impossible relationship helps them endure the day-to-day struggle in the fated settlement of Port Royal.
ISBN 0-88780-544-2

### The Sea is So Wide
In the summer of 1755, Barbe Comeau offers her family home in the lush farmland of the Annapolis Valley as overnight shelter to an English officer and his surly companion. The Comeaus are unaware of the treacherous plans to confiscate the Acadian farms and send them all into exile. A few weeks later, as they are crammed into the hold of a ship and sent south. In Virginia she patiently rebuilds their lives and opens a bakery. The last thing she expects is to see is the friend whom she believed had betrayed her and her family walk through the door, having given up everything in the search for her.
ISBN 0-88780-573-6

## By W. Albert Hickman

### The Sacrifice of the Shannon
In the heart of Frederick Ashburn, sea captain and sportsman, there glows a secret fire of love for young Gertrude MacMichael. But her interests lie with Ashburn's fellow adventurer, the dashing and slightly mysterious Dave Wilson. From their hometown of Caribou (real-life Pictou) all three set out on a perilous journey to the ice fields in the Gulf of St. Lawrence to save a

ship and its precious cargo — Gertrude's father. In almost constant danger, Wilson is willing to risk everything to bring the ship and crew to safety.
ISBN 0-88780-542-6

## By Alice Jones (Alix John)

### The Night Hawk
Set in Halifax during the American Civil War, a wealthy Southerner — beautiful, poised, intelligent and divorced — poses as a refugee in Halifax while using her social success to work undercover. The conviviality of the town's social elite, especially the British garrison officers is more than just a diversion when there is a war to be won.
ISBN 0-88780-538-8

### A Privateer's Fortune
When Gilbert Clinch discovers a very valuable painting and statue in his deceased grandfather's attic, he begins to uncover some of his ancestor's secrets, including a will that allows Clinch to become a wealthy man, while at the same time disinheriting his cousins. His grandfather's business as a privateer and slave trader helped him amass wealth, power and prestige. Clinch has secrets of his own, including a clandestine love affair. From Nova Scotia, to the art salons in Paris and finally the gentility of English country mansions, Clinch and his lover, Isabel Broderick, become entangled in a haunting legacy.
ISBN 0-88780-572-8

## By Charles G.D. Roberts

### The Forge in the Forest: An Acadian Romance
Jean de Mer, an "Acadian Ranger," returns, after three years' absence, to his lands on the shores of Minas Basin to find his son Marc in trouble with the Black Abbé — a French partisan leader. Marc is waiting to be tried as a spy. Together father and son make a daring escape but Marc is wounded and Jean must endure a perilous canoe journey with a young English woman to rescue her child from the Black Abbé. This historical romance takes place before the Acadian deportation, when tensions between the English and French were running high. The Acadians, while refusing to take sides, were nevertheless drawn in, accused of disloyalty by both sides.
ISBN 0-88780-604-X

### The Heart That Knows
On her wedding day a young girl is suddenly abandoned. Standing on the Bay of Fundy shore she watches her husband's barquentine sail away without a word of explanation. Weeks follows days and she is left to face life as an outcast, scorned by her neighbours and family for being a mother, but not a wife. Over the years her son, like many sailors' children, grows up without a father.

Confronted with the truth, the young man sets off to sea, determined not to return to his New Brunswick home until he sought vengeance on the man who treated his mother so heartlessly.
ISBN 0-88780-570-1

# By Margaret Marshall Saunders

## Beautiful Joe
Cruelly mutilated by his master, Beautiful Joe, a mongrel dog, is at death's door when he finds himself in the loving care of Laura Morris. A tale of tender devotion between dog and owner, this novel is the framework for the author's astute and timeless observations on farming methods, including animal care, and rural living. This Canadian classic, written by a woman once acclaimed as "Canada's Most Revered Writer," has been popular with readers, including young adults, for almost a century.
ISBN 0-88780-540-X

## Rose of Acadia
One hundred and fifty years have past since the Acadians were sent into exile; now, Vesper Nimmo, a Bostonian, sets out for Nova Scotia's French shore with the intention of carrying out his great-grandfather's wish to make amends to the descendants of Agapit LeNoir. Nimmo finds himself immersed in the struggles of the Acadians to preserve their culture and language while the lure of city life, including money and modern conveniences, draws young people to the Boston states. He meets beautiful, angelic Rose à Charlitte, the innkeeper where he makes his temporary home. When he becomes ill she cares for him, but when he falls in love with her, she cannot marry him — not until she is freed from her past.
ISBN 0-88780-571-X